UNSEEMLY FATE

BOOK 7 OF THE CONCORDIA WELLS MYSTERIES

K.B. OWEN

CONTENTS

Unseemly Fate
Book 7 of the Concordia Wells Mysteries
Copyright © 2019 Kathleen Belin Owen

Published in the United States of America

ISBN-13: 978-1-947287-08-2 (paperback)
ISBN-13: 978-1-947287-07-5 (ebook)

DEDICATION

For my Aunt Lorraine,
with love and gratitude for her support.

CHAPTER 1

HARTFORD, CONNECTICUT, SEPTEMBER
1899

*F*or those who subscribe to the adage *idle hands are the devil's tools and an idle mind his workshop*, then Mrs. David Bradley—formerly Professor Concordia Wells—might well be headed for trouble. Not that finding herself in awkward predicaments was unfamiliar territory for Concordia. In her single life, she'd had a tendency to "meddle," as a certain police detective of her acquaintance was wont to say. And we all know a leopard cannot change its spots, married or not.

Letitia Wells, Concordia's mother, was well acquainted with her—well, perhaps *proclivities* would serve as the kinder term—which was why she was knocking upon the weathered-trim screen door of the Bradleys' converted farmhouse one bright morning to take her daughter shopping.

"Oh, thank heavens it's you and not Aunt Drusilla come to fetch me," Concordia said, ushering her in.

To say that David's elderly aunt was not particularly pleasant company was like saying a bed of nails wasn't particularly soft. Drusilla Fenmore, a vocal woman of *fixed opinions*, preferred her female relations the way she preferred her corsets—rigid and straight-laced. In Drusilla's view, Concordia was sadly wanting in that regard, and not even the loan of the old woman's favorite books on female comportment had made a speck of difference.

"We'll call for her on our way to Brown Thomson's," Letitia said.

"*Must* she come along?"

"That's no way to talk about a new family relation." Letitia gently brushed a strand of bright-red hair from her daughter's pale, freckled forehead. "Get your hat. I'll help you re-pin your hair. I cannot think what possessed you to get it cut so short this summer. Oh, and your spectacles are crooked, dear."

Concordia pushed them up. "It's a wonder they stay on at all."

Letitia sniffed. "Is something…burning?"

"Something *was* burning." With a sigh, she led the way to the kitchen.

Atop the old stove—which hadn't been replaced since Mr. Lincoln had freed the slaves—sat a pitted, blackened pan, still smoking.

"It's our last good pan," Concordia said.

Her mother clucked her tongue. "It *was* your last good one. How fortunate we're already going out today. Give it a good soak in the sink, fetch your hat, and let's go."

Concordia would much prefer a trip to the bookseller's, but at least she was getting out of the house. The unaccustomed idleness of newly married life made her restive. It was not a physical idleness, of course—the old, rambling farmhouse and grounds needed plenty of upkeep, and they were short-staffed as it was, with only the boy who came daily to feed the chickens and take care of their new gelding, Domino.

No, Concordia realized, it was more of an idleness of the mind, only briefly allayed by chance opportunities to read. As a married woman, she was not allowed to keep her former teaching position at the college—at any college—and certainly could no longer *live* with the young ladies in the cottage dormitory. How she missed it all—the engagement of the classroom, the fun of the school clubs, and even the challenge of staying ahead of the lively young ladies she'd had in her charge. Chasing chickens who'd escaped their pen seemed rather tame in comparison to keeping up with girls who cooked fudge in their rooms, stayed up past lights out, played pranks upon the staff and each other, and even, on occasion, tried to sneak out of the dormitory to see a beau.

Brown Thomson's department store was a massive building that dominated the corner of Main and Temple Streets. It sported a three-story brick façade laid out in a series of tall arches, topped with an ornamental, crenellated parapet at one end and a grand spire at the other.

"Where to first?" Concordia asked, as the doorman opened the door for them.

Drusilla Fenmore, a rigid-backed woman still attired in unrelieved mourning two years after her husband's demise, squinted at Concordia under heavy, hawkish brows. "I would think a wider-brimmed hat would be the first order of business. Your face is more freckled than when I saw you last week. One would think you don't wear a hat at all." She prodded her with the umbrella she insisted upon carrying, no matter the weather. Sun and rain were equal adversaries.

Concordia gave her mother a pleading look, but Letitia shook her head. "You do seem more, *er*, speckled than usual."

Concordia waved a dismissive hand. "The spots will fade, never fear." She wasn't about to admit to forgetting her cap when she went cycling yesterday. Didn't Drusilla have better things to worry about than another lady's complexion? *Mercy.*

"A woman should never become complacent about her appearance," Drusilla declared, "married or not."

Before Concordia could formulate a retort, Letitia intervened. "We'll browse the drapery silks first. I believe something in olive or gold would suit. Then we can stop at the kitchenware counter for a new pan."

"New pan?" Drusilla asked. "Georgeanna and I bought you an entire set of cookware as a wedding gift. How is it you need more? You've only been married a few months."

Concordia flushed. "It was a generous gift, but the old stove at the farmhouse has been hard on our cookware."

Drusilla raised an eyebrow but said nothing more.

After finding the fabric they required—they settled on a figured silk in deep olive—and securing a modestly priced replacement pan, delivery was arranged, and the women were finally free to go to lunch.

"Shall we go to Markham's Tea Room?" Letitia suggested. "It's right around the corner."

Concordia's breakfast of tea and scraped-off burnt toast seemed ages ago. She was willing to eat anywhere.

On their way out of the department store, they passed a table display of soft, ready-made infant sacques. Concordia's mother lingered. "Oh, look—matching bonnets," Letitia murmured, fingering the lace edging of the yellow satin cap. "Aren't they sweet?"

Drusilla, eyebrow raised, glanced at Concordia, who kept her expression neutral. Although she and David were indeed expecting their first child, the doctor had cautioned them about sharing the news this early. Mother was the only other one to know.

Concordia's pulse quickened at the thought of a *baby*. But was it excitement about starting a family or dread that her life would once again change? Marriage had changed things enough, though she was grateful to President Langdon for skirting the college rules by quietly appointing her a "lecturing fellow." Starting in October, she would conduct monthly literature seminars and mentor senior students.

It was a temporary position, of course. Motherhood was

permanent.

Drusilla broke into her thoughts. "Shall we go?"

Concordia gave a wan smile. "Yes, of course."

Markham's was doing a brisk business during the lunch hour, but the maître d' finally escorted them to a table.

"Why, Drusilla Fenmore—what a surprise to see you here!" a tall, silver-haired gentleman exclaimed. He stood from his chair at a nearby window table.

Drusilla stiffened. "Isaiah," she returned coldly. "I'd heard you were back from South America."

The smile froze on his lips. "For more than a month now." He gestured to the other man at the table, who'd stood politely during the interchange. "Drusilla, you remember Ernest Richardson."

Richardson bowed. He was a good bit younger than his elderly companion—late fifties, Concordia guessed, though the receding iron-gray hairline suggested perhaps a few more years than that. He had a pleasing aspect, with a patrician nose, light eyes, a strong, cleft chin.

"Care to introduce us to your lovely companions?" the old man —Isaiah—went on. His gaze swept over Concordia in particular, and he gave her a broad smile from a face darkened from years spent out-of-doors.

For some reason, he seemed familiar to her, although she'd never laid eyes on him before. The shock of wavy gray hair that fell across a crevassed forehead, the dark brown eyes, the dimpled grin—it stirred an association she couldn't quite place.

Drusilla shifted her umbrella, ostensibly to free her hand, though the tip came suspiciously close to spearing Isaiah's foot. "Mrs. Wells, Mrs. Bradley—may I present Mr. Isaiah Symond, my uncle," she muttered.

Ah, so that was it. Now she could see the resemblance to her father-in-law, who would be Isaiah's nephew. The likeness ended with the face, as Isaiah possessed a tall, rangy frame instead of the compact, muscular build of the Bradley men.

"Pleased to meet you, sir," Concordia said.

"Ah," he exclaimed, "so you're David's new bride! A pleasure."

"And Mrs. Wells"—Drusilla gestured to Letitia, who inclined her head and murmured a greeting—"is her mother."

The maître d' shifted restlessly, and Isaiah Symond waggled a hand in his direction. "The ladies will be joining us. Three more place settings."

As they were seated, Concordia discreetly gave Isaiah's table companion—Ernest Richardson—another look. He, too, seemed familiar, though not because of a family resemblance. Where had she seen him? He was certainly a well-groomed gentleman, his graying mustache and sideburns neatly trimmed and his hair smoothly tamed by the application of pomade—though perhaps too much pomade, as he covertly scratched his head from time to time. He wore a well-tailored gray pinstripe suit, with not a crumb or a speck to be seen.

Richardson turned and caught her staring.

"I beg your pardon," she said hastily. "You look familiar. Have we met?"

"Perhaps, ma'am." He smiled. "You used to be affiliated with Hartford Women's College, I understand. I'm teaching a class there. Filling in for Professor Mercer. Poor man broke his leg last month."

"I heard about that. Now I remember where I've seen you—we passed in the stairwell of Founder's Hall one evening. How do you like the school?"

He inclined his head. "I'm settling in quite well, thank you."

In the lull after they'd placed their orders, Concordia asked, "Do you teach at another school as well, Mr. Richardson?"

"Actually, I'm an attorney by profession."

"*My* attorney, specifically," Symond retorted, giving him a sharp glance.

"Naturally, Isaiah. We've known each other far too many years for it to be otherwise." Richardson adjusted the spoon beside his cup. His emerald-and-gold cufflink caught the light briefly. "*You* are my most important client."

Concordia didn't doubt it. Isaiah Symond could obviously afford to pay him well.

A general silence ensued after their food arrived.

Concordia picked up the conversational thread again. She was quite curious about this attorney-turned-instructor. "How do you find the time to teach, Mr. Richardson?"

"It's only the one class in economics, and I recently hired another clerk to help at the office. You know him. Your brother-in-law, Lawrence Bradley. I took him on at Isaiah's recommendation."

She sat back in surprise. "Lawrence?"

More than three years ago, Lawrence Bradley had led a dissolute life in Hartford—drinking, gambling, even visiting houses of ill repute. His family could do nothing with him. Finally, to get him away from the bad influence of his ne'er-do-well friends, John Bradley had packed him off to his uncle's sheep ranch in Brazil. Concordia had just become acquainted with David in those days.

So, Isaiah Symond was the relation who'd taken responsibility for David's brother. Drusilla had mentioned South America. Now it was making sense.

But David had said nothing about his brother being back in town. She didn't know quite what to make of that.

Isaiah Symond chuckled. "You haven't seen him since our return, have you, Mrs. Bradley? He's straightened out nicely...became my right-hand man in running the ranch. Very able, responsible fellow."

Letitia Wells leaned forward. "If you are both here, who's managing your ranch now?"

Symond waved a dismissive hand. "Oh, I've sold it. I'm back for good, ready to rest my head in the welcoming bosom of my family." He winked at Drusilla.

Drusilla's scowl deepened, if that were possible, and a flush tinged her cheeks. Concordia imagined Symond was teasing the woman—some family joke she had no insight into. But she knew enough to see that Drusilla didn't like it one bit.

"Speaking of family," Symond continued, leaning back to allow the wait staff to remove their plates, "I sent out dinner invitations to everyone last week. I've been back since August, and I have yet to re-connect with the whole Bradley clan." He smiled at Concordia. "That includes you, too, dear, as our newest family member. But I haven't received your response."

She'd glimpsed an invitation of some sort last week. David had taken possession of it before she'd had a chance to look it over. *A tiresome dinner invitation,* he'd said. "I regret the oversight."

"Can you come?" Symond pressed. "It's tomorrow night at seven."

Concordia bit her lip. She knew they were free. It should be all right, she reasoned. They would certainly eat better there than at home. "Of course. We'd be happy to attend."

"Excellent!" Symond turned to Letitia Wells. "My dear lady, you must excuse my lapse in not sending you an invitation. I'm still catching up since my return, and I don't have a wife to consider all of the niceties. I do hope you would be available? It's terribly late notice, I know."

She glanced at Concordia. "I should be delighted. Thank you."

Symond's grin widened as he turned to Drusilla. "You will attend, I trust? John, Georgeanna, and, of course, Lawrence are coming as well."

Drusilla inclined her head in agreement, though her look could freeze water.

"Is there an occasion in particular you're celebrating," Concordia asked, "or merely a general homecoming?"

He grinned. "I want a chance to toast the new bride, since I couldn't attend the wedding. I have a gift for you, too."

Richardson cleared his throat. "And an announcement to make, I believe."

Symond made a shushing gesture. "That's a surprise, my good man."

"You're very kind, but a gift is not at all necessary," Concordia demurred.

He laughed. "You, my dear, are one of the few family members to feel that way. Most of my relatives are out to curry favor in some form or other."

She suspected Isaiah Symond was given to exaggeration, as she'd seen no evidence of money-grubbing behavior on the part of her in-laws. David's father made a tidy income from real estate ventures, they had a comfortable townhouse in the city, and they wanted for little. Perhaps Symond was referring to distant Bradley relatives she had yet to meet.

Letitia Wells checked her watch and touched Concordia on the arm. "We should be getting back."

"Yes, of course."

The gentlemen rose politely as the ladies took their leave.

"It was a pleasure to meet you, Mr. Symond," Concordia said, "and you as well, Mr. Richardson."

Symond reached over and clasped her gloved hand. "Please, call me Uncle Isaiah. We're family now."

Everyone ignored Drusilla's snort.

Concordia knew exactly where to find David for the evening meal on Thursdays—the school dining hall. His solid schedule of afternoon classes and laboratory sessions, followed by the weekly meeting of the student Chemistry Society—David was the faculty sponsor—meant he'd be grabbing a quick repast on campus rather than stopping at home.

She spied him at a table with three other department colleagues. They all looked to have finished their meal. One of the men had cleared a space for his notepad and was avidly sketching something as the others leaned close.

Perhaps it could wait. She could intercept him on his way out. She headed instead for the Willow Cottage tables.

"Mrs. Bradley!" Charlotte Crandall exclaimed, jumping up and pulling over an empty chair. "Come, join us. It's been an age since we've seen you."

Charlotte, a former student at Hartford Women's College, was now a junior faculty member who'd taken over Concordia's position as Willow Cottage's teacher-in-residence. Though she looked older than her years in a high-buttoned plain shirtwaist and with her smooth brown hair snugly gathered at the nape of her neck, the spark of humor in her brown eyes softened the effect.

Concordia took a seat. "I keep missing you when I visit the library and the staff lounge."

Charlotte grimaced. "I can't manage to stay in one place very long. I've been so busy."

How well Concordia remembered—clubs, classes, grading, faculty meetings, and most of all, the senior play.

Seated beside Charlotte was a new student, Madeline Farraday. She was taller than most, but her blond hair and frank gray eyes made her an attractive girl. At twenty-four, she was one of the oldest students at the school, nearly of an age with the younger teachers.

Concordia knew Miss Farraday quite well. They'd first met at the Dunwicks' cottage in the Hamptons last summer. At Concordia's urging, the young lady had applied to the college, secured a scholarship, and quit her job as a nursemaid. It was a brave move, Concordia knew. The girl's funds were extremely limited.

"Miss Farraday, how is your semester going so far?"

"I like my classes fine, and I'm certainly grateful my entrance exams allowed me to be placed in the sophomore year." She blew out a breath. "But my lodgings are another matter." She glanced at Charlotte.

"Miss Farraday's boarding house in town suffered a roof collapse," Charlotte explained. "She's staying with us at Willow Cottage until repairs are completed. Probably another week."

Madeline winced.

Charlotte gave the girl a pointed look. "I know it's cramped, but we must all make the best of it."

Across the dining hall, Concordia saw David get up from his chair. She waved. He brightened and started toward them.

"Ooh, Mrs. Bradley!" One of the girls leaned past Madeline. "When are we having our first meeting of the Literature Club?"

Concordia stood to greet David.

"This is a surprise," he murmured.

"I won't keep you long," Concordia said.

"Mrs. Bradley?" the girl persisted. "Can we set a date? Tomorrow evening, maybe?"

Concordia looked back over her shoulder. "I'm afraid that won't do. Mr. Bradley and I have plans."

David shot her a look.

Drat. She didn't intend to tell him this way. "There are a few evenings next week that should work," she went on. "I'll send a note around."

As they left the dining hall, David asked, "Exactly what plans do Mr. and Mrs. Bradley have tomorrow night?"

"I met your great-uncle Isaiah today," she began.

He took her arm and led her to a bench. "How on earth did that happen?"

She described their lunch in the tea room.

He scowled. "I take it he pressed you to answer the invitation on the spot? I'd hoped to avoid the man's company."

11

She folded her arms. "Drusilla shares your sentiment, though that isn't saying much. Do *all* of the Bradleys hate Isaiah Symond?"

"*Hate* is too strong of a word," David said. "It's more of a—an aversion to his company. Nothing to worry about, dear." He checked his watch. "I have to go." After making sure no one observed them, he planted a kiss on her forehead. "See you at home."

She watched him hurry away, her mind awhirl with questions.

A note for Concordia arrived at breakfast the next morning.

"Something wrong?" David asked, as he brought his coffee cup to the sink.

"Lady Principal Pomeroy wants me to come to her office at eleven o'clock." She looked up and met David's eye. "Miss Farraday has gotten herself into some trouble."

"Trouble? What have you to do with the girl? You're not responsible for her behavior."

"No one thinks that," she reassured him, "but Miss Pomeroy knows I'm interested in her welfare, as I was the one who encouraged the young lady to apply. I recommended her."

He rolled his eyes. "And so it begins."

"Begins? What do you mean?"

"My dear, it's as inevitable as combining chemicals known to produce an exothermic reaction. Step one—you are interested in a young lady's welfare. Step two—that young lady finds herself in trouble. Step three—you intervene. Then...*boom!*" He fanned his hands apart.

She sniffed. "That's rather patronizing. Besides, it doesn't apply here. I'm not related to the girl, nor do I have any official standing at the college. There will be no...*boom*."

~

The lady principal's office was located in Founder's Hall—dubbed simply "the Hall" by students and staff. All of the faculty offices were in the three-story building, one of the original structures built when the school started out as a ladies' seminary nearly fifty years before. As the Hall also housed the library, group study rooms, and the antiquities gallery, the addition of another wing was being considered.

Miss Pomeroy left her office door open on this warm, mid-September day to create a cross-breeze with the window. Loose papers skittered across the surface, which she promptly anchored with a gray-rimmed china teacup borrowed from the faculty lounge and never returned.

Charlotte Crandall was waiting there, too, but as Concordia greeted her, her smile didn't quite reach her eyes.

Uh-oh. Something serious was afoot.

"Thank you for coming, Concordia dear," Miss Pomeroy began. "I don't quite know how to start. There's something we wanted to ask you...." Her voice trailed off as she glanced at Charlotte.

"We should tell her what happened last night," Charlotte prompted.

"Ah yes, of course." Miss Pomeroy straightened the silver-rimmed spectacles that listed crookedly upon her nose. "There was an incident late last night involving Miss Farraday."

Oh dear. "What happened?"

The lady principal wearily gestured to Charlotte.

"I heard someone moving around in the front hall just after midnight," Charlotte said. "When I opened my door, there was Miss Farraday putting her shoes on."

Concordia took a breath. "And she was sneaking out to—"

"To meet a young man," Charlotte finished.

"What young man? A Trinity student?" The boys from nearby

Trinity College were permitted to accompany the young ladies for certain on-campus functions at Hartford Women's College— strictly chaperoned, of course. But at midnight? Never.

"Mr. Lawrence Bradley," Charlotte said, watching Concordia carefully.

Concordia blinked. "You mean...David's brother?"

"You didn't know of it?"

"I only just learned Lawrence returned with his great-uncle from South America—last month, I understand—but I haven't had occasion to converse with him yet, much less be privy to his romantic activities. I'm sure David doesn't know. How on earth did Miss Farraday and Lawrence become acquainted?"

Charlotte shrugged. "Not here at the school. Miss Farraday said they've been seeing one another for several weeks. Her land-lady apparently permits him to visit in the parlor set aside for her boarders."

Concordia nodded. A boarding house was a bit more lax in its rules than a women's college, especially regarding how much time a young lady could spend with a gentleman. It would have been properly chaperoned, of course. She knew Mrs. Carr ran a respectable establishment. She turned to the lady principal. "I assume you've spoken with Madeline about her behavior?"

Miss Pomeroy groped for the pencil wedged in her frizzy, gray-brown topknot. "This morning. I warned her she's at risk of being expelled. I don't wish to do so. Miss Farraday's studies thus far had been exemplary."

"What was her response?"

"Oh, she seemed penitent enough. She promised to comport herself better in the future. And to keep her busy and out of trou-ble, I've assigned her to help Miss Cowles in the library a few hours per week."

"Punishment enough," Charlotte murmured.

Concordia's lips twitched. Jane Cowles was a well-known taskmaster.

"The problem is more deep-seated than this incident," Charlotte said. "Miss Farraday seems determined to distance herself from the other students—declines to involve herself in clubs or join in other doings. She's not well-regarded by her peers."

"No doubt the age discrepancy makes it difficult for her to get into the spirit of things," Concordia said. "She's unaccustomed to such a life."

Miss Pomeroy grimaced. "She's not exactly our ideal of a demure young lady looking to better herself with a college education."

"I do appreciate you giving her the chance, all the same," Concordia said. "I know it was a risk to accept her in the first place."

"Indeed, it was," a surly male voice chimed in. Dean Maynard stood in the door, heavy black eyebrows lowered in his customary scowl. The man had a disagreeable habit of listening in on conversations and intruding his opinions—and his eyebrows—where they were not welcome.

"What Edward was thinking in allowing it," he went on, "I'll never know."

"Our president has obviously discerned academic potential in the young lady," Concordia retorted.

His eyes narrowed in a slant to join the brows. "I hold *you* to account for this, Mrs. Bradley. You have been a deleterious influence, intruding these modern sentiments upon a respected institution such as ours. Now we have a married woman employed at the school and a brazen, older girl insinuating herself in the college life of young, impressionable young ladies. Neither belongs here."

Concordia bristled. Who was he to decide such a thing? But she knew the argument was pointless. She took a breath. "I'm sorry she's causing trouble. I'll speak with her."

A student tapped lightly on Miss Pomeroy's open door. "Mr. Maynard? The bursar sent me to find you."

Maynard muttered, "Another upstart female," then turned on his heel and left. Charlotte got up and closed the door firmly behind him.

Except for the audible sigh that escaped the lady principal, the room was quiet for a few moments.

Concordia looked from one lady to the other. "I *am* sorry," she repeated.

"I'm not saying it was a poor experiment," Miss Pomeroy said. "In many respects, Miss Farraday is suited to academic life. But she needs to be taken in hand."

"Perhaps I can encourage her to become more involved in campus activities," Concordia said, "so she's not throwing herself at the first eligible gentleman she meets." She shook her head. Lawrence Bradley, of all people.

"Perhaps you can also ask your husband to speak with his brother about the situation and press upon him the need for propriety," Miss Pomeroy said.

"Of course," Concordia said. "And while Miss Farraday is staying at Willow Cottage, you'll have stricter control over her activities."

Charlotte gave an unbecoming snort. "I have my hands full already. Her presence creates friction among her fellows. And with another week or more before the repairs to her boarding house are completed..." She flashed a meaningful look at the lady principal.

"Concordia, dear," Miss Pomeroy said, "Miss Crandall has a possible solution, should you agree to it."

Concordia already had an idea of what they had in mind and knew David wouldn't like it one bit.

CHAPTER 2

WEEK 2, INSTRUCTOR CALENDAR,
SEPTEMBER 1899

That evening, the ride to Letitia Wells' house to collect her on the way to Isaiah Symond's dinner party was a quiet one. In the gloom of the carriage, Concordia caught only glimpses of her husband's face as the vehicle passed the occasional street lamp.

"Your thoughts seem distinctly elsewhere," she observed.

He gave a rueful smile. "Sorry. I'm not looking forward to spending time with Isaiah."

"Why is that? He seems agreeable enough."

"Oh, he can be charming when he wishes. But one must have a care for his temper. His wealth has spoiled him. He assumes he can control people with his money."

"How do you mean?"

He waved an impatient hand. "Never mind. The family decided long ago about that."

"Has he never married?"

"No. Not that he didn't have the young ladies eager for his attentions in his younger days. Perhaps it's just as well."

"David," she said impatiently, "what troubles you about your great-uncle? You're annoyingly cryptic in reference to him."

"There's bad blood between him and my father. Even I don't know the full extent of it."

"Then why would your father send Lawrence to live with him these past three years?"

"He was desperate to get Lawrence away from the bad influence of his friends. Of course, we're grateful for Isaiah's willingness to take on that responsibility, but now that my brother has a job as a clerk for Isaiah's lawyer, our indebtedness to the man continues. We must maintain at least the veneer of politeness during these little social functions, no matter how onerous."

A change of topic was in order. "Speaking of your brother, I was hoping you could have a word with him."

He listened, brow furrowed, as she related what Charlotte and Miss Pomeroy had told her.

"I'll certainly impress upon Lawrence the importance of discretion."

"Can you find out if his intentions toward Miss Farraday are... honorable?" she asked. "I mean no disrespect, but—"

"Given his past behavior, you wish to protect the lady," David finished. "Naturally."

"There's something else, regarding Miss Farraday. She's doing fine academically, but she's not fitting well into cottage dormitory life."

He smiled. "The students are a harum-scarum bunch."

"No one is happy with the situation, apparently, and Miss Pomeroy asked—well, it was Charlotte's idea, actually..."

"Yes?" he prompted.

"The general consensus is that Miss Farraday would be better off in a private home, so they asked me—I mean, *us*—"

"They want Madeline Farraday to live with us?" he interrupted.

"Only until Mrs. Carr's boardinghouse is habitable. About a week."

"But the young lady actually *living* with us…that is wildly inappropriate."

"You'll be leaving for the chemistry symposium in a few days. She can stay with me while you're away."

"True, but it sets a precedent I don't care for. We are not a boarding house, subject to the whims of the college. This is our *home.*"

"Of course it is, dear. But it would give me an opportunity to mentor the girl and perhaps involve her in one of the groups I sponsor. She may not find the Bicycling Club all that appealing, but perhaps the Literature Club would suit. We're supposed to have our first meeting this week at the farmhouse. The timing would be ideal."

"Of course this was all Miss Crandall's idea," he muttered.

"Do you want me to convey our regrets to Miss Pomeroy, then?"

He hesitated. "You really want Miss Farraday to come?" When she didn't answer, he took her hand gently. "Do you feel lonely when I'm away on campus?"

"That's not quite it. I can find plenty of company if I wish. Mother visits often…as does your Aunt Drusilla."

He made a face. "The latter is hardly an agreeable diversion. You know you're welcome to visit with the teachers in the staff lounge."

"I have upon occasion, but…"

"So what's wrong?" he asked.

How could she describe the last two weeks, since the start of the school semester? Swallowing the lump in her throat as she said goodbye to him each morning, watching him take the path leading to campus, leaving her at home?

Of course she kept herself occupied—effecting small repairs to the old house, mending shirts, checking with the lad who took care of the few barn animals they had, feeding Caesar, their newly adopted cat, practicing her cooking. Important tasks, to be sure, but not what she was trained to do, any more than David was.

"I don't feel of *use* anymore," she said, finally. "Before our marriage, my days were filled with activity, responsibility, and intellectual challenge."

The words of Lord Tennyson's poem came to mind:

> How dull it is to pause, to make an end,
> To rust unburnish'd, not to shine in use!

She sniffed and fumbled for her handkerchief. "I don't have a place at the school anymore. Oh, I know, Mr. Langdon has created a small position for me, and I'm grateful for that, but how much work will I actually be doing? Nothing as yet."

"It's early days in the semester," he pointed out. "Be patient."

"But there's more that troubles me. I am woefully unprepared for tasks of a domestic nature. It's a wonder I haven't burned down the house." Whoever said *practice makes perfect* had never seen her in the kitchen.

He chuckled. "A few blackened pans...hardly worth mentioning."

"My point is, whether at home or at the college, I feel as if I'm a liability."

"Oh, it's not as bad as all that." He patted her hand. "I grant you, the unaccustomed idleness is vexing to someone of your active nature, but soon enough"—he put a gentle hand to her abdomen—"there will be little ones to occupy you."

She was spared the necessity of a response by their arrival at her mother's house, followed by the short ride to their host's establishment.

The ordinary nature of Isaiah Symond's brick-front, three-story townhouse in the Frog Hollow neighborhood belied the startling interior. As the maid took their wraps, Concordia tried not to gape at the elephant-foot umbrella stand taking up the entire corner by the stairs, a stuffed mongoose under a glass dome, and a pair of iron spears mounted on the foyer wall.

The drawing room was even more extraordinary. Vying for attention were glass cases containing bric-a-brac from far-flung continents—Venetian glass bud vases, brass temple bells from the Far East, a wood mask of tribal origin, a set of Russian nesting dolls...

She managed to tear her gaze away to greet her fellow guests. Lawrence and John Bradley stood politely as they entered, Drusilla nodded from her position on the sofa, and Concordia's mother-in-law, Georgeanna Bradley, hurried over to greet them.

"Our apologies for the late arrival," David said.

John smiled at his son. "Perfectly understandable. None of us would be here if we could help it."

"Indeed." Drusilla sniffed. "The things one does for family."

Georgeanna led Concordia over to the sofa. "Sit down, Concordia dear. Plenty of room here."

"Where's our host?" David asked.

Lawrence waved a hand vaguely toward the door. "In the study with Mr. Richardson. We brought over some documents for his signature."

Concordia studied him covertly. Lawrence was David's older brother by two years, and the similarity between the sons and their father was evident in the compact build, wide shoulders, dark eyes, and thick, wavy hair—though their father's was now touched with gray. Lawrence's appearance was much improved since Concordia had last seen him, drunken and disheveled, at the women's suffrage rally several years ago. His dinner jacket fit smoothly across his shoulders, and his collar was straight and pristine white. He looked around the room with a sharp, clear-eyed gaze. She felt her spirits lift at the transformation in the gentleman.

"I don't believe we've been introduced," Letitia Wells said, inclining her head toward Lawrence.

"Oh, I beg your pardon!" Georgeanna exclaimed. "This is my other son, Lawrence Bradley. Lawrence, this is Mrs. Wells, Concordia's mother."

Lawrence gave a small bow. "A pleasure, ma'am."

Letitia Wells inclined her head politely, then turned away to scrutinize the art on the walls. She gestured toward a particularly hideous black-and-red painted wood mask, its features garishly distorted, its edges bristling with raffia and feathers. "Mr. Symond has unusual taste in art."

John Bradley snorted. "'Taste' is not the word I would use. There is nothing tasteful or cohesive about what you see on the walls or in the cases. Isaiah enjoys collecting mementoes of his travels, whether they come from Italy, China, Egypt, or the Congo."

Lawrence's lips twitched. "Uncle Isaiah even has a shrunken head. He keeps it in his study. No idea how he came by such a thing."

"Heavens," Letitia said.

"Well, then." Georgeanna shifted upon the sofa cushion. "Concordia, how is your household setting up? Are you two settling in?"

"Mostly, though we have yet to hire a domestic."

Each Bradley male assumed a freakishly similar look of collective boredom. Concordia smiled to herself. Mind-numbing domesticity could squelch any gruesome topic, to be sure. Just to be sure, she went on. "My friend Sophia Capshaw—I believe you met her at one of our luncheons last year—has offered to refer someone suitable to live in, cook, and do light housekeeping."

"Sophia?" Letitia's face brightened. "How kind. She and I shall have to compare notes as to what is needed."

Concordia smiled. Mother had long possessed a soft spot for Sophia. Ironic, given Sophia's tireless efforts on behalf of women's causes, including suffrage. Not even her marriage to police lieutenant Aaron Capshaw had deterred her from the progressive causes close to her heart.

"Oh?" Georgeanna said. "Does your friend know of someone?"

"She helps out at Hartford Settlement House. Many women there are looking for employment."

Drusilla raised a hawkish eyebrow. "The settlement house? All you'll get from there is some bone-lazy foreigner who hasn't a clue about keeping a clean house. They are accustomed to living in squalor, after all."

Concordia blinked. The widow was in a fine pucker this evening. Perhaps her corset was too tight.

"Well, if Sophia recommends her, that's good enough for me," Letitia said placidly. She glanced at her daughter. "Though you'll have to make sure she can manage that ancient stove of yours."

"Oh yes, definitely," David said, winking when Concordia shot him a look.

Sunday's chicken had not been *that* dry.

David drifted over to the pianoforte near where his brother was seated, idly flipping through pages of sheet music. "How do you like working for Richardson?" he asked Lawrence.

"Well enough." He shrugged but didn't look up. "The hours are longer than I like."

"It takes away from spending time with a certain young lady," Georgeanna interjected, giving Lawrence an indulgent smile as he flushed. "Not that I blame him. She's a charming girl."

David glanced at Concordia. She gave a slight shake of her head. *Not here.*

Drusilla sniffed. "You are far too gullible, Georgeanna. There is something about the young woman I do not care for."

Lawrence shot her a look of irritation. "What's that supposed to mean, Aunt Drusilla?"

She'd opened her mouth to reply when Symond and Richardson walked in.

"Ah, good!" Symond exclaimed. "We're all here. Dinner should be ready shortly. I've invited Mr. Richardson to stay."

"Much obliged," Richardson said with a little bow. He passed a hand self-consciously over his brown paisley vest. "I'm afraid I'm not in proper dinner attire."

"I don't stand on ceremony where that's concerned," Symond said dismissively.

An awkward silence settled upon the room as the gentlemen sat.

Concordia cast about for a topic.

"Mr. Richardson, how is your economics class proceeding? I hope the young ladies haven't been giving you trouble." It was safe to assume that conducting a class was not at all the same as managing a law practice.

"They are charming girls, though prone to going off on tangents with a barrage of questions."

Concordia smiled. "It can be a challenge to keep them on topic." Personally, she enjoyed many of those tangents. Moving away from the lesson plan occasionally could be beneficial.

Isaiah Symond shifted restlessly in his seat. "I'm sure you can keep them in line, Ernest." He added, nearly under his breath, "You excel at deflecting *my* questions when they don't suit you."

Richardson appeared not to have heard. "Though the girls who race ahead of the lesson, reading chapters in advance, tax me a bit. I'm not ready for those questions."

Concordia and David exchanged a look. Here, perhaps, was the essential difference between a passionate academic and a dilettante instructor. The academic would already know the textbook by heart, and more beyond that. The academic was delighted by unexpected questions.

John Bradley waved a dismissive hand toward Richardson. "Well, I'm sure you're doing your best."

Aunt Drusilla's disapproving frown had deepened to a scowl. "What on earth do girls need with *economics*? By all means, teach them to keep track of household expenses so they can run their homes when they marry, but the rest is wasted upon them."

Concordia eyed her mother. In the past, her mother would have agreed with such a view—she'd been a vociferous opponent of her own daughter getting a degree and making her way in the world—but now she was oddly silent. Had her opinions changed, or did such notions seem less agreeable coming from the querulous widow?

As if sensing her daughter's look, she smiled but didn't turn her head.

Concordia wasn't sure what to expect of a bachelor's dinner spread—particularly considering the man's taste in room décor—but Isaiah Symond's staff had laid a most tasteful table. The white damask cloth, shot through with gold thread, draped smoothly, the matching napkins were folded in the traditional three-corner pyramid shape to hold the dinner roll, and tiny salt-cellars of bone china were interspersed beside spotless crystal goblets. The one jarring note was a pair of matching brass candlestick holders, their wide bases thickly encrusted with what looked to be emeralds and rubies. She found her eyes straying to them, as the gems gleamed in the warm glow of the candlelight.

"Ah, you like them?" Symond asked. "The emeralds were mined in Brazil. The candle holders cost me a pretty penny, but I beat out the fellow who originally commissioned them. Found himself suddenly without the ready cash at hand, so I swooped in." He sat back with a contented smile.

Drusilla sniffed. "Rather gaudy, if you ask me."

Out of the corner of her eye, Concordia noted David's clenched jaw. She was beginning to understand what he'd meant about Isaiah Symond. Ownership seemed the old man's primary objective, and if someone was bested in the process? All the better.

She was reminded of Duke Ferrara's boast in a Robert Browning poem:

Notice Neptune...
Taming a sea-horse, thought a rarity,
Which Claus of Innsbruck cast in bronze for me!

The conversation lagged during the main course, with only the sound of cutlery against china punctuating the silence.

Letitia Wells turned to David. "I understand you're traveling next week?"

He set aside his spoon. "Yes, I'm to be a guest speaker at the Yale symposium on the role of chemistry in our modern world."

"Wasn't it supposed to be a historical focus?" Concordia asked.

"That was Dr. Hayden's original concept, and I'll give a separate panel presentation on the eighteenth-century contributions of Lavoisier, but the overall theme has changed."

David's father leaned forward. "Oh? Why is that?"

"Hayden and his colleagues are troubled by recent work in the field of organic chemistry—specifically, an upsurge of research into poisonous compounds for use as weapons." David's brows lowered in a troubled expression. "Concern has grown internationally over the trend. No doubt you've read about the Hague Convention a few months ago?"

"Ah, yes. The Tsar's idea originally," John Bradley said. "I understand several declarations were signed as a result, including a prohibition on the use of poisonous gas as a weapon."

Georgeanna, whose attention had been occupied with the roll she was buttering, dropped it and clutched a hand to her bosom. "Heavens."

"That's right," David said, ignoring her outburst. "But *our* country did not sign that particular declaration. We were the only major power to refuse to do so."

"So there's concern that the United States will develop its own chemical weapon," John said. "That *is* worrisome. But what has your symposium to do with that?"

"Hayden is certainly no politician," David said, "but he knows that a government needs its scientists in order to make such a weapon a reality. He's hoping the symposium could go a long way toward prevailing upon his fellows to direct their priorities elsewhere. Scientists from all over the country will be in attendance. There will be panel discussions on the ethics and the grim realities of developing a poison to use against men in battle."

Drusilla coughed into her napkin.

Georgeanna patted her back and glared at her husband and son. "May we please refrain from such horrid subjects? You forget there are ladies present."

"My dear," John Bradley murmured, "I doubt I would ever be permitted to overlook a lady."

Fortunately, it was soon time for the women to retire to the drawing room while the gentlemen headed for the study to smoke in peace and discuss whatever subjects they pleased. Concordia envied them the latter.

As she passed beyond the dining room doors, she noticed David pulling Lawrence aside.

Good. She was sure he would impress upon his brother the need for discretion where Madeline Farraday was concerned.

John Bradley approached them, a worried frown tugging at his brow.

David waved him off. "You go on ahead, Papa. We'll be along in a moment."

John hesitated, then followed the other gentlemen toward the study, casting one last look over his shoulder at them.

Odd. Did he fear his sons would quarrel?

Concordia was brought out of her reverie when her mother touched her on the elbow. "Coming, dear? Georgeanna says they are serving those lemon snaps you like."

"I'll join you momentarily. I have a—um—detour to make."

Letitia's forehead cleared in understanding. "Yes, of course."

Concordia actually needed some fresh air. Her head ached, and an uncomfortable clenching sensation in her abdomen had developed since they'd sat down to dinner. With a relieved sigh, she stepped out a side door of the front porch.

The cool night air helped, but she knew she couldn't stay long. She'd just decided to go back inside when she heard a man cough.

"Hello?" she called out into the gloom.

After a muffled exclamation, the voice of Mr. Richardson called back. "Over here, Mrs. Bradley."

She followed the sound around to the side of the house, where the library opened onto a small patio. Richardson's short, wide-shouldered form emerged from the shadows. He politely bowed. "I regret startling you, ma'am. Didn't realize anyone was out here besides me."

"What *are* you doing here?" Concordia asked. "I assumed you were in the study with the other gentlemen."

He gave her a sheepish smile. "I'm not much of a smoker. It was getting too thick for me in there."

Concordia chuckled. "I'm surprised my husband didn't follow you out. He isn't much of a smoker, either."

"He had the benefit of being near the window, as I recall." In an abrupt change of subject, he asked, "Do you know anything about Lawrence's latest love interest? Miss Farraday is her name, I believe? Isaiah's curious about the lady's background, after Lawrence introduced her last week. Although she's a student in my economics class, I know little of her."

"She's a private person. I don't wish to speak out of turn," Concordia said cautiously. "Why is Mr. Symond interested in the young lady?" If anyone should be checking into the girl's pedigree, it would be Lawrence's parents, not his great-uncle.

"He considers Lawrence practically a son, after their years together in Brazil. I imagine he's merely protective of him."

There seemed to be a lot of that going on, Concordia thought, recalling her father-in-law's reluctance to leave the brothers to talk alone. "I'm sorry I cannot be of help. I'd suggest Mr. Symond ask the lady directly."

"Of course."

"I had a question for you as well, Mr. Richardson, if I may."

He raised an eyebrow.

"As I've only recently married into this family," she went on, "I'm unfamiliar with previous dealings between its members. But you've been Mr. Symond's attorney for quite some time, is that correct?"

"Indeed, several decades now."

"Then perhaps you can clarify something."

He inclined his head. "If I'm able."

"I cannot help but notice that Mr. Symond's relations exhibit a degree of—well, not hostility, exactly—more of a stiff civility toward him. Do you know why?"

"He's not the easiest man to deal with, frankly, Richardson said. "The family was relieved when he moved to South America, but he made sure they wouldn't forget him. Each year he'd return for a month-long visit. He had practically an itinerary—attend board meetings, sign business papers, harass relatives, and change his will yet again, cutting off one relation to favor another."

Concordia remembered David's words. *He thinks he can control people with his money.*

"You may have noticed," the lawyer continued, "he isn't all that satisfied with me, either."

She nodded. So, he *had* heard Symond's remark earlier.

"He complains continually," Richardson went on, "claiming I haven't explained things sufficiently, or I haven't warned him about certain investment risks, or I've given him too many documents to read and not enough time to do it. All unmerited, of course. He threatens to fire me an average of two to three times a year. Then he retracts it, often with a gift or a bonus to sweeten the pot. No doubt he knows he's wrong but is too proud to admit it." He scratched his head and sighed.

"Why do you put up with such a mercurial man?" she asked.

"He pays me well." He smiled and twisted a gold signet ring on his little finger. "'With the rich and mighty, always a little patience,' as the proverb goes."

"Is he really that rich? This house doesn't seem as grand as one would expect under the circumstances." Nor was it in one of the more fashionable neighborhoods, such as Governor's Row or Asylum Hill.

"This isn't one of his properties," the lawyer said. "It's a short-term lease while he looks for something suitable. I cannot, of course, go into detail about his affairs, but trust me when I say he is a wealthy man."

"He accumulated his wealth while ranching in Brazil, I suppose?"

"Oh no. Long before that. He inherited a tidy amount upon his father's death when he was still a young man."

"Wait, wasn't David's grandmother Isaiah's sister?" Concordia hoped she was remembering the family tree correctly. "Did she also receive a share when the father died?"

"She didn't see a dime," Richardson said. "Was cut off when she married against her father's wishes."

Concordia wondered if that was the source of the "bad blood" between John Bradley and Isaiah Symond. Did John resent the treatment of his mother? But John Bradley had become a successful businessman and affluent in his own right.

"All that was before my time," Richardson said. "Isaiah hired me to manage his affairs a few years after he'd inherited. A large sum like that requires a lot of upkeep."

Something else confused her. "Why would Mr. Symond go to a South American ranch and stay there for twenty years? He could have had a life of comfort and leisure here."

Richardson shrugged. "Said he needed a new adventure. He's always been the restless type. Traveled all over before he settled down to ranching. The usual places in Europe, of course, but exotic locales as well. Hong Kong, Egypt, Siam... In the years I've

UNSEEMLY FATE

served as his attorney, there were any number of occasions when
getting correspondence to him was a challenge."

"We noticed the…décor," she said.

He chuckled. "Hideous stuff, isn't it? The man cannot resist
picking up items, especially if it means getting the upper hand
over someone else."

So he'd come to that conclusion as well.

"You're quite frank about it," she said.

"It's no secret. He has no intention of changing his ways."

"I'm curious—why did Mr. Symond decide to return to Hartford for good?"

The lawyer had just drawn breath to speak when a cheerful
female voice chimed in. "There you are, Concordia!" Georgeanna
Bradley waved a be-ringed hand as she stepped out to the patio.
"We were getting worried."

Why did ladies feel compelled to keep track of one another so
closely? After all, none of the male guests was hunting down the
errant Mr. Richardson. "I needed some air," Concordia said. "I
regret causing concern."

Georgeanna's nod was so vigorous that her side ringlets bounced.
"Of course, dear. The gentlemen are joining us now in the parlor.
Come, Isaiah has an announcement for us. Then we can go home."

Concordia suddenly realized how very tired she felt. And the
heavy pulling sensation in her abdomen was becoming difficult to
ignore. Yes, best to get the evening over with.

"Ah!" Richardson brightened. "The surprise. We cannot miss
that." He gallantly held the door open for them. "After you, ladies."

The sight of her smiling husband waiting for her in the parlor
cheered her considerably.

"David and Concordia," Isaiah said, "you two sit together on
the divan. He handed her a flat white box tied in blue ribbon. "Go
ahead, open it."

Inside was a heavy silver frame that held his photograph.

"I had that taken about ten years ago."

Time had not changed him much, though the brows and whiskers were more of an iron-gray in the photograph than their current silver. Perhaps, too, the forehead was less crevassed.

"I wanted you to have that, to add to your gallery of family pictures," Isaiah said.

David leaned in for a closer look. "At least it will scare the moths away," he murmured in her ear. She coughed.

"John has one as well," Isaiah added.

Concordia noticed John and Georgeanna exchange a look and wondered what dusty recess the picture had been relegated to.

"*That* is your surprise wedding gift?" Drusilla asked, lip curled.

Isaiah scowled. "Patience, woman." He handed Concordia another box.

Inside was a small, engraved plaque which read: "The William Blake *Descriptive Catalogue*, courtesy of Mr. and Mrs. David Bradley."

"I'm bestowing it in your honor," Isaiah said.

"You have one of the Blake *Catalogues*?" Concordia asked incredulously. "A rare find after all this time." When artist-poet William Blake sold copies of his *Catalogue* in 1809 as the discounted cost of admission to his public art show, less than one hundred were printed. She had no idea how many might remain, ninety years later.

Isaiah puffed his chest. "One came my way a number of years ago, but it had been languishing in Richardson's safe. Your college has it now and is making the necessary arrangements to display it properly."

"A generous gift," David murmured.

Isaiah beamed at Concordia. "When I learned you were to be married"—he gestured toward Georgeanna Bradley, which earned her a black look from her husband—"I considered what you would enjoy most, my dear. Imagine my astonishment when I learned you were a teacher of English literature. Quite an unconventional lady my grandnephew was marrying! I took the liberty of writing to your president in order to get to know you better." He gestured toward Richardson. "Ernest made all the arrangements with the school, including the purchase of additional pieces to round out the display. I've visited there this week to be sure the exhibit is up to snuff. Dorothy Phillips and her handyman have been working hard. They are nearly done."

Concordia didn't quite know what to make of it all. "This is… quite a surprise, sir."

Isaiah gave a nod of satisfaction. "Quite a college you have there. An impressive campus for its size. I never paid attention to its existence before now. And lovely young ladies, too. If I were a college fellow again, I would undoubtedly relish studying Shakespeare with a bevy of such beauties." He winked. "Though I don't know if I would be able to concentrate." He laughed at his own joke.

"That is why no male students are allowed in our classrooms," Concordia reproved mildly.

But the old man was enjoying himself too much to pay her any mind. He gestured toward David. "I had a feeling you would be too pig-headed to accept a monetary gift, young man, but something that benefits the institution you both care about seemed the perfect choice. How could you refuse that?"

She and David exchanged a look. Indeed, how could they?

Isaiah tapped the box. "This plaque is a memento for you to keep. The full-sized version will be prominently displayed beside the exhibit itself."

Concordia felt a brief wave of dizziness. She blew out a breath.

Letitia Wells crossed the room. "May I see the plaque?" She glanced at it briefly, her eyes mostly upon her daughter.

Concordia felt a stronger clenching sensation in her abdomen, then something more. "Excuse me a moment." As she turned to leave the room, her mother passed the plaque to Georgeanna, made her own excuses, and followed her out. David stood, but Letitia waved him back into his chair.

"Concordia dear," her mother said, putting an arm around her waist when they had reached the empty corridor, "what's wrong? You've gone quite pale."

"Mother, I—I feel my cycle coming on." She hesitated. "That's not supposed to happen, is it?"

Letitia eased her onto the hall bench. "No. It's not. We need to get you home. Wait here. I will make our excuses."

Concordia didn't need any prompting to stay on the bench. She clasped her hands over her abdomen and prayed.

Finally, their carriage pulled away from Symond's house, and Concordia was alone with David and her mother. She slumped in her seat and blinked back tears.

"Concordia." David clasped her hand and leaned close. "I'm so sorry you're unwell." He looked over at Letitia. "What's wrong with her?"

Letitia sighed. "I fear she's losing the baby."

CHAPTER 3

WEEKS 3-4, INSTRUCTOR CALENDAR, SEPTEMBER 1899

Some are born to sweet delight, some are born to endless night.

— WILLIAM BLAKE

*D*avid stood in the foyer of their farmhouse, valise at his feet. "You're sure you'll be all right here without me?"

It was the third time that morning he'd asked the question. Concordia stifled a sigh. "I told you, dear, I'm feeling much better. And you heard the doctor—I wasn't that far along. I should make a complete recovery."

She was starting to feel more like her old self every day, except for a persistent, dull ache of loss, felt in her psyche as strongly as if her body had received a blow. But no need to tell him about that. No doubt he felt it in some way himself.

She smoothed the collar of his houndstooth jacket. "There isn't anything you could do for me here except hover. Mother has promised to come to check on me regularly, Madeline Farraday arrives later today, and Mrs. Houston is taking care of everything else." Concordia's mother had insisted on sending their long-time family housekeeper to stay at the farmhouse while she recuperated. "I've never been fussed over so."

She gave him a gentle push toward the door. "Don't worry about me. Focus on the symposium."

So, with a final embrace and a kiss on the cheek, David was gone.

Madeline Farraday arrived that afternoon, trudging up Rook's Hill with her satchel and valise. Mrs. Houston led her into the spacious family common room, where Concordia was reading by a bright window.

She got up to greet her. "Welcome. I'm so glad you could come to stay while my husband's away."

"Well," Miss Farraday said briskly, "you're the one doing me a favor, Mrs. Bradley. I don't know if I could stand another night with those screeching girls and their carryings-on. You have a lovely home," she added, surveying the space. She went over to the deep mantel set into the stone fireplace.

For want of a better place for framed photographs—a pianoforte was not in their budget at the moment—the family photographs were propped there, amid the candlesticks and David's favorite duck decoys.

Madeline picked up a photograph of David and Lawrence. "I see the family resemblance."

Concordia knew that picture well. The brothers, ten years younger, wore matching Yale sweaters and wide smiles. Lawrence posed with his arm draped protectively over David's shoulders. She hoped they might find that easy camaraderie once again.

Madeline next picked up Isaiah's picture. "I've met this gentleman. He's Lawrence's great-uncle, from Brazil?"

"That's right," Concordia said, surprised. "How did you—ah, yes, I heard you were introduced."

"About two weeks ago. We ran into him quite by accident at

the Atheneum. I don't think he liked me much. He frowned at me continually."

"I wouldn't put much store in that."

"Lawrence said much the same," Madeline said, "that it's probably because his great-uncle wants him to settle into his new job as Mr. Richardson's clerk, without any romantic distractions."

"I suppose that's understandable," Concordia said.

She knew she should ask Madeline how serious she and Lawrence were. That's what a proper matron would do.

Well, she wasn't a proper matron yet, it seemed. And she'd grown weary of standing all the while.

Madeline's brow smoothed in sympathy as Concordia sank onto the sofa and propped her feet on the ottoman. "I hope I am not an inconvenience during this troubling time. I heard of your misfortune. I'm sorry."

Concordia flushed. "You're not an inconvenience. And I'm fine, thank you. Who told you?" *Land sakes*, she hoped it wasn't spread all over campus by now.

"Miss Jenkins. Don't worry, she spoke to me in confidence—wanted to be sure I don't overtax you."

Hannah Jenkins was the college's infirmarian—as well as its basketball coach—and had been of great help these past few days. Concordia nodded. "She's the soul of discretion."

The young lady took off her hat and gloves and perched on the ottoman. "Perhaps it's indecorous of me to continue with the subject, but you should know...a trouble such as yours is not uncommon. It happens to many women, I understand. Don't be disheartened. It doesn't mean that you won't be able to have perfectly healthy children later on."

"The doctor told us as much." She raised an eyebrow at the girl. "But how do *you* come by such knowledge, Miss Farraday?"

"I was the Gemmers' nursemaid, remember? It happened to Mrs. Gemmer, in between Serena and her baby brother."

"Well, I'm looking forward to being fully up and around soon,"

Concordia said. "The doctor says I'll be able to resume normal activity tomorrow, and that is what I plan to do." Except for riding her bicycle, which he said would have to wait at least another week. With the ever-watchful Mrs. Houston close by, she didn't dare bend that rule without her mother and David hearing about it. And now Miss Jenkins had her own confederate in the house.

A large ginger tabby strolled in, spied the newcomer, and headed straight toward her.

Miss Farraday's face brightened. "And who is this?"

The cat took that as an invitation to flop on the floor at the girl's feet.

"That's Caesar. We inherited him from Miss Banning, who used to teach history at the college before she passed away."

"He's quite...large." Miss Farraday leaned over and scratched him under the chin.

"Miss Banning kept him indoors and indulged him terribly with treats. He's actually sleeker than he used to be. He has the barn and grounds to explore now." Concordia had to admit, the beast had become a good hunter. She hadn't seen a mouse in the pantry in weeks.

"So tell me, Miss Farraday," Concordia went on, "how do you like Hartford Women's College so far?"

"Oh, I like it fine. It's a luxury to be able to read for as long as I like, believe me."

"Have you joined any clubs?"

"We-ell, the Literature Club is the only one that holds any appeal."

"Wonderful!" She decided to take the half-hearted comment as a full endorsement. "We plan to host a tea here this week, to welcome new members."

Madeline plucked at her skirts.

"Has the adjustment been difficult?" Concordia asked.

"Not exactly. The rules are tiresome. Most of the teachers aren't such sticklers, but some of the administrators... One in particular keeps a sharp eye on me, watching to see if I make a mistake. May-Not."

Concordia's lips twitched. "You mean the dean, Mr. Maynard?" *May-Not* was the student nickname for the man—not in his presence, of course. It was hard to blame them, as he dropped many a *may not* when exhorting students about the rules.

"That's the one."

"I wouldn't worry. He is more bluff and bluster than anything else." In a change of subject, she asked, "Have you made any friends?"

"Maisie seems nice. Even though she's a senior and I'm just a soph, she's introduced me around and helps me with trigonometry. And she's on scholarship here, too, so she knows what it's like."

"What it's like?" Concordia echoed.

"Come now, Mrs. Bradley." Madeline rolled her eyes in impatience. "When one's clothes are not new and one has no social connections of consequence, it's very difficult to fit in."

"Maisie has no difficulty in that regard," Concordia said. "Her fellows set little store by which cotillion she might or might not have attended. They *do* value her fellowship—well, there's also her ability to construct an illegal tabletop stove for cooking fudge. The key is to become more involved. The school is rich in traditions and activities that allow the girls to bond."

Madeline gave a derisive snort. "I've seen some of those 'traditions'–freshies and sophs playing pranks upon each other, switching signs, alarm clocks going off in the middle of the night… No, thank you."

Concordia grinned. "They can be a mischievous bunch. What about Founder's Day preparations? The committee could always use a hand."

"Perhaps."

It was like talking to a wall. This was not at all what Concordia expected. Why wasn't the young lady happy—*grateful*—for this opportunity? Why didn't she launch herself into activities with eagerness? Girls from across the country traveled to their nearest city—many having a trip of several hundred miles—to take the entrance examinations for Hartford Women's College and vie for the few scholarships available. A spot at the school was highly sought after.

She bit her lip, remembering a particularly avid student who was forced to drop out when she could no longer afford the tuition. Victoria Lester. She'd been saving for that very opportunity. Then she'd died. Now it was too late.

Too late for Victoria, but not for Madeline Farraday. Perhaps a bit of a talking-to was in order.

Concordia blew out a breath. "If you prefer to sit and stew over your past misfortunes, Miss Farraday, so be it. But I suspect that you deride the girls who enjoy their friendships and activities here because you cannot, or will not, enjoy them yourself." She gave a bitter smile and stood. "Or *may-not*. You and the dean actually have much in common."

Madeline gaped.

And with that final shot, Concordia walked out.

Mrs. Houston's firm management was finally bringing cleanliness, order, and regular meals to the farmhouse. The pans stayed intact.

Although Concordia missed David, she was beginning to settle into a comfortable routine—household chores and letter-writing in the morning, visits to campus in the afternoon to peruse the library or visit the faculty lounge, and student gatherings at the farmhouse after the evening meal. Most of the latter involved preparations for Founder's Day, a school holiday set aside to honor the foundress of Hartford Women's College, Theodora Blake. The entire campus took the day off to celebrate. Festivities included a special chapel service, the collective weaving of the long chrysanthemum chain by the students, a grand picnic lunch on the quadrangle—weather permitting—and a bonfire in the evening. Each year, the flower chain grew longer and the bonfire larger.

She and David wrote each other daily. In her current missive, she was regaling him with tales of the escaped chicken huddled in the laundry basket—startling Mrs. Houston no end—and Caesar's recent "gift" of a field mouse left on the front porch. She also shared details of her upcoming lecture on synesthesia in Keats's poetry. He may be a chemist and have no idea what she was talking about, but it was to be her first seminar since returning to Hartford Women's College and she was bursting with excitement at the prospect.

She re-read the letter she'd drafted so far. Chickens, cat, Keats. *Mercy*, what an odd collection. Married life was not at all what she'd anticipated.

Madeline Farraday came into the kitchen, teacup in hand. "Good morning, Mrs. Bradley." She rinsed her cup and put it on the sideboard.

Concordia checked the clock. "You'd better hurry off to chapel."

The girl gave a snort. "Let's hope it's calmer there today." At Concordia's questioning look, she went on to explain, "Yesterday morning, we found the hymnals upside down in the racks and the freshmen pews smeared with molasses."

"Oh dear."

"Guess who had to clean it up?" Madeline went on. "The sophs." She pointed a hand at her chest. "*I* certainly had nothing to do with it, and I don't think it was a soph trick to begin with."

Concordia raised a skeptical eyebrow. "Freshmen are the customary target of the sophomores, you know."

"That's what May-Not assumed. He categorically ordered us to scrub the entire chapel. But I think the juniors pulled the trick to get the sophs in trouble."

"The juniors?" Students usually settled down and stopped indulging in such tomfoolery by their third year. There were exceptions, of course. Basketball team rivalries between junior and senior classes, for example, were rather intense. "Why would the juniors want the sophomores to be blamed?"

"Well, a couple of sophs stole the banner from the junior class study room last week. So I'd *heard,*" she emphasized.

"I see. Nonetheless, you'd better get going."

"Heavens, yes," the girl exclaimed, grabbing her book satchel. "'Bye!"

Concordia turned back to her letter. She hadn't yet told David about Madeline's extended stay. The repairs to Miss Farraday's boarding house were finished, but she'd invited her to remain a bit longer. It was more convenient for the girl than hopping the trolley every day.

"Miss Farraday is staying on until you return," she wrote. "It's nice to have company in the house besides Mrs. Houston. The girl seems to be coming out of her sulks. More of the students have been visiting from Willow Cottage, which livens up the place and encourages Miss Farraday to get involved. She and Maisie are becoming fast friends."

She hesitated, then added: "It helps that Lawrence hasn't been around to provide a distraction."

She wondered how long the young man would exercise restraint in that regard.

It was the night before Founder's Day, and the house was filled with the mingling sweet-and-spicy scents of Mrs. Houston's pumpkin pies cooling on the sill and cut chrysanthemum stalks for the flower chain. Deadwood branches had been pruned and cleared from the old orchard and were loaded on the farm cart for the bonfire tomorrow evening, and nearly all two dozen of

Willow Cottage's students were sitting in Concordia's large common room, twisting raffia and twirling ribbons into bows to adorn the dining hall tables for tomorrow's feast. The ever-motherly Mrs. Houston had made sure the young ladies were well supplied with cider and doughnuts as they worked.

Concordia plied the scissors to snip lengths of ribbon for the girls to work with and glanced over at the sound of Miss Farraday's chuckle. Her lap was currently heaped with bows, tossed there by giggling young ladies as they finished and started upon the next. Madeline was trying to keep up, arranging them in baskets so they wouldn't be crushed when carried back to campus.

The group was so lively, in fact, that Concordia nearly missed the knock on the door. Given its persistence, the caller must have been at it for a while. Since Mrs. Houston had already retired for the evening—she was an early riser—Concordia answered the door.

"Mr. Richardson, hello!" she exclaimed. "What brings you here?"

"I hate to disturb you all at this late hour"—he cocked his head at the sudden sound of laughter coming from within—"but I learned Miss Farraday was staying here. She left this behind in the classroom today." He tapped the thick, gray textbook under his arm.

Concordia stretched out a hand. "That's quite kind of you. I'll make sure she gets it."

He hesitated. "I would like a word with her, if I may. She expressed some confusion over an assignment that I did not have time to clarify. I won't be but a moment."

"Oh, I see. Of course."

She ushered him into the front parlor and went to fetch Madeline.

$\sim$

The party soon broke up—the "ten o'clock rule" in effect even on the eve of a school holiday—with the girls calling their goodnights to Concordia and Madeline as they carried the large baskets of decorations between them and tottered down the hill.

"Whew!" Concordia collapsed on the settee and propped her feet. "That was a lot of work, but worth it."

Madeline gave a noncommittal grunt. She picked up the textbook Richardson had brought, idly flipping the pages.

"Is something on your mind, dear?" Concordia asked.

Madeline kept her head down, but in the light of the lamp Concordia caught a gleam of tears on her cheeks.

"What's wrong? You seemed to be having a fine time a little while ago."

"Yes, I know." Madeline sniffed, angrily swiping at her face with the back of her hand. "I cannot explain. It—it's complicated."

"It doesn't have to be. I believe the girls are warming up to you. After all, you're not so different than they are. Just a bit older."

Madeline abruptly stood. "With all due respect, Mrs. Bradley, you don't know what you're talking about. My life will never be like that of these girls. *Never.*" And with that, she ran out of the room.

CHAPTER 4

FOUNDER'S DAY, SEPTEMBER 1899

Better to shun the bait than struggle in the snare.

— WILLIAM BLAKE

---

*I*t was a chilly, overcast start as the students and staff
filed into the chapel for morning services. In honor of
Founder's Day, they sang the school anthem, "Forward, Woman,
to Thy Calling," and listened to President Langdon's dramatic
recitation of the winning student poem.

Thankfully, the sun broke through the cloud cover and
warmed them up nicely as the girls hurried to the quadrangle.
They tossed their gloves in a collective heap beside the fountain to
work on the chrysanthemum chain that would adorn the dining
hall's balusters. Concordia offered to help Miss Pomeroy and
Miss Jenkins group the students into teams and divide the flowers
between them, but Hannah Jenkins waved her off. "No need. The
staff has it well in hand." She turned back to the clamoring girls.
"Patience, ladies!" she snapped.

Concordia stepped back. *Why am I here?*

Still, she enjoyed watching the students laugh and chatter as they worked. No matter the class—freshman or sophomore, junior or senior—the pranks and rivalries were set aside on Founder's Day. She closed her eyes and breathed in the mingling scents of fallen leaves and bruised chrysanthemum stems. It was a wonderful season to be at the college.

She stifled a sigh. Even if she wasn't a full-fledged member of it anymore.

The Willow Cottage girls were grouped at the far end of the fountain, where Maisie Lovelace was showing an unenthusiastic Madeline Farraday how to bunch and wrap the stems along the rope. The girl seemed little improved in temperament from last night, as if the weight of the world was upon her shoulders.

"Mrs. Bradley?" a man's voice murmured.

She turned to see George Lovelace, Maisie's uncle, attired in his customary workman's twill overalls and faded plaid shirt. He swept the cap from his head. "Do you have a bit of time? Miss Phillips was hoping she could ask you about the new exhibit."

Concordia glanced back at the quadrangle. She wasn't needed here, and she would love an early look at the display. "Of course."

The college's Gallery of Antiquities had opened only a few years ago, after a valuable seventeenth-century European bodice dagger turned up among the stage props. The discovery that the rhinestones at the base of the knife handle were in fact *diamonds,* and that the weapon was a rare artifact, prompted the idea of starting an antiquities collection. The gallery brochure, however, omitted the fact that the knife only came to light after Concordia had the misfortune to find it plunged in the chest of a staff member.

Pieces had trickled in from local donors over the years—most notably Colonel Adams's entire collection of Egyptian artifacts, which was why Egyptologist Dorothy Phillips had been hired as curator. She also served as one of the history professors.

Isaiah Symond's donation did not quite approach the scope of the colonel's gift, but it was attracting attention nonetheless. Tomorrow's exhibit opening promised to be quite the affair. There were sure to be tedious speeches aplenty and no room to sit down. Lucky David—he was going to miss all the *fun*, Concordia thought wryly. He was still in New Haven, having been invited to stay on after the symposium's end for an additional week of talks with the organizers.

She followed George around to the side door of the stairwell to avoid passing through the library. The gallery occupied the remainder of the first floor, where one entered through a set of interior double doors trimmed in polished brass and mahogany. Inside, rows of tall, pointed Gothic windows that reached almost to the ceiling provided natural light. The original oak wainscoting lent the space a collegiate dignity. *Rest assured*, the wainscoting seemed to say to prospective donors, *this place will remain for the century to come.*

Dorothy Phillips came through the far door that led to her office beyond. She was of middling age and sturdily built, with barely a hint of gray in her unfashionably short brown hair. Her skin was also more spotted than fashion dictated, doubtless from repeated time in the sun.

"Ah, Concordia, so nice to see you, dear," Miss Phillips said. "You're looking well. Married life seems to be agreeing with you."

Concordia blushed. "Thank you. It's an adjustment. I do miss being here."

The lady made a face. "I should like to 'miss' the place for a while." She motioned toward the stack of envelopes she carried before passing them to the handyman. "Administrative tasks are the most tiresome of all. Can you send these out when you head home, George? My latest report to members of the funding committee."

She turned back to Concordia, squinting from behind narrow, gold-rimmed spectacles. She either needed stronger lenses or, as

Concordia fancifully preferred to believe, it was a habit acquired from years of peering into dark, long-forgotten tombs.

"Let us work on something far more interesting. Come see what we've set up." She dodged an old leather bag of tools—George's, no doubt—with the ease of practice and drew Concordia over to a small glass case. Beside the case, easels held mounted lithograph reproductions of William Blake's better-known tempura and watercolor paintings. A sign upon a side table described his body of work as an artist and poet.

Miss Phillips opened the case and gently extracted a slim, light-brown octavo booklet propped upon the apricot-velvet-lined interior, then frowned. She turned it right side up. "George? Whyever would you put the book in the wrong way?"

He shook his head. "I haven't touched it, miss."

"Well, I know I didn't set it like that." She leaned closer, squinting into the case. "And the bulb is gone. Did you remove it?"

"Gone?" George came over. "It weren't me. Maybe it fell out." He dropped to his knees and started groping under the table.

"Who else has been in here?" Concordia asked.

The lady pursed her lips as she thought. "Several people stopped by for an early look. I couldn't very well refuse President Langdon, Lady Principal Pomeroy, or Dean Maynard. Then the librarian and Miss Crandall wanted to see it, too."

"I can't imagine any of them making mischief," Concordia said. Of course, the absent-minded Miss Pomeroy would likely replace a book upside down, but steal a light bulb? Hardly.

"The doors aren't kept locked during the day," George said. "Maybe a student slipped in. Someone pulling a prank?"

Miss Phillips nodded. "That's more likely, especially after the chapel incident the other day."

"Well, don't you worry, miss," George said. "I have a spare bulb in my shop."

"Good. We'd better check the rest of the cases. And I suppose I should inform the dean next time I see him." Miss Phillips passed the booklet to Concordia. "Here it is. The *Descriptive Catalogue*. I'll be right back."

Concordia had of course handled historical books and documents before, but the thrill never abated. The entire booklet was barely larger than the size of her hand and only sixty-six pages in total. On the cover was a brown woodcut print, faded now. It was one of the plates from *Jerusalem, the Emanation of the Great Albion*, with "W. Blake" inset in the middle.

Miss Phillips returned. "Everything else looks in order, thank goodness." She squinted over Concordia's shoulder. "What pages would you like open for display?"

"Oh, definitely the Canterbury Pilgrims." Concordia turned the pages carefully—the paper itself was of cheap quality and rather fragile—until she found the spot.

Number III.
Sir Jeffery Chaucer and the Nine-and-Twenty Pilgrims on their journey to Canterbury.

Blake's original purpose in creating the *Catalogue* was to advertise sixteen of his best temperas, watercolors, and sketches, describing them in the booklet in great detail. However, it was the artist-poet's ensuing commentaries that attracted the most attention to the *Catalogue*, then and since—particularly his exposition on the Canterbury Pilgrims. Blake had devoted more than a third of the *Catalogue* pages to them. She skimmed a few more pages before looking up. "Charles Lamb, one of Blake's own contemporaries, considered it the finest criticism of the poem he'd ever read." She handed back the booklet.

"True," Miss Phillips said, "though Blake's contemporaries, generally speaking, dismissed him as a bitter, erratic genius. Possibly insane."

Concordia lifted an eyebrow. "William Blake is a far cry from the tombs and monuments of Ancient Egypt."

Dorothy Phillips flushed. "A dear friend of mine is an avid Blake scholar." She gripped the *Catalogue* a bit more tightly than was perhaps prudent and looked down at the page, though Concordia suspected that wasn't what she saw.

"Miss Phillips? Are you all right?"

"Hmm? Yes, yes, I'm fine." The lady blew out a breath. "Well then, we shall have it open to the Pilgrims." She settled the *Catalogue* inside the case and locked it.

George leaned over with his cleaning rag and polished the glass. "How do you like the cabinet, Mrs. Bradley? Made it m'self, all oak trim, not a nail-hole in sight."

"Impressive. Did it take you long?"

"A bit of time, but Mr. Symond and that lawyer of his got me started on it right at the beginning of the semester. The hardest part was dealing with the problem of heat from the electric bulb. I've built in vents to allow it to dissipate."

"Indeed?" Concordia leaned closer to see the smooth-cut, even slats near the top, on either side of the empty bulb socket.

"Even so," Miss Phillips said, "we'll have to keep the use of the bulb to a minimum to avoid fading the ink even further."

"You've gone to so much trouble, Mr. Lovelace," Concordia said.

He smiled. "Not at all, ma'am."

"I'm grateful to you. And to Mr. Symond, of course. It's an incredibly generous gesture."

Miss Phillips sighed.

No doubt Concordia's expression matched the puzzled look she noted on the handyman's face. The lady was working too hard.

"If you'll excuse me," George said, "I should be getting home. I'll be sure to mail those reports for you, Miss Phillips." He rummaged in the pocket of his overalls. "Oh, and I brought you back some of that tea you like, the kind you said you had trouble finding?" He passed over a small linen sack.

Miss Phillips's eyes brightened as she reached for it. "Why, thank you, George. How thoughtful. What would I do without you?"

He cleared his throat awkwardly and left.

"Bless the man, his timing is perfect. I could do with a cup of tea," Miss Phillips said. "Would you care to join me, Concordia? I'm sure I can scavenge another cup."

Concordia realized she'd appreciate a chance to sit down for a bit. And of course, she'd never turned down a cup of tea in her life. "Excellent idea."

Dorothy Phillips's office always made Concordia smile. It had a comfortable, crammed orderliness that she'd come to associate with faculty spaces—bookshelves so overloaded with meticulously sorted volumes that they sagged in the middle, stacks of scholarly papers neatly corralled into crates set in the corner, open shelves lined with expedition artifacts from the lady's collection.

As the history professor rummaged the desk drawers for a second cup, Concordia's eyes strayed to the windowsill. Miss Phillips kept her favorite artifacts in that spot, including a little stone figurine of a black cat that Concordia especially liked. It was only six inches high, but there was a delicacy to the carving she found appealing.

It wasn't there, though the other pieces remained.

"Where's your cat statuette?"

"Hmm?"

Concordia repeated her question, adding, "You usually keep it there." She pointed.

Miss Phillips glanced over at the sill. "Oh dear, I never noticed. The cleaning staff insisted upon coming in here to dust yesterday. I'd been putting them off long enough as it was. I'll have to ask them." She set a clean mug in front of Concordia, then blew into a gaudy floral cup with a chip in the handle. "Apparently they didn't dust everything, but it will do. Shall I pour?"

"Yes, please. Perhaps whoever put the *Catalogue* in upside down and took the bulb also made off with your figurine?"

"I'm reluctant to suspect a student of outright theft. Besides, my office door is locked when I'm out. Don't worry about it, dear. It will turn up, I'm sure."

After a few moments of quiet sipping—the tea was more of a tisane, infused with citrus peel and quite good—Miss Phillips set her cup aside. "I'm glad you could come by. I have a project in mind to go along with the new display, something that might draw more visitors and perhaps future donors. I believe we can expand the Blake exhibit in the future, but it would be wise to not rely upon a single patron for that. Mr. Symond has been most generous, of course, but who knows when he would tire of the endeavor?"

Concordia smiled behind her cup. Miss Phillips was perceptive to have recognized the dilettante nature of Isaiah Symond's pursuits. The man's own home was evidence of that. He grew easily bored.

"What sort of project?"

"A series of lectures open to the public, upon the subject of William Blake's works. Perhaps you could start with the Canterbury Pilgrims entry." Miss Phillips paused. "If you're available, of course. I know so little about married life and how busy you might already be...."

Concordia leaned forward. "That's a wonderful idea. As far as academic responsibilities, I have only the one seminar in October. To be perfectly honest, I've been feeling distinctly underutilized."

Dorothy Phillips smiled. "Well, we cannot have *that*. We would have to settle the details quickly, however. For maximum effect, we should announce the series at tomorrow night's exhibit opening."

"Perhaps we could start small—say, a two-part series, the first in a few weeks' time, and the second prior to Thanksgiving, before things get really busy at the end of the semester."

"Excellent," Miss Phillips said. "Can you write out lecture titles and brief descriptions right away? I'd need it by tomorrow morning. Then I'll have a student who's skilled at calligraphy put together a small sign."

"Of course."

"Wonderful! We'll announce it at the opening. The mayor and his wife will be attending, along with the trustees, and if I know Edward Langdon, he'll ask a reporter from the *Courant* to cover the event."

Concordia couldn't decide if the tingling sensation along her spine was nervousness or excitement. "I'll have it to you first thing tomorrow, if not sooner."

By the time she stepped out of Founder's Hall, the picnic was well underway. The quadrangle and the grounds beyond were dotted with blankets, hamper baskets, young ladies in bright dresses, and college boys in jaunty straw boaters.

One of the girls stood and waved in her direction. Maisie Lovelace. Madeline scrambled to her feet beside her, turning aside and briefly putting a handkerchief to her face.

Concordia made her way over, dodging sprawled legs and sandwich wrappers. She had just reached them when Lawrence, dressed in a pale gray seersucker jacket, approached quickly from the other side.

"Sorry I'm late," he said breathlessly. "Richardson kept me past the lunch hour with a box of filing." He tipped his cap to Concordia.

"There, you see?" Maisie said, prodding Madeline. "I told you he'd come."

Madeline sniffed. "I don't know if I feel like a picnic anymore."

What a contrary girl. Not satisfied with the rules about restricting young men visiting and yet not happy when the young man *did* visit. Perhaps Madeline had not the inner character she thought.

One thing Concordia knew for sure. All this drama was making her head hurt.

"Are you all right, Mrs. Bradley?" Maisie asked.

"A bit of a headache, that's all." Mercifully, as she was not a chaperone, she was free to come and go. Perhaps the married life *did* have its advantages. "I'll catch up with you later. Have fun."

After a cheese sandwich and an apple at the staff buffet, she felt considerably better. She headed to the library. Why not start on the project for Miss Phillips?

The interior was orderly and mercifully quiet. Only a few students lingered.

She browsed the Chaucer section, pulled out a couple of books, and made her way to the scholars' alcoves, a space designated for upperclassmen and visiting teachers. The librarian, Jane Cowles, had set aside an alcove for her this semester.

She waved to the librarian as she passed the circulation desk but didn't stop to chat. Miss Cowles, a fixture at the school for the past twenty years, was a wiry, intense woman, with a habit of regarding the world along the end of a narrow nose that often quivered over some imagined slight. Concordia found her more than a bit intimidating.

The alcove, though small, was equipped with a small mahogany writing desk, comfortable chair, a shelf, and writing implements.

She plunked her books on the desk and groped for her seat. Abruptly, the rear legs of the chair buckled and she fell backward with a crash.

"Heavens!" Miss Cowles exclaimed, hurrying over to rescue the flailing Concordia, whose knees were tipped in the air, her skirts in her face. "Are you all right, Mrs. Bradley?"

Concordia heard a young lady giggle somewhere behind her,

but she and the librarian were too busy getting her upright to see who it was.

"What happened?" Concordia winced and rubbed the shoulder she'd fallen upon.

Miss Cowles clucked her tongue. "This is the second chair to collapse in as many days." She crouched down to examine the pieces. "I think I see the problem. Several screws have been taken out, where the legs join with the seat."

"It was deliberate, then?"

"I'm afraid so. I regret that I didn't look carefully at the one that broke yesterday. I thought it was simply an old chair that had finally reached the end of its utility. But of course, it's obvious now. Someone sabotaged them." She led Concordia over to a sturdy, upholstered chair. "Sit and catch your breath while I check the other chairs. I'll bring you a reliable one." She hurried away.

Concordia sighed. There were most certainly pranksters on the loose this semester.

Once she was re-settled upon another chair, Concordia spent the rest of the afternoon perusing books, compiling notes, and writing up topic descriptions for Miss Phillips. She looked up from her work finally when Miss Cowles approached and cleared her throat. "I'm sorry, but we have to lock up. I'm needed to help supervise the students around the bonfire."

Mercy, it was already dark outside. "Of course," Concordia said. "I remember how nerve-wracking the bonfire can be." Darkness, flames, and long skirts were not a good combination, but the tradition was stubbornly entrenched.

Miss Cowles's thin nose quivered. "The conflagration grows bigger every year. Count yourself lucky you don't have to worry about such things anymore."

Concordia gave a rueful smile and tucked away the sheet she'd prepared for Miss Phillips. "Just give me a moment while I put the books away."

"No need." Miss Cowles waved a hand. "I'll have a student clean up in the morning."

Concordia took the staff cut-through in back of the library. It was supposed to be a fire exit, really, though teachers regularly used it to get from the library to the Hall stairwell that led up to their offices. The librarian had long ago given up trying to get people to leave through the front doors and go around to the outside staff entrance.

It should only take a minute to drop off her notes to Miss Phillips. And a good thing, too. Her rumbling stomach reminded her she was overdue for supper at home.

She crossed the stairwell and went through the other door to reach the little corridor leading to Miss Phillips's office.

The door was locked. No one was within. Concordia slid the paper under the door in case she returned tonight.

Miss Phillips might be at the bonfire. Once outside, Concordia followed the sounds of laughter and the scent of wood smoke to the pond.

The girls were standing back from the flames, tossing the wood collected from the Bradley farm onto the pile, along with old school papers, stray sticks...anything that would burn. She squinted through the play of firelight. No sign of Dorothy Phillips, though she did see Miss Jenkins, who paced along the perimeter waving a long stick. She headed toward her.

Miss Jenkins had been put in charge of overseeing the bonfire ever since the Singed Skirt Incident of '96. If ever there was a time when the lady's basketball coaching skills were needed to keep the students in line, it was now.

"Not so close!" she called out sharply.

Concordia jumped back instinctively, but she wasn't the object of the reprimand.

"Miss Bonner!" Miss Jenkins clarified, giving Concordia a sideways glance.

The young lady in question dutifully stepped away after tossing a clump of leaves onto the fire.

Miss Jenkins rolled her eyes. "Why must you girls add leaf litter? It is invariably damp and creates far too much smoke. Have you never built a wood fire before?"

All that was missing was the coach's whistle around her neck.

The girl sheepishly dropped the rest.

Concordia hid a smile from the sharp-eyed matron. "Good evening, Miss Jenkins. Have you seen Miss Phillips?"

Hannah Jenkins snorted. "I haven't the leisure to look away from this inferno, believe me." She turned to an older girl who was employing a stout branch to push the glowing bits back into the pile. "Go around to the far side and make sure the freshies are keeping their distance."

The girl hurried off.

"The stack is so large this year I can't see the other side." Miss Jenkins brushed a strand of damp hair from her forehead. "Now, what was it you asked?"

"Miss Phillips," Concordia prompted.

"Ah. She's busy with preparations for the exhibit opening tomorrow. Asked to be excused from the bonfire festivities."

Concordia watched the dancing flames. There seemed little point in finding Dorothy Phillips tonight. She may as well go home.

As she left the pond and took the lighted path toward Rook's Hill, Concordia noticed movement in the shadow of the gazebo off to her right. Two figures, male and female.

Oh-ho-ho, that would not do at all. She changed direction toward the gazebo path. Even though she wasn't a teacher anymore, she certainly wasn't going to allow some dalliance to take place in the shadows.

As she approached the gazebo, she slowed, caution overriding her initial impulse. What if it was a confidential talk between staff members? She'd been too far away to see if the figures were students or teachers. She should first make sure.

As she sidled closer, shielded by the ivy-covered lattice screen, she heard a male voice.

"I'm telling you, it cannot be true. He's playing at some kind of game."

Concordia frowned. Lawrence. Which meant the lady must be—

"He has no reason to lie."

Concordia nodded to herself. Yes—Madeline.

"Well, I don't believe it for a minute," he retorted. "I'm going to talk to him again. We'll settle this once and for all."

The young lady's answer was indistinguishable.

Concordia drew closer, no longer interested in playing glowering matron to a lovers' tryst. Besides, she reasoned, they could not be kissing if they were talking. But what distressed them so? What "he" did they mean?

"I really do care for you, you know." Madeline's voice was tight with anguish. "I'm sorry."

"I will not allow some malicious old man to come between us," Lawrence said. "I'd kill him first."

Concordia sucked in a quiet breath at the ferocity of his tone.

Madeline was weeping now. "Don't talk like that, please. Can't you see it's no use? We cannot change the facts. There is nothing more to be done."

"Maddy. Maddy, don't cry." Lawrence's voice was muffled.

Concordia risked a peek through the vines and saw that he'd embraced the girl.

But she quickly pushed him away. "We can never see each other a—again."

Concordia flattened herself against the vegetation as Madeline ran out. Lawrence did not follow. Curious, she squinted through the gap to see him collapsed on the bench, head in his hands.

Unsure what to do, she left him, quietly resuming her path

toward home. The "old man" Lawrence referred to must be Isaiah Symond. She remembered Madeline saying that Symond seemed distant when they'd first met, possibly disapproving of an *affaire de coeur* just as Lawrence was embarking upon his career.

Had Symond interfered more forcefully? How had he persuaded Madeline to break off the relationship? Had he told her about the young man's profligate past?

Even so, Madeline had no living parents to object to the courtship, and Concordia doubted the girl would break off the romance based upon Lawrence's history. By all appearances, he was a reformed man.

But a man with a temper, she reminded herself.

I'd kill him first.

She shivered.

Perhaps she could get Madeline to confide in her. Or David could speak with Lawrence when he returned. How she wished David were here now, so she could hash it over with him.

Ah, but if David were here, what would he say about her interference?

Step two—the young lady finds herself in trouble. Step three—you intervene. Then...boom!

She wrinkled her nose. Maybe it was better for him to be away at the moment.

Mrs. Houston had left a lamp burning in the kitchen beside a covered plate of cold ham and leftover biscuits. Bless the woman. They'd all be spoiled if this kept up much longer.

After Concordia had eaten, she climbed the stairs to Madeline's room. The door was closed. No light shone underneath.

In the quiet, she thought she heard... She leaned closer. Yes, snuffling sounds. Madeline was crying. Should she knock? Better not. The girl would not appreciate being disturbed. There would be time tomorrow for a talk.

CHAPTER 5

WEEK 4, INSTRUCTOR CALENDAR, SEPTEMBER 1899

I will not be fooled by you into opinions that you please to impose.

— WILLIAM BLAKE

"Whew! I'm glad that's over," Miss Phillips murmured, passing her cloak to the maid at Sycamore House, the residence for the college's president and other male administrators. The building was well suited for social events at the college—receptions, dinners, dances, and the like—as it possessed a spacious dining room, ballroom, terrace, and expanded kitchen facilities.

Concordia handed over her own wrap. "I'd call it a resounding success, thanks to your efforts. The mayor and his wife were quite impressed with the new exhibit. All of the exhibits, actually."

"So long as that reporter from the *Courant* writes a favorable account," Miss Phillips said. "He asked a great many questions about the provenance of the *Descriptive Catalogue*."

"That *was* odd," Concordia said. And Isaiah Symond had not

cared for the reporter's persistence. His answers had been terse and not entirely forthcoming. It did cause one to wonder….

"Shall we go in?" Miss Phillips asked.

"Yes, of course. Are we the last to straggle in?" Concordia, not blessed with tall stature, stood on tiptoe for a better view of the dining room. "I don't see Miss Cowles."

"I doubt she's coming. I overheard the dean berating her for not attending to a new shipment of books. Apparently, there are so many boxes they don't fit in the library storeroom, and he tripped over one of them today. I assume that's where she is now."

"I can't say I blame her for putting it off," Concordia said, as they joined the company in the dining room. "The storeroom is a dreary, windowless space."

Randolph Maynard was the only man she could ever imagine taking the crusty librarian to task. But nothing ever happened fast enough for Maynard's liking. He abhorred disorder.

At the long table of polished cherry, Concordia found herself seated between Ernest Richardson and Isaiah Symond, with Miss Phillips, Miss Pomeroy, and Dean Maynard immediately across from them. Symond was solicitous of the ladies in general and Miss Phillips in particular as she was finding her chair, gallantly pulling out her seat for her and fetching her handkerchief when it dropped to the floor. Judging from the lady's mottled flush and clenched jaw, she did not appreciate such attentions.

"So, Miss Phillips, congratulations on a job well done," President Langdon said. "But tell me, what's this about a Blake lecture series? The mayor's wife showed me the placard."

Dorothy Phillips craned her head toward the head of the table. "A series of two lectures are planned for now. The goal is to create more interest in the new exhibit and generate further donations to the gallery."

Langdon's expression brightened. "Excellent idea!" He gestured to Concordia. "And you are to conduct them? I can think of no one better suited."

Concordia flushed, ever grateful for Langdon's faith in her, which had remained steadfast over the years.

Maynard reached for his wine glass. "Far too much trouble over a musty old book no one cares about."

The staff was used to such sulky mutterings and paid him no attention. Ernest Richardson flashed him an amused glance but said nothing.

Symond took the bait, however. He leaned toward Maynard. "I'd say a great many folks *will* care about it. The notion of a lecture series to bring in outside attention is a splendid idea." He hesitated. "However, shouldn't the college engage a professor to lead it? A man, I mean. What do you think, Mr. Langdon?"

Every female academic in the room stiffened.

"*Ahem.*" President Langdon tugged at his collar as if it had suddenly grown tight. "We don't make that distinction here, Mr. Symond. All the professors at this institution are well qualified, no matter their sex."

Symond spread his hands in apology. "Yes, yes, of course. I misspoke. I meant that one would consider it inappropriate for a married woman—who is naturally no longer associated with the school, save for ties of nostalgia—to give the talks."

"I *am* associated with the school," Concordia retorted. "I'm a lecturing fellow."

Symond sat back. "I beg your pardon?"

Maynard rolled his eyes. "It's an honorary title, Symond, in gratitude for the help Mrs. Bradley has provided to the institution over the years. The position is just enough to keep the lady busy— and out of trouble—until the inevitable little ones come along." He glanced briefly at Concordia, who made no attempt to hide her disdain.

Out of trouble, indeed.

Dean Maynard turned in his chair to meet Langdon's eye. "I have to agree with Mr. Symond in this instance, Edward, if only for the fact that the college shouldn't broadcast the hiring of a married woman in any official capacity."

"Two lectures hardly qualify as disrupting social mores," Miss Phillips interjected. "And Mrs. Bradley is eminently suitable. She was awarded the Romantic Poetry Studies Medal at Vassar and has since published several well-reviewed articles on the Romantics." She nudged the lady principal sitting beside her, who seemed to be in a doze. "Miss Pomeroy, tell them about Concordia's qualifications."

"Huh?" The lady looked up, blinking. "Ah—I regret I've not been attending to the conversation. I'm sure whatever you decide will be suitable." She rose. "If you'll excuse me, it's getting late. I wish you all goodnight."

The gentlemen stood politely. Concordia wondered if she should leave, too, but would it appear churlish? Maynard, at least, would attribute it to a fit of sulks.

How she missed David. He would have found a way to make such unpleasantness easier to tolerate, with an irreverent quip and a surreptitious wink.

A change of subject was in order.

As the plates were removed, she said, "I'm grateful the exhibit opening went smoothly and the prankster didn't strike again."

Miss Phillips was the only one to nod in agreement. The others looked at her blankly.

Dean Maynard folded his arms and glowered. "Mrs. Bradley— what strange contortion of logic would lead one to believe a sophomore prank in the chapel would be duplicated in the gallery?"

"First of all," she retorted, "I doubt the blame for the chapel lay with the sophomores."

President Langdon lifted an eyebrow. "Indeed?"

"I would look to the juniors for that," Concordia said. "From what I understand, they had their reasons to cause trouble for the sophomores. What better way than to play a trick on the sopho-mores' favorite targets—the freshmen?"

Maynard's lip curled in a sneer. "You've been talking to Miss Farraday, I assume. She told me her theory, but I find it highly questionable."

"We should look into it all the same," Langdon said.

"And the pranks have not been confined to the chapel." Concordia explained the sabotaged chairs in the library and the missing bulb and upside-down book in the gallery. Then she glanced over at Miss Phillips. "I wonder, too, if your missing cat statuette is connected."

Miss Phillips shrugged. "I doubt it. I'm sure it will turn up."

Maynard leaned forward. "You're missing something, Miss Phillips?"

The lady gave a reluctant nod. "From my office."

"Aside from the chapel prank," Concordia said, "the remaining incidents have occurred on the first floor of the Hall."

Symond's brows lowered. "Should we be concerned about the security of the Blake exhibit?"

"Not at all," Langdon assured him. "The lock on the double doors of the gallery is new and, unlike the outer doors of Founder's Hall, unique to the gallery. Only three people possess copies of the key—Miss Phillips, the custodian, and myself."

The maid appeared in the dining hall doorway. "Coffee and dessert are now served in the library, Mr. Langdon."

"Excellent!" Langdon got up and tugged his vest down over his wide middle. He gestured toward Symond and Richardson. "You gentlemen are in for a treat. Cook's madeleines are divine."

As they made their way to the library, Concordia noticed Miss Phillips lagging behind, her brow furrowed and her air one of general distraction. Concordia hung back to walk beside her.

"Is something troubling you?" Concordia asked. "It's not the lecture series, is it?"

"Hmm?" She looked up. "Oh—no." She leaned in closer, a flush creeping up her cheeks. "I'm not sure I *locked* the gallery doors."

Concordia's eyes widened. "Oh, dear."

Even though they kept their voices low, Symond, who'd been waiting politely for them to precede him into the library, sucked in a breath. "What's this? The gallery has been left unlocked, with a prankster on the loose?"

As he didn't trouble to keep his voice low, every head turned.

Miss Phillips flushed and met his eye, though Concordia could see a flinching sort of wariness there. "I'm afraid that is a possibility. I should go see." She turned to the maid. "Can you get my cloak, please?"

"I'm coming with you," Symond said.

"That isn't necessary," she said quickly.

"Nonsense," he snapped. "I haven't gone to this much trouble and expense to have something happen to my exhibit."

Miss Phillips sighed. "Nothing is going to *happen*. It's merely a precaution."

Richardson came up behind them. "Want me to come along, Isaiah?"

"No need. It shouldn't take us long."

Concordia put a hand on the lady's arm. "I'll walk out with you. I should be getting home anyway."

Miss Phillips's forehead smoothed in relief.

As they approached the Hall, Concordia noticed all the windows were dark, as would be expected at this late hour. Miss Phillips led the way around to the side door to the stairwell, but Symond hurried ahead of her. He hesitated when the door opened easily. "Isn't this supposed to be locked, too?"

"We usually leave it open for junior staff to access the stairwell to their offices," Miss Phillips said. "I'm more concerned with the gallery doors."

"We should lock this nonetheless," Symond said.

"If you wish." She groped in her reticule. "Where are my keys?" she murmured. "Oh no."

"No keys?" Symond growled.

"When did you have them last?" Concordia asked.

"I honestly cannot remember. My office?"

Symond held the door open. "Well, woman?" he demanded. "Let's get them and lock up. It's getting late."

Even in the narrow light cast by the electric wall sconces, she could see Miss Phillips flush again.

Someone was running toward them across the quadrangle. Even from this distance, Concordia recognized the tall figure and fair hair of Madeline Farraday.

"Mrs. Bradley," the girl called out as she approached, "can you come home quick? Mrs. Houston took a tumble down the stairs. I fetched Miss Jenkins to tend to her. She told me you'd be here. I don't know how badly she's hurt. Her ankle—" She stared at Isaiah. "Oh."

He looked equally startled, then tipped his hat. "Ah, Miss Farraday."

Without another word, the girl turned on her heel and walked away. With a murmured apology, Concordia hurried after her.

It was close to midnight before Mrs. Houston was dozing comfortably in her bed, ankle wrapped and propped on a cushion. Concordia closed the door behind them as she and Miss Jenkins stepped out to the front porch.

"I gave her a draught to help her sleep," Hannah Jenkins said. "Make sure a doctor looks in on her tomorrow. It appears to be a simple sprain, but it's wise to be cautious. I only run a school infirmary. I'm not a physician."

"I'll contact my mother in the morning," Concordia said. "She'll arrange it and likely bring her back to her house to finish recuperating." On a selfish level, she was going to miss the wonderful dinners Mrs. Houston made.

"You'll want to keep that cat out from underfoot in the future," Miss Jenkins said, mouth twitching.

Madeline stepped out to join them on the porch, shawl wrapped around her. "Mrs. Bradley? I'd like to accompany Miss Jenkins back to campus, if I may. I'm missing my notebook. I must have dropped it somewhere between here and the quadrangle. It would be ruined if I don't get it before it rains."

It did, indeed, smell like rain, but Concordia didn't like the idea of a student being out so late. "Miss Jenkins can look for it on her way back to campus."

"I'll bring it inside if I find it," Miss Jenkins promised.

Madeline's brows drew together in distress. "It has all my medieval French poetry translations! I have more studying to do before tomorrow's test. Please?"

Concordia blew out a breath. Mrs. Houston's accident had disrupted everyone's schedule, so she was not about to remonstrate with the girl about the late hour.

Hannah Jenkins no doubt had the same idea. "I'll help her look. The gatekeeper can walk her back here."

"All right," Concordia said. "But don't be long, Miss Farraday. I'll be waiting up for your return."

Concordia awoke with a start in the wingback chair. She glanced at the mantel clock. One thirty! Surely Madeline would have woken her when she returned. She ran up to check the girl's bedroom. It was empty, the bed still made.

It shouldn't have taken this long.

Concordia hesitated. She didn't want to leave Mrs. Houston alone, but she had to find Madeline. She peeked in on the housekeeper. The woman was sleeping soundly.

If she was quick about it, she could be back before Mrs. Houston awoke.

Just in case, Concordia scribbled a note, put it on the house-keeper's side table, and made sure the crutches Miss Jenkins had provided were within easy reach before grabbing a jacket and lantern.

She put up her hood. They'd been right about the rain. At least it was only a light drizzle at the moment. When she reached campus, she kept to the main path, passing the network of side paths leading to the pond, the gazebo, Sycamore House, and the student cottages. Her brisk steps ringing upon the pavement and the gentle *pish* of the rain were the only sounds on this still night. No sign of Madeline.

She reached the quadrangle, bordered on three sides by the chapel, student dining hall, and Founder's Hall. She stopped. A light shone through a side window of the first floor of the Hall. It wasn't coming from the library, but toward the back, where the antiquities gallery was located.

Could Madeline be there?

Concordia hurried over to the side door, expecting it to be secured by now, but the knob turned under her hand.

She took a breath for courage, ignoring the prickle of unease at the base of her neck. Lifting her lantern high, she stepped into the gloom of the stairwell.

And promptly collided with George Lovelace.

"Mrs. Bradley!" he exclaimed. "Lord, you scared me to death." He passed a shaking hand over his mustache and blew out a breath.

"What are you doing here, George? What's going on?"

"Looks like trouble at the gallery." He jerked a thumb over his shoulder, and she pushed past him. "No…wait! You shouldn't go in there."

She ignored him, then wished she hadn't as she stepped through the open gallery doors. She only vaguely noticed the chaos of the room—a glass case tipped over, a table pushed out of position, various exhibit items littering the floor—before she saw Isaiah Symond, sprawled face-down on the floor, unmoving. By the light of the wall sconces, it was obvious he'd been struck on the back of the head. His silver hair was matted with blood.

She knelt beside him, touching him gingerly, as George caught up to her.

She looked up. "He—he's dead."

George helped her up. "Yes. I wanted to spare you, ma'am. Come. This is no place for a lady."

"I—I'm all right. But we should send for the police right away."

He nodded vigorously. "And at least one thing was stolen." He pointed to the glass case on the table that was out of position. It was empty, the door ajar.

The *Descriptive Catalogue* of William Blake was gone.

CHAPTER 6

In the universe, there are things that are known, and things that are unknown, and in between, there are doors.

— WILLIAM BLAKE

George volunteered to stay with the body while Concordia hurried to DeLacey House. It would have been quicker to go straight to see President Langdon at Sycamore House, as they had the only telephone, but she was frantic to find Madeline now. The lady principal could go to Sycamore House with the necessary message. As Miss Phillips and Miss Jenkins also lived at DeLacey, more of the people involved could be roused at once. Miss Phillips should be informed of what had happened at the gallery, and Miss Jenkins would be needed to look at the body. Isaiah Symond was beyond her ministrations, of course, but Miss Jenkins was the only person on hand with medical experience until the police arrived. And Concordia wanted to ask what she knew of Madeline's whereabouts.

At Concordia's sharp knocking, the maid flung open the door. "What on earth—?"

Concordia pushed past her and bounded up the stairs, rapping on each lady's door and moving to the next.

Miss Cowles was the first to step into the hall, even though Concordia hadn't knocked upon her door. She was fully dressed but had taken her hair down and braided it for the night.

The lady narrowed her eyes. "Have you lost your mind, Mrs. Bradley? You are dripping all over the floor."

Before Concordia had a chance to apologize, Lady Principal Pomeroy and Miss Jenkins stepped out of their rooms, each clad in a nightdress, hair tousled from sleep. Miss Pomeroy's spectacles barely sat upon the tip of her nose.

"I'm sorry to disturb you all, but it's quite urgent." Concordia quickly explained what she and George had discovered in the gallery.

Amid the exclamations, Jane Cowles shook her head. "I don't know what this school is coming to," she muttered. She went back in her room and shut the door.

Well, then. Concordia sighed.

"I'll have Mr. Langdon call the police," Miss Pomeroy said. "Give me a moment." She turned to Miss Jenkins. "Would you accompany Concordia to the gallery in the meantime?"

"Right. I'll be dressed in a minute," Hannah Jenkins said, already pulling back her white hair in a topknot as she nudged the door shut with her foot.

"Better take Dorothy with you," Miss Pomeroy called.

"I already knocked on her door," Concordia said, heading back down the hall to tap on it again. "Miss Phillips?" The door was unlocked, and she tentatively opened it.

Concordia had never been in Dorothy Phillips's private quarters before. The study was as orderly as one would expect, except for an open valise propped on the hardback chair in front of the desk.

She quickly passed through and knocked on the bedroom door before pushing it open. "Miss Phillips?"

The history professor was fast asleep in a wingback chair, fully dressed, face mashed against the side. She was beginning to rouse, squinting up at her in confusion as she groped for her spectacles.

"Concordia?" She smoothed her hair and shook out her skirts as she stood. "What are you doing here?"

"Something terrible has happened."

While Miss Pomeroy hurried to rouse President Langdon and telephone the police, Concordia, Miss Jenkins, and Miss Phillips headed to the gallery.

Concordia touched Miss Jenkins on the elbow. "Madeline didn't return to the farmhouse," she murmured. "I've been looking for her. Do you know where she is?"

"The girl found her notebook fairly quickly," Miss Jenkins said. "It was on a bench by the fountain, as she'd thought."

"What then?"

"She thanked me and headed for the gatehouse."

"What time was this?"

"No more than half an hour after we'd left you. Twelve thirty, I'm guessing."

Concordia stopped. More than an hour ago. She didn't like this at all. Where could Madeline be? "I'm going to talk to the gatekeeper. I'll catch up to you later."

Miss Jenkins nodded. "Of course."

The gatekeeper, Mr. Clyde, lived in a small cottage adjoining the gatehouse. Concordia knocked repeatedly, pushing the wet hair out of her eyes as she waited.

Finally, he opened the door as he finished thrusting a burly arm into an overcoat to cover his nightshirt. "What in blazes is goin' on? Do ya know what time it is?"

"I do indeed, and the police would have woken you soon enough," she retorted. She related the discovery of the body in the gallery.

He sucked in a breath. "Lordy, not again? Ev'ry year, it's more o' the same."

Concordia rolled her eyes. Not *every* year. "But there's something else. Have you seen Miss Farraday? She was supposed to ask you for an escort back to my house tonight. Twelve thirty or so. We haven't been able to locate her."

His eyes widened. "Ya don' think she was murdered, too?"

"Nonsense," she snapped, although she was distinctly uneasy about the two incidents happening on the same night.

"Sorry, ma'am. Nobody came knocking at my door until you showed up."

"Did you see anyone pass by, perhaps headed for one of the paths up Rook's Hill?"

"I locked up at ten o'clock on the dot"—he gestured to the iron gate built into the tall, fenced hedgerow—"and went to bed. Didn't see a soul. Mebbe she went out the east gate? It stayed open late, 'cause of the reception tonight."

The east gate, located near the stable, was the private entrance for the residents and visitors of Sycamore House. There was no gatekeeper there, as Langdon, Maynard, and the stable master each had a key and could come and go at will. Concordia shook her head. "That would take her well out of the way of the farmhouse."

The gatekeeper scratched his head. "Don' know what to tell ya, ma'am."

"All right, if you see her—" She broke off at the sound of carriage wheels approaching. A black coach, driven by a uniformed policeman, was pulling up to the gate. The gatekeeper muttered under his breath as he grabbed the key from a hook.

Concordia watched as Mr. Clyde turned the key and swung

the gate wide. The vehicle proceeded through, then stopped again when it reached her.

Even in the dim light of the coach lanterns, the unmistakable, melancholic face of Lieutenant Capshaw came into view through the drizzle. He was already shaking his head as he stepped out of the coach.

She could practically read his thoughts. *So. Another body, Mrs. Bradley?*

She couldn't blame him, of course. There had been a shocking number of bodies over the years of their acquaintance. And since his marriage to her best friend Sophia, that acquaintance had deepened to a friendship of sorts, though neither was quite ready for Christian-name familiarity.

But he didn't say a word until he was close enough for her to see the rain roll off his cap brim as he tipped it courteously toward her. His eyes narrowed as he looked her up and down.

She knew she must be a sight, wet hair plastered to her head and dripping down her neck, soaked hem dragging below her coat —which she only now realized was misbuttoned. *Drat.*

"When the precinct sergeant told me a teacher had found the body," Capshaw said, "you were certainly *not* the person I expected. In retrospect, that should have been my first assumption."

Concordia folded her arms to suppress her shivering. "It wasn't solely *my* discovery, Lieutenant. Mr. Lovelace was with me at the time."

"Lovelace...the school's handyman?"

"Yes, you met him last year."

He raised an eyebrow. "Indeed. When will this school cease to be embroiled in trouble?" The last was muttered under his breath. He gave a short bow and held the coach door wide. "Let us talk on the way, Mrs. Bradley."

She took his proffered arm and stepped in.

Inside the coach, another uniformed man sat on the bench across from them. His burly form took up most of the seat.

"Hello, Sergeant Maloney," she said.

He touched his cap brim politely in her direction. "Ma'am."

Heavens, how many policemen did she know by name? And from other parts of the country, too. Best not to start listing them all. It was a wonder David had worked up the nerve to marry her.

"Now then," Capshaw said, as the vehicle proceeded down the drive toward Founder's Hall, "how did you and Mr. Lovelace come to discover a dead man, and at this hour? Although perhaps the time is immaterial, as I have been called to this establishment at all sorts of odd hours. It fails to surprise me now."

"I couldn't sleep," Concordia began, deciding to leave Madeline Farraday out of it for now. "So I went for a walk."

"At two in the morning? And in the rain? Doesn't Mr. Bradley object to his wife roaming the school grounds alone at night?"

"Mr. Bradley is out of town," she retorted.

He rubbed his neck wearily. "That explains plenty."

In the dim light of the carriage, she saw Maloney put up a hand to unsuccessfully hide his smirk.

Talk of David reminded Concordia of something important. "Lieutenant, have the Bradleys been informed yet?"

Capshaw blinked. "Informed?"

"The dead man is my husband's great-uncle, Isaiah Symond. Mr. Langdon was supposed to have told the police that when he called."

"Word of it didn't reach me. I'll take care of it when we're finished. But first, tell me what the man was doing here at all. Does he hold a position at the school?"

"No. He was here for the opening of the new exhibit and attended the reception that followed."

She had just finished explaining Symond's donation to the school when the coach pulled up to Founder's Hall.

Several people hovered uncertainly in the vestibule in front of the double doors of the gallery—President Langdon, Lady Principal Pomeroy, Dean Maynard, Miss Phillips, and George Lovelace.

Edward Langdon brightened at the sight of Capshaw. "Ah, Lieutenant. We weren't sure where to wait. We didn't want to go inside and disturb anything, although I did ask Miss Jenkins to have a look at Mr. Symond, to—*ahem*—make sure... Here she is." He shifted his bulky frame as the door opened behind him and Miss Jenkins stepped out.

Capshaw gave a short bow toward the lady. "Quite dead, I trust?"

"Oh, yes. Quite," the lady said. "Struck in the back of the head."

Capshaw gave a dismissive nod and started to move past her.

"His nose is bloody, and there are bruises under his eyes, as if he'd been punched as well," Miss Jenkins went on. "I wonder if he was struck in the face first, then hit the back of his head as he fell?"

Not much flustered the infirmarian, Concordia marveled.

Capshaw's face took on a pained expression. "If you please, Miss—Jenkins, the sergeant and I must get on with our work." He gestured to the patrolman. "Escort Mrs. Bradley and Mr. Lovelace upstairs. There's a staff lounge on the third floor where they can wait. Oh, and Miss Phillips—you're the curator here? You, too, if you please."

"I'd rather go home and wait there, lieutenant," Concordia said. "I have an injured housekeeper who shouldn't be alone." And she wanted to be there when—*if?*—Madeline turned up.

"Sorry, ma'am. I want the three of you at hand when I'm finished," Capshaw said.

The lady principal stiffened and exchanged a glance with President Langdon.

"I'll go to the farmhouse and stay with Mrs. Houston until you're back," Hannah Jenkins offered. "After all, I'm not needed here, as a witness or a nurse."

Capshaw frowned. "You shouldn't walk all that way alone. We don't know who's responsible for Mr. Symond's death and where that person might be now."

"Don't worry. I'll wake Miss Cowles and take her with me." Miss Jenkins smiled. "The lady is fearsome enough if crossed."

A truer word was never spoken. Concordia remembered Miss Cowles's fury at the condition of her beloved library after the Horse Prank of '97. The miscreants were scrubbing and re-shelving for a week.

Capshaw shook his head. "That won't do, miss, even with two of you ladies." He blew out a breath. "All right, I can briefly spare the patrolman who drove us here. Tell him to be quick about it, and return as soon as he's seen you safely to the farmhouse."

Miss Jenkins inclined her head. "Of course."

Concordia passed her the house key. "You have to give the screen door a hard tug to get it open—it sticks." *Mercy*, they'd meant to fix that weeks ago.

The staff lounge was a homely, comfortable room. A hodge-podge of rockers, settees, upholstered chairs, and mismatched occasional tables filled the space. Concordia rummaged in the cabinets for a tea towel to dry her hair and hem, then got the kettle going. Dorothy Phillips sank wordlessly into a chair. George Lovelace sat across from her, nervously twisting his tweed cap in his hands.

The awkward silence was mercifully broken when Miss Pomeroy, Mr. Langdon, and Mr. Maynard walked in.

"Did the lieutenant ask you to stay as well?" Concordia asked.

"We decided to keep you company," Miss Pomeroy said.

Miss Phillips shifted over on the settee for the lady principal. "That's quite kind."

Langdon settled into a wooden rocker, which creaked alarm-ingly under his bulk. "I should be on hand. I'm responsible for what goes on at the school. I can't imagine going back to bed now, with that poor man lying dead in the Hall."

Miss Phillips winced.

Maynard offered no explanation for why he was staying, however. With a silent scowl, he took a seat by the door, crossing his elegantly trousered legs and drumming restless fingers upon one knee. Even at this hour, he managed to look perfectly groomed, especially compared to President Langdon, whose collar was askew and vest wasn't completely buttoned.

Of course, Concordia was not one to criticize.

There is only so much tea one can drink and mindless small talk one can engage in—avoiding the one topic that brought everyone here at this hour, of course—before smiles thinned, polite nods grew fewer and farther between, and silence prevailed.

Randolph Maynard was the first whose patience cracked. He abruptly quit the room to pace the hallway. He knew better than to go downstairs to the gallery, of course. George soon joined him in the corridor. She could hear their quiet murmur of conversation, but nothing of what was said.

Concordia confined her own restlessness to pacing from her seat to the window to look out. The rain had stopped, and the blackness was gradually taking on a grayish tint. Her thoughts turned to Madeline. What was she up to? Had she returned to the house at last?

She hugged her arms across her chest. There was far too much mischief afoot tonight.

Finally, Capshaw and Maloney returned to the lounge, Maynard and Lovelace trailing behind.

"The doctor has arrived to examine the dead man," Capshaw said. "I have some questions in the meantime."

"Would you care for some tea?" the lady principal offered.

"Thanks, miss. That would be welcome," Capshaw said, with a

nod to Maloney.

Everyone else gritted their teeth and waited.

Once the policemen were settled with their cups, Maloney in a chair beside the door—did he think someone would attempt an escape?—and Capshaw seated across from Concordia, the lieutenant began.

"I need to understand the events of last night and this morning and establish the last person to see Isaiah Symond alive."

Maynard snorted. "The murderer was the *last one*, Lieutenant. Obviously."

Capshaw ignored the jibe, though Concordia, having known him for some years now, could see by his deliberate movements—carefully setting aside his cup, smoothing his reddish mustache, extricating his oft-folded wad of notes, and slowly thumbing the pages—that he was keeping a firm check on his temper. Maynard could test the patience of a saint.

"Mrs. Bradley has explained Mr. Symond's donation to the gallery," Capshaw said. "The exhibit opening took place last night, I understand. What time did it conclude?"

"It was rather late," Miss Phillips said. "A little after nine o'clock, I believe."

"What happened after that?"

President Langdon answered. "We returned to Sycamore House for a reception dinner, in honor of Mr. Symond and those involved in working on the exhibit."

"Who attended?" Capshaw's tiny nub of a pencil was poised over the page.

"Let me think." Langdon leaned forward, ticking off the list on his fingers. "Miss Pomeroy—though she left a bit earlier than the rest—Miss Phillips, Mrs. Bradley, Mr. Richardson, Mr. Maynard, Mr. Symond, and myself."

"When did Mr. Symond leave the gathering?"

Langdon glanced over at Dorothy Phillips.

She shrugged. "I'm not sure exactly when we left. Ten thirty, perhaps?"

"'We'?" Capshaw echoed.

"I wanted to make sure the gallery was locked up," she said. "We'd had trouble with campus pranks lately. Mr. Symond and Mrs. Bradley offered to accompany me."

Capshaw flashed a look at Concordia, who shook her head.

"I'm afraid I'm not a good witness for you, Lieutenant. A student intercepted me just as we reached the Hall. Our house-keeper had fallen down the stairs. I left Mr. Symond and Miss Phillips in order to get home quickly."

"I see." Capshaw turned back to Miss Phillips. "What happened then?"

"Mr. Symond and I checked the doors, and they were indeed unlocked." She looked down at her hands. "That was my lapse, I'm afraid."

"Which doors do you mean?" Capshaw asked. "The outer doors of the building?"

"Those were locked, except for a side door to the stairwell," Miss Phillips said. "We customarily leave that one open, you see, in case a junior faculty member needs to work late in her office. They don't have building keys."

"So you mean the inside double doors that lead directly into the gallery."

"Yes," Miss Phillips said. "I had, indeed, neglected to lock those."

"So you and Symond locked the doors and left?" Capshaw asked.

The history professor sighed. "I couldn't find my keys. At the time, I wondered if I'd accidentally locked them in my office." She glanced at George.

"It turns out I'd taken them by mistake," he said. "That's why I was returning to campus. I knew Miss Phillips couldn't lock the gallery doors without them—unless she fetched the custodian. I planned to lock up and then leave them for her."

"I'll get to you momentarily, sir," Capshaw said. "I have a number of questions for you in particular."

George swallowed.

"Go on, Miss Phillips," Capshaw prompted. "Did you locate the custodian to lock up?"

She shook her head. "He'd already gone for the day."

"What did you do then?"

"Mr. Symond and I went into the gallery to check that everything was in order."

"And was that the case?"

Miss Phillips stiffened. "Yes. Of course."

"Then what happened?"

"I went to DeLacey House to borrow another senior staff key. My belief was that, once all the outer doors of the Hall were locked—as I said, the side door was the only one open—the gallery would be secure enough until morning. "

"Did Mr. Symond accompany you?"

"No." The lady's forehead creased. "He was quite angry with my carelessness and insisted upon standing guard at the gallery."

Capshaw raised an eyebrow. "Indeed?"

"He is—was—a very stubborn man," Miss Phillips said. "Once a notion was fixed in his mind, there was no budging him."

"So you fetched a building key and locked the door?"

"Yes." She turned to the lady principal. "You'd left yours on the hall table in DeLacey House. I hope you don't mind. You'd already retired. I didn't want to disturb you."

"I wondered if they'd been moved," Miss Pomeroy said, "but I often lose track of such things. No matter, dear."

"And yet the side door was unlocked a little while ago," Concordia said. "Unless"—she glanced at George—"you unlocked it when you let yourself in?"

The handyman hesitated. "I didn't need to. It was already open."

Capshaw shifted in his seat. "Mrs. Bradley, I will ask the questions, if you please. Now then, Miss Phillips, your account doesn't make any sense. If you accomplished your objective and the door was secured, why was Mr. Symond *still in the gallery?* Wouldn't he have left with you?"

She blushed and looked down at her hands. "I didn't tell him. I simply locked the door from the outside…and left."

"You left him there?" Capshaw's tone was incredulous.

"The man was intolerable, Lieutenant. I thought it would serve him right to waste an hour or so of his time before he realized what was going on. Oh, he wasn't trapped in there," she added hastily. "The stairwell door opens from the inside, locked or no. Of course, I had no idea he'd be in any danger, alone in the gallery."

"What time did you leave him?"

"A short time after eleven, I'd say."

Capshaw tapped his pencil upon the page. "And Mrs. Bradley and Mr. Lovelace discovered him dead close to two in the morning. Nearly three hours later. But if it was locked as you say, no one should have been able to get in without a building key. And if Mr. Lovelace's account is correct, someone *did* unlock that door sometime after you left."

"My account *is* correct, sir," George said gruffly.

Capshaw looked across the room at Sergeant Maloney. "The doctor should be finished by now. Fetch him for me, if you please."

After Maloney left, Capshaw nodded toward the handyman. "You say you returned at this ungodly hour to bring back Miss Phillips's keys?" His voice dripped with skepticism. "Why not wait until the morning?"

The man self-consciously stroked his raggedy, graying mustache. "At the time, it didn't seem so outrageous. I was worried about the campus mischief-maker. I couldn't sleep."

"There seems to be a great deal of that going around,"

Capshaw muttered, shooting at quick look in Concordia's direction. "Would someone tell me about these pranks?"

Miss Phillips detailed the incidents.

"All right then." Capshaw turned back to George. "You were concerned about the gallery exhibit and wanted to make sure the keys were restored to Miss Phillips, correct?"

"That's right."

"What time did you get here, Mr. Lovelace?"

"At the same time as Mrs. Bradley. We encountered each other in the stairwell."

Concordia shifted in her chair. "Not quite. Mr. Lovelace was already inside the building. I ran into him as he was coming out."

Lovelace shot her a look. Annoyance? Dismay? She couldn't tell.

"I was going for help," he said.

Maloney stuck his head in and gestured to Capshaw, who stood.

"Excuse me."

As hard as Concordia strained to hear through the cracked-open door, it was no use. Capshaw and the doctor kept their voices low.

Soon Capshaw and Maloney came back in and resumed their seats.

Capshaw now carried an object wrapped in a large handkerchief. He regarded George thoughtfully. "Symond was struck in the back of the head with this." He unwrapped a heavy, metal wrench and held it up. A dark substance adhered to one end. Concordia's stomach twisted. It was blood.

"Is this yours?"

George blew out a breath. "Yes. But I certainly didn't kill him! Why would I? Anyone could have picked that up. I left my tools here all week, tucked out of the way. With all the work needed doing at the gallery, it was more convenient." He turned pleading eyes toward Dorothy Phillips.

84

Miss Phillips stared at him for a long moment. Was her faith in George shaken?

Finally, the curator nodded. "It's true, Lieutenant. I gave him permission to leave his tools."

"When were you last at the gallery, Mr. Lovelace?" Capshaw asked. "Before you ran into Mrs. Bradley this morning, I mean."

"Yesterday afternoon, before the exhibit opening. I was replacing the bulb and cleaning up the work area before the guests arrived."

"And then what?"

"I went home."

"At what time?"

"Four o'clock."

"And that was the last time you were at the gallery, before you and Mrs. Bradley discovered the body?"

George shifted impatiently. "I have told you so already, sir."

Dorothy Phillips leaned forward. "Lieutenant Capshaw, why all the questions? I left Mr. Symond entirely alone at eleven. There was absolutely no one about, including Mr. Lovelace."

Capshaw flipped a page and studied it briefly. "Mr. Langdon, when did the rest of the party leave your residence to head home?"

"Not long after Symond did, perhaps another thirty minutes. Except for Mr. Maynard and myself, of course, as we live there. Why is that significant?"

"The doctor tells me Mr. Symond was killed several hours ago." He gave Dorothy Phillips a penetrating look. "Shortly after you left him, Miss Phillips."

She shuddered.

Dean Maynard waved a hand in irritation. "It seems to me you are flailing about for a suspect, Lieutenant. First the handyman, and now our curator. This isn't some outré sensation novel. The *Descriptive Catalogue* is gone, and a man is dead. The two are obviously connected. The answer is simple—we have a thief who was after the new exhibit item. He entered the gallery, panicked when he saw Symond, and attacked him. Symond was well advanced in years. Probably didn't stand a chance against a young, desperate criminal."

"I agree it's possible," Capshaw said. "However, according to Miss Phillips, she locked the last of the outer doors. None appear to have been forced. No scratches or other damage."

"What if the man used a lockpick?" Concordia asked. "After all, if it was a professional thief..." Her voice trailed off at the sight of the dean glaring at her.

"And what would you know about lockpicks, Mrs. Bradley?" Maynard growled.

Capshaw's mustache twitched as he glanced down at his notepad. "News of the exhibit was widely disseminated, I trust?"

Everyone nodded.

"Was the book very valuable?" he asked Miss Phillips.

She pursed her lips as she considered. "In specific collectors' circles, it might fetch a couple hundred dollars."

Capshaw made a note. "It's an enticement, although any decent sneak thief could make as much in a week with less effort and risk."

"Setting aside for the moment the absurdity of juxtaposing 'decent' and 'sneak thief,'" Maynard snapped, "what do you mean by 'less effort and risk'?"

"Selling such an item would be fraught with risk, as its theft would be widely publicized. Then there is the difficulty of obtaining it in the first place. You must concede that a strange man sneaking around a ladies' campus would attract notice. Further, such a man would be unfamiliar with the building and what sort of locks he would encounter."

"What if he'd attended the opening earlier that evening, to ascertain those details?" Concordia asked.

Capshaw turned to President Langdon. "If you would provide a list of the exhibit attendees, we'll look into that."

"Of course," Langdon said.

"More likely, the culprit is someone known to Symond and familiar with the campus. We have much to learn about the victim." He passed his notepad and pencil to Concordia. "You say Isaiah Symond has relations in town? Write down the addresses, if you please. I'll want to interview them. They may have additional information as to motive. It may not be connected to the gallery at all."

Concordia scribbled John Bradley's townhouse address. "I don't know if his relations will be much help. The family was not especially close to the man." She passed back the notepad. "However, he had a long-time friend and associate, Ernest Richardson. He may be able to tell you more."

"Business associate?" Capshaw asked.

"Mr. Symond's lawyer, actually."

"What is his address?"

"I've never been to his home," Concordia said. "He teaches here at the school, however."

Langdon straightened. "I can get it for you, Lieutenant."

Capshaw insisted upon having the patrolman drive Concordia home. It was after four o'clock in the morning by the time she opened her front door.

Miss Jenkins was reading in the parlor, a tea tray on the ottoman. "Welcome back. The itinerant Miss Farraday has returned."

Simultaneous sensations of relief and anger washed over her. "How long ago?"

"She was already here when I arrived. Couldn't have been long, however, judging from the dripping coat in the hall. The girl was bursting with apologies, naturally, and had a story to beat the band."

Concordia sank onto the settee. "And what story was that?"

"She claims that, after she found her notebook, she encountered a friend and spent the next hour in conversation. When she realized the time, she decided not to disturb the gatekeeper and hurried back here alone."

"That's a rather thin story."

Miss Jenkins snorted. "Quite. And where would she and this 'friend' have gone to talk? It's too cold and dark for a prolonged out-of-doors conversation."

"The more likely explanation is that the notebook was a ruse all along. It gave her an excuse to slip out to meet Lawrence."

"Lawrence?"

That's right, the infirmarian didn't know about Madeline and Lawrence. Concordia gave her an abbreviated explanation. "But what's odd," she finished, "is that I overheard them arguing yesterday. She was breaking it off with him."

Hannah Jenkins rolled her eyes. "You know these young ladies. On again, off again. One might as well be watching table tennis."

"I suppose. I assume you sent her to bed?"

Miss Jenkins nodded.

They were both quiet for a while, staring at the dying fire. "I don't know what I'm going to do about Madeline," Concordia said finally. "This behavior will get her expelled."

"She's not your responsibility," Miss Jenkins pointed out, covering a yawn behind her book. "She's only staying here temporarily, correct?"

"True. She returns to her boarding house tomorrow, in fact. But it's difficult not to feel a sense of responsibility toward the girl. After all, she's here at the college because of my intervention. Miss Jenkins, do you think—"

She broke off as she noticed the infirmarian's chin had dropped to her chest. The lady was snoring softly.

Concordia quietly got up, covered her with an afghan, and turned out the light.

CHAPTER 7

One thought fills immensity.

— WILLIAM BLAKE

$\mathcal{C}$oncordia's sleep was deep, dreamless, and all too brief, as Lieutenant Capshaw showed up at her door only a few hours later.

"Heavens" was all the startled Concordia could manage, as an equally sleepy Hannah Jenkins came to wake her with the news. "Who else did you say accompanied him here?"

"Your father-in-law and brother-in-law, along with Mr. Richardson." Miss Jenkins passed over a dressing gown as Concordia felt for her slippers. "I pointed them toward the parlor. The policeman asked to see Miss Farraday as well."

Why on earth was Capshaw bringing them all *here*? And why talk to Madeline? Concordia glanced at her mantel clock—seven. What new information could he have collected in such a short time?

"Madeline's still asleep?"

Miss Jenkins nodded. "Mrs. Houston as well, although the medicine I gave her should wear off soon."

"All right, let's leave Mrs. Houston undisturbed. I'll wake Miss Farraday."

"I'll tell them you'll be down in a few minutes." Miss Jenkins passed a weary hand behind her neck. "Then I should be heading back to campus."

"Yes, of course, there's no need for you to stay," Concordia said. "I'm grateful to you for helping out last night."

After a quick brush of her short, red hair, Concordia dressed in her simplest house gown and hurried to Madeline Farraday's room.

Her knock was met with a faint *hummh* on the other side of the door.

Concordia opened it. Madeline was making a half-hearted attempt to prop herself upright.

"Mrs. Bradley, I—I'm so sorry about last night—"

"We'll address that later." Whatever the excuse, this wasn't the time. "We have company. I also have sad news to relate." She quickly filled her in on finding Isaiah Symond dead in the gallery and the *Catalogue* missing.

Madeline looked at her blankly.

"You must be quick," Concordia prodded. "Lieutenant Capshaw, John Bradley, Lawrence, and Mr. Richardson are all waiting for us downstairs."

The girl flung back the covers. "Lawrence! He's *here*? Why?"

How odd that the young lady focused her attention upon Lawrence's presence rather than the policeman's. And made no comment on the fact that a man had died.

"I can't explain why any of them are here," Concordia said impatiently. "Best to dress now, and we'll find out what's going on."

As they entered the parlor, Concordia noticed Capshaw first, as he stood in the far corner conferring with Sergeant Maloney.

Capshaw nodded toward Maloney. The sergeant left, tipping his cap and bowing in their direction on his way out.

Although Capshaw's fatigue was evident if one looked for it—the shadows under his deep gray eyes, the slower stride—he gave Madeline a sharp, assessing look as she crossed the room. The girl kept her eyes lowered, not looking up at anyone. She perched beside Concordia on the settee.

"Now then, Miss Farraday," Capshaw began briskly, settling himself upon the ottoman across from her, "Mrs. Bradley has no doubt informed you of Mr. Symond's unfortunate demise?"

"Just now." Madeline glanced, finally, at Lawrence Bradley, who drummed upon his knee with restless fingers.

"There is a valuable exhibit item missing as well," Capshaw went on. "We have not yet determined if that's directly connected to his death."

Madeline tucked a blond strand back into her hastily arranged chignon. "What have I to do with either one?"

"I'll get to that in a moment." Capshaw gestured to Concordia. "Mrs. Bradley, have I your permission to search the premises?"

She stiffened in surprise. "You're looking for the *Catalogue*, I assume? You must know it cannot be here."

"We're searching the entire campus, and you're quite close," he said.

Concordia shrugged. "Of course, if you feel it necessary."

"But why did you search *our* house, Lieutenant?" John Bradley retorted. "We are nowhere near the college. Poor Drusilla had an attack of the vapors at the sight of a policeman pawing through her possessions in the wee hours of the morning."

"You must not take it personally, Mr. Bradley," Capshaw said. "Anyone with an interest in the victim's welfare—or demise—is being questioned and searched. We've gone through Mr. Richardson's living quarters and office as well." He waved a hand toward Ernest Richardson, who appeared irritatingly alert and well-groomed for the early hour—every hair, button, and seam in place.

Of course, he had not discovered a corpse in the middle of the night.

"Does David know yet?" Concordia asked her father-in-law.

"Not yet," John said. "I plan to send word as soon as the telegraph office opens." He flashed a look at the policeman. "Although my son may not be eager to return to the ignominy of a murder charge against his family."

"There is no murder charge, sir." Capshaw turned back to Madeline Farraday, who sat listless, barely paying attention to the conversation. "Miss Farraday, I understand that you were the one who fetched Mrs. Bradley last night, when the housekeeper suffered a mishap?"

Concordia gave a start of surprise. She hadn't told Capshaw the name of the student who'd come to get her. A most thorough man.

"That's right," Madeline said.

"What time was that?"

The girl glanced at Concordia. "It was after curfew. I'm not sure of the exact time."

"I'd already told you, Lieutenant," Concordia said impatiently. "Ten thirty."

"Miss Farraday," Capshaw said, "you returned here to the farmhouse with Mrs. Bradley and Miss Jenkins, correct?"

"Yes."

"And you stayed here the rest of the night, I assume?"

Madeline flashed Concordia a pleading look, but Concordia shook her head. She was not going to lie for the girl. "Go on, tell him."

Madeline explained her errand.

Capshaw's eyebrows nearly met his hairline. He gestured to Concordia. "You gave permission for this?"

"Miss Jenkins was heading back to DeLacey House anyway, so they returned to campus together. The young lady's study routine had been disrupted by Mrs. Houston's unfortunate tumble down the stairs, so I bent the rules a bit. The plan was for her to ask the gatekeeper to escort her back after she found her notebook."

The room grew quiet as Capshaw scribbled notes. Concordia glanced over at Lawrence, who was trying, unsuccessfully, to catch Madeline's eye. In the meantime, her father-in-law, John Bradley, perched upon the edge of a rocker, watching his son intently.

Finally, Capshaw looked up. "Miss Farraday, did you find your notebook?"

"Yes."

"And what time did you return with it to the Bradley house?"

Madeline looked down at her hands. "Almost two o'clock," she mumbled.

"We must have missed each other," Concordia said. "I was setting out to look for you around one thirty. I didn't see you at all."

"I took the sheep tracks instead of Rook's Hill," Madeline explained. "It's longer, but I didn't want to navigate the steeper slope in the dark." She grimaced. "I *am* sorry for worrying you, Mrs. Bradley."

Capshaw brought them back to the topic at hand. "It seems a long time to search for a notebook, Miss Farraday." He fixed her with a piercing look. "Is that *all* that transpired in that time?"

"Well, no...I was engaged in a confidential conversation with... a friend."

"Ah." Capshaw's pencil hovered over the page. "And that friend's name?"

She shook her head. "I promised not to say anything."

"Why fix your attention upon Miss Farraday?" Concordia interrupted. "As I said before, she had no association with Isaiah Symond."

Capshaw's expression grew more melancholy, if that was possible. "On the contrary, Miss Farraday has a rather *close* association to Mr. Symond." He leaned toward the girl and met her eyes. "You know to what I refer?"

She bowed her head. Concordia saw tears glinting upon her eyelashes.

"Have I your permission to explain it to Mrs. Bradley?" he asked.

She waved her hand, not looking up.

"Explain what?" Concordia asked impatiently.

"According to the dead man's attorney here"—he gestured to Richardson—"Isaiah Symond recently discovered that Miss Farraday was his daughter."

Concordia's mouth dropped open. Madeline's anguished words from two nights before came back to her.

Can't you see it's no use? We cannot change the facts. There is nothing more to be done.

So that was why they could no longer see one another. Lawrence and Madeline were blood relations.

Concordia glanced over at Lawrence, who had crossed the room to pass his handkerchief to Madeline. He tried to pat her hand, but she waved him away.

Concordia remembered his words to the young lady.

I will not allow some malicious old man to come between us. I'd kill him first.

But surely, it had been spoken in the heat of the moment. Lawrence wouldn't really kill his great-uncle. Would he?

"As Miss Farraday is enrolled in my economics class and she already knew me," Richardson continued, "Isaiah asked me to break the news to her and to see if she would be willing to meet with him. He wanted to explain the reasons for his neglect and his plan to make things right."

"Was that when you came here to see her?" Concordia asked.

"That's right."

Madeline looked up at last, cheeks flaming. "I wanted nothing to do with Isaiah Symond. Just when I was making something of my life and was happy, he comes to ruin it. Again."

Lawrence leaned forward in his chair. "We still don't know if it's true, Maddy. The old man could have been mistaken."

Richardson's brow furrowed. "The similarity to the girl's mother is striking. Isaiah showed me a photograph." His expression softened as he watched Madeline dab her eyes. "He meant you no harm, Miss Farraday. He wanted you to know, before your relationship with his grandnephew progressed any further."

"*This* is why Miss Farraday is a suspect?" Concordia asked Capshaw. "You believe that in a fit of rage she clubbed Mr. Symond over the head because he was her long-lost father?"

"Rage or revenge," Capshaw said calmly. "It's a working theory. And young Bradley here is a possibility. Or the two of them together."

John stood. "I have already told you, Lieutenant, my son could not possibly have harmed Isaiah. Besides, he had no opportunity. He was at home, with me, the entire evening."

"Not the entire evening," Capshaw said. He flipped back a page and scanned it. "According to Symond's parlor maid, your son showed up at his house late last night, close to ten thirty. She says he was clearly intoxicated and exceedingly upset when she told him her master was not home. Further, she'd told the young man exactly where Symond was that evening—at the college."

John paled, glanced at his son, then back at Capshaw. "You didn't say anything about this before."

"The sergeant just informed me of it." Capshaw folded his arms and sat back, as if he had all the time in the world for a cozy chat. "So, do you either of you wish to amend your statements?"

Lawrence shifted restlessly. His father put a staying hand on his arm. "So what if my son went off in a huff to Isaiah's house? As the maid told you, the old man wasn't there, so no harm done. It doesn't mean anything."

Capshaw's nostrils flared. "It means that you gave a deliberately misleading statement, sir, when you said your son was with you all evening. That is a prosecutable offense. Mr. Richardson here can tell you that the courts frown upon lying to the police."

John flushed. "Very well." His voice was stiff. "Lawrence was home when I retired at ten o'clock. I concede I did not know for a fact whether he remained there the entire evening when I made that statement. I apologize."

Capshaw turned to Lawrence. "What did you do when you left Symond's house?"

"I returned home," Lawrence said. He passed a hand over his wavy, dark hair—so much like David's—leaving it standing on end.

"Can anyone in the house corroborate that? The staff, perhaps?"

"I used my key. Both family and staff had retired."

Capshaw *tsked* under his breath. "That is problematic, sir."

"How so?"

"You knew Mr. Symond was on campus for the gallery opening and reception. The maid had told you so. If you had gone straight there from Symond's house, you could have arrived in time to see Miss Phillips leave your great-uncle alone in the gallery to guard it. We already know you were upset by his role in disrupting your romance with Miss Farraday. By the maid's account, your temper was inflamed by excessive liquor. A heavy wrench was at hand. Easy enough to impulsively grab the tool and strike him."

"But what about the missing exhibit piece?" Richardson asked. His expression took on an eager, meditative quality, as if it were a mere puzzle to be sorted out. Concordia was simultaneously envious and irritated by the man's detachment. "If the young man was as flagged as you say, would he have had the wherewithal to break into the case and steal the book? And if so, where is it now?"

Concordia's irritation faded. She gave him an appreciative glance. He'd cut right to the heart of the matter.

"We're still searching for it," Capshaw said.

"Ha! There, you see?" John Bradley folded his arms. "It's absurd to suspect my son. If anger toward a relation were sufficient motive for murder, nearly all of us would be locked up."

But Capshaw didn't seem flustered by the setback. "I didn't say that was the only motive. Are you aware of how rich your uncle was, Mr. Bradley?"

John Bradley shrugged. "No idea. We had no interest in his money."

Capshaw inclined his head toward Richardson, who spoke. "Between Isaiah Symond's holdings and accounts, over four million dollars."

"Mercy," Concordia muttered.

"Do you know who stands to gain the most by his death?" Capshaw turned his question back to John Bradley, who let out a bark of laughter.

"You are asking the wrong man. Isaiah changed his will so often—from spite, pique, or to get something he wanted—I doubt even Richardson would know without checking."

The lawyer nodded. "John's right about that. Not to speak ill of the dead, but Isaiah changed his will quite often, as someone or other fell in or out of favor. He had drafted a new will only last week, but hadn't yet signed it." He looked over at Miss Farraday. "That one would have given his entire estate to you, miss."

Madeline swallowed. "You did say he was changing it in my favor."

"However, I'm afraid it is not valid without a signature," Richardson said.

She sighed. "I never wanted his money." She glared at the lawyer. "You were supposed to tell him so at the time."

"I did. Perhaps that's why he delayed signing it."

Capshaw shifted impatiently. "Tell them who actually inherits, if you please, Mr. Richardson."

The lawyer's brow briefly creased in irritation before he spoke. "It turns out that last month's will is the valid one. I checked it before coming here this morning, to be sure."

"Who are the beneficiaries?" Concordia asked. She hoped it was not David. The honorary exhibit had been trouble enough.

Richardson cleared his throat. "There are two principal co-heirs. Mr. John Bradley and Mr. Lawrence Bradley."

Once Concordia had seen Richardson and the Bradleys out, she went to check on Mrs. Houston. The housekeeper was already dressed and tidying the bedroom, maneuvering by hopping on a single crutch.

Upon hearing the news that policemen would be searching the house, her face took on a mottled-red hue. "They believe us to be thieves and murderers? Outrageous. Your mother would never stand for such goings-on." She gave a little hop and thumped her crutch for emphasis.

Concordia suppressed a smile. The woman was, literally, hopping mad. "My mother is not mistress of this household. I am. Besides, it's a mere formality. Our house is situated just beyond the school grounds. The lieutenant is being thorough."

The woman's eyes narrowed. "It's that girl, isn't it? Miss Farraday. That's who the police suspect."

Concordia shook her head. "Surely not, Mrs. Houston."

"I'd be careful around her, if I were you. Too moody and independent-minded for my taste. Back in *my* day, girls conducted themselves as demure young misses should. They didn't put themselves forward like that...young lady."

"Times have changed" was all Concordia said. Privately, she was glad they no longer lived back in Mrs. Houston's day.

The housekeeper was too busy muttering to herself to pay her any mind.

For want of a better place to wait, Concordia and Madeline sat on the porch swing, quietly taking in the distant view of the school grounds. Every once in a while, they heard the strident tones of Mrs. Houston and the *thump* of her crutches as she followed Capshaw from room to room.

"I'm surprised you didn't wish to oversee the lieutenant going through your belongings," Concordia said to Madeline.

The girl waved a dismissive hand. "I'm used to it, frankly. When one has been in domestic service, it's a common occurrence. I had very little expectation of privacy while I was a nursemaid for the Gemmers."

"How distasteful." Concordia could not imagine such a life.

"Besides, the police won't have much to go through. I'd brought only a suitcase and a book satchel with me." She gave a bitter laugh. "No Blake *Catalogue*."

They were quiet for a time. A breeze ruffled the leaves. A crow cawed in the distance.

"I hope you don't mind my asking," Concordia said hesitantly, "about Isaiah Symond?"

Madeline gave her a quick glance before looking away, her cheeks tinged pink. "It's natural that you'd be curious. Go ahead."

"I assume you never met your father. But your mother must have spoken of him, surely?"

"Mama died when I was very young. I don't recall her speaking much of my father. Once she told me he had to sail far away and couldn't be with us."

She grew quiet. Concordia waited.

"After she died," Madeline said finally, coming out of her reverie, "they couldn't find any other family, so I was sent off to a home for orphaned girls."

"And he never contacted you?"

"No."

"What do you know about your mother? Did she grow up in Hartford?"

"I don't know if she came from here. Her name was Rebecca Farraday. She earned her living in New York City as a singer. She had a lovely voice." Madeline smiled. "I remember her singing to me when she'd tuck me in at night."

"Do you believe Isaiah Symond was indeed your father?"

"It's very likely. Mr. Richardson showed me the photograph Symond kept. It *was* my mother. On the back was written, 'To my darling Isaiah.'" Madeline looked over at Concordia, her expression fearful. "But I—I didn't kill him. I wanted nothing to do with him or his money."

"The money would have profoundly changed your life. Why wouldn't you want it?"

She shrugged. Concordia had to wonder if the lady *doth protest too much*. She remembered the girl's small sigh when Richardson said the will in her favor was invalid. Had she been disappointed? Concordia felt a sudden chill. Had she assumed the will in her favor was already signed and done? It would be a powerful motive.

The silence dragged on.

"You believe me, don't you?" Madeline asked.

"I certainly want to. You have to concede that you are not making it easy to do so. Why be so secretive about your whereabouts last night? You must know how that looks."

Madeline tipped a defiant chin. "I don't care about that. I don't want to get someone else in trouble. But as I said, we were only talking. No pranks and certainly no murder."

Concordia gritted her teeth. What to do about such a stubborn young lady? How she wished David was here.

Capshaw and his assistant stepped out on the porch.

"All finished," Capshaw said, writing one last note in his pad. "Thank you for your cooperation."

Madeline Farraday got up and headed for the door. "If you'll excuse me, I have packing to do."

Capshaw opened it politely, but she brushed by without meeting his eye.

"I take it you found nothing of note, Lieutenant?" Concordia asked. "I could have saved you the time, had you believed me."

He smiled. "Eliminating Miss Farraday as a suspect is not a waste of my time."

She raised an eyebrow. "Despite her refusal to name the person she spent time with last night?"

"My impression of Miss Farraday's temperament leads me to consider her unlikely to act on impulse."

Except where romantic feeling was concerned, but she kept that thought to herself.

He tucked his notepad and pencil into his tunic. "If Mr. Symond had died after signing the new will in the young lady's favor, we would be having a different conversation."

"You consider the attack on Symond and the theft of the *Catalogue* to be impulsive acts?"

"Exactly. With that in mind, Lawrence Bradley is the most likely suspect."

"Aside from a common thief," Concordia reminded him.

He inclined his head in acknowledgment.

"Why search our home?" she asked.

"In case Lawrence took the book to divert us and then gave it to Miss Farraday to conceal for him."

"Fair enough. So what happens next?"

Capshaw looked over at the patrolman who had taken a seat in the police coach, patiently waiting to leave. "For you and the Bradley household? Nothing." His lips twitched. "We have scandalized your housekeeper enough."

"But you *will* be investigating the possibility of it being a thief, will you not?" Concordia called out, as he walked away.

He stopped and turned to her with narrowed eyes, his expression as gloomy as ever. "I thought marriage would cure you of meddling in police affairs."

"Meddling?" Concordia gave him her most wide-eyed, innocent expression. "Surely not."

He shook his head. "Events will soon become unpleasant for several people in your life."

Her stomach clenched. "You mean Lawrence?"

"And your father-in-law."

"Because they are Isaiah Symond's co-heirs?" she asked incredulously. She had difficulty imagining her in-laws, separately or together, plotting to kill the old man for his money.

"More than that. John Bradley strikes me as a man who's desperate to protect his son at all costs. I'm not confident he's told me the whole story of Lawrence's whereabouts. His reticence may cost him dearly."

Concordia stiffened. "I refuse to believe either one is capable of murder. You're after the wrong men, Lieutenant."

His brows drew together in a steely expression as he hoisted himself into the coach. "I'm warning you, Concordia," he called. "Stay out of it."

She watched them drive away. *The devil I will.*

CHAPTER 8

As a man is, so he sees. As the eye is formed, such are its powers.

— WILLIAM BLAKE

Concordia returned to the kitchen to find the housekeeper leaning on her crutch, scrubbing the counters with the single-minded fury of a beleaguered woman.

"Mrs. Houston, you're supposed to be staying off your feet until the doctor gets a look at that ankle," she chided.

The woman shuffled toward the sink, sliding the sponge ahead of her. "I'll be fine, so long as no more policemen come tearing the house apart. Besides, I cannot abide a dirty sink."

Concordia doubted it was dirty at all, but left her to it and headed up to Madeline's room.

As she expected, the girl was busy pulling shirtwaists out of drawers and stacking textbooks. She laid out everything gently, with a subdued, preoccupied air.

Concordia tapped on the open door. "Madeline?"

She didn't turn around. "I'll be done and out of here shortly, Mrs. Bradley." Her hands clenched around the satchel handles. "I *am* sorry to have brought you nothing but aggravation in return for your kindness."

"This isn't your fault. It will get straightened out, don't worry."

Madeline finally met her eye and gave her a wan smile. "Thank you for that."

"When you're finished packing, could you keep Mrs. Houston company for a while? I'm heading to campus to send a telegram to my mother about her mishap. Mrs. Houston's doctor should have a look at her."

"Of course, though I have to warn you, she doesn't like me much."

Concordia waved a dismissive hand. "She's slow to warm up to everyone. I have other things to tend to on campus"—such as a bit of snooping—"but you're free to leave when my mother gets here. It shouldn't be long."

Back in her room, she had a thought. Why not ride her bicycle to the school? She felt a thrill of anticipation as she dug around the armoire for her cycling outfit. Mrs. Houston, despite voicing her disapproval of the shortened skirt and close leggings necessary to such a costume, had nonetheless sponged out the old mud stains in the skirt and pressed the blouse.

She hadn't ridden since her illness. The distress of that time came flooding back as she dressed. Would she always have difficulty carrying a child? Was David disappointed in her? She blew out a breath as she tucked her hair under the cycling cap. Those were worries for later.

Caesar was prowling the storage shed as she extricated her machine. She backed the bicycle out through the narrow door, just missing his swishing ginger tail. "Go hunt somewhere else."

The tabby looked at her with his golden eyes, gave a token *mew* of protest, and trotted off towards the meadow.

Under an expansive blue sky, she drew a deep breath full of

early-October warmth and the tang of reds and golds. It called to mind one of her favorite Browning poems:

days decrease,

And autumn grows, autumn in everything.

She felt her shoulder muscles relax as the sun warmed her back. This was exactly what she needed.

She walked her machine beyond the steeper decline of Rook's Hill, then steered toward the gentler-sloped sheep tracks that led to the campus pond. How wonderful it felt to be riding again—the *whir* of the pedals, the steady rhythm of exertion, the easy responsiveness of the steering as she swerved to avoid the rock or fallen branch she'd come to anticipate after dozens of trips along this path.

She smiled as she crossed a small stream. She and David had first met near here, when she had—almost—run him down with her bicycle. Amazingly, it had proved to be the beginning of the love and deep kinship that had eventually resulted in their marriage. She couldn't wait until he returned tomorrow.

She propped her bicycle against the railing beside the front steps of the Hall and headed for the mail room beside the library. The school's messenger boy was busy sorting letters and stuffing them into pigeon-hole slots for the staff.

"Hello, Sam. I need to send a telegram when you have the time to spare."

The sixteen-year-old's eyes lit up as he turned around, and a smile widened upon his freckled face. "O' course, Miss—er, Mrs. Bradley! Jes' give me a minute. Almost done."

Jane Cowles came through the door, gave Concordia a quick nod, and veered to the column of letter receptacles to the left.

"Two for you today, miss," Sam called out to the librarian. He tossed the empty canvas mail bag into a corner and fished out a pencil and pad. "All right, Mrs. Bradley. Ready."

After she'd dictated the telegram to her mother, the boy

flipped the notepad closed and put on his jacket. "I'll get right over to the telegraph office, ma'am, don't you worry."

"Thank you." She passed him a coin.

He flashed another toothy grin and was off.

Miss Cowles looked on, her thin nose quivering in curiosity. "I was not aware that you continue to receive mail at the school."

Concordia flushed. "I do not." Surely the librarian must know that.

Miss Cowles slit her letters. "Ah. How convenient that you can avail yourself of Sam's services, nonetheless. But I must be getting back to work." Her gaze swept over Concordia's bicycling attire. "Enjoy your day."

She blinked in surprise as the librarian stalked out the door. What bee was in that lady's bonnet? Why should she care if the messenger boy performed a small errand for her?

Miss Jenkins might know. She and Jane Cowles had been colleagues at the school for the past two decades. Perhaps there was a way to get on the librarian's good side.

Later, of course. At the moment, she had a more pressing task.

It felt strange to knock on the door of Willow Cottage, which had been her home in recent years before her marriage.

Ruby Hitchcock answered it. "Why, Miss—Mrs. Bradley, so nice of you to come see us!" She opened the door wider. "Are you here to see Miss Crandall? I'm afraid she's in class all morning."

As Charlotte Crandall was the teacher-in-residence at Willow Cottage and had become one of Concordia's close friends, Ruby's assumption was natural enough.

"Actually, I want to speak with Maisie. Is she here?"

"She is, but I can't say if she's on her way to class, too. Why don't you wait in the parlor while I fetch her."

Concordia grimaced. The parlor was a formal space for welcoming visitors. "I'd rather wait in the kitchen, if you don't mind."

"O' course! I'll make us a nice cup of tea, if you can stay on for a bit."

Concordia would have preferred to conduct her conversation with Maisie Lovelace in private, but she knew she could trust the matron. She might even be of help. "Thank you. Tea would be most welcome."

"I'll be back. You know the way."

Ruby's heavy tread made the floorboards creak overhead as Concordia navigated the narrow hallway. Although much of Willow Cottage had been rebuilt since last year, she had the sensation of stepping back in time, to her first year at Hartford Women's College as a new lady professor in charge of the well-being of two dozen high-spirited girls. It was just as she remembered—brass wall hooks crammed with scarves and hats hanging cheek-by-jowl, books stacked next to sewing baskets on the long hall table. She sniffed the air. It even smelled the same—a mingling of lemon polish, ironing starch…and was that a hint of illegally cooked fudge? She smiled.

Ruby soon returned with the senior, a dark-haired, ruddy-cheeked, energetic girl.

Maisie plunked herself into a chair while Ruby got the kettle going for tea. "I'm so glad you came. You heard, I suppose?"

"Heard?"

"Uncle George had to go to the police station."

"Really?" Capshaw had left her house an hour and a half ago. Not even he was that quick.

"I was here when it happened," Ruby chimed in. She jerked a thumb over her shoulder toward the cook stove. "He came to see to that this morning—the second burner in't working proper—when the policeman came lookin' for him."

"Which policeman, do you know?" Concordia asked.

Maisie stuck a hand in her skirt pocket and passed over a card. "Here."

Sergeant James Maloney, Hartford Police Department, Kinsley Street Station.

The sergeant must have sought out Lovelace as soon as he'd finished reporting to Capshaw at the farmhouse.

Ruby clucked her tongue. "Them police have gone too far, I say."

"Did Maloney say your uncle was under arrest?" Concordia asked.

The girl propped her head on her chin. "Not yet. Only if he 'refuses to cooperate.' Uncle didn't want to go. He'd had a hard enough night after you two found...well, you know."

Concordia passed back the card. "I'm sorry. I had no idea."

"Then why did you come?" Maisie asked.

Concordia hesitated. The Bradleys might object to her discussing confidential family matters, but Lawrence and John Bradley suffering the disgrace of possible arrest was far worse. She had to get answers.

Taking a breath, she recounted Capshaw's interview of Madeline and herself, the search of her house, and the policeman ultimately fixing his suspicions upon the Bradleys as the co-heirs. She told them the basis of Capshaw's reasoning—the gaps in Lawrence's accounting of his time that night and his father's false statement to protect him.

For the sake of Madeline's privacy, she left out the part about the young lady possibly being Symond's daughter. Concordia knew Madeline found it mortifying enough that she was thereby related to Lawrence, her former beau.

But Maisie was too quick-witted by half. "But why did the lieutenant come to your house and question Madeline, of all people?"

"That will take some...explaining. I'll get back to that later," Concordia said, stalling for time.

"Land sakes, ma'am, that's ter'ble," Ruby interjected. "Everyone's been sayin' it was a thief that broke in an' was caught in the act by the elderly gentleman. Doesn't that make more sense than some relations out to get the inheritance? Even if your father-in-law told a little white lie to keep his son from looking suspicious to the police—what father wouldn't protect his son?"

"Still," Concordia said, "it's troubling that no one can corroborate Lawrence coming directly home after going to Symond's house."

"But why do something so wicked on the campus of a girls' college? If you're always spending time wi' your family anyways, why wait to do it in a strange place?"

The kettle whistled, and Ruby got up to tend to it.

"True." Concordia suppressed a shudder at the thought of sitting beside one's hearth with a family member who had murder in his heart.

"What does your husband have to say 'bout his brother and father being suspected?" Ruby asked over her shoulder.

"He's still out of town." She looked over at Maisie. "Did the sergeant go through your belongings?"

The girl's nostrils flared. "He certainly did. Uncle George said they'd already searched his shop and residence, too. The policeman didn't find what he was looking for, of course."

Concordia nodded. "The *Descriptive Catalogue*." Where was it? And why steal it? While the book had commercial value in certain esoteric academic circles, there were far more profitable items in that very gallery for the taking.

Maisie rolled her eyes. "I never had a chance to see the book in the first place, much less make off with it. I was too busy finishing a research paper last night to attend the opening." She accepted the tea Ruby pressed on her and reached for the sugar tongs.

Concordia took a sip. Bless the matron for remembering that oolong was one of her favorites. She circled her fingers around the sturdy brown porcelain cup and cradled its warmth. Finally, she looked over at Maisie. "I wanted to speak with your uncle, but obviously that will have to wait. I was hoping he remembered some little detail since last night. Did he share anything with you?"

"Not really. He wasn't exactly eager to tell me about it. 'Not fit for a lady's ear,' he said. But you could always ask Miss Phillips. If he remembered something, he may have gone to her about it." Maisie's mouth quirked. "He seems rather sweet on her."

Concordia sat back in surprise. "Really?" Those two were an unlikely pairing, though she would never say so in front of the girl. She glanced over at Ruby, who raised an eyebrow.

"What's so strange about that?" Maisie demanded. "They're the same age. They've worked together a lot lately."

There seemed no good answer to that. Ruby quickly brought them back to the more pressing subject. "What do you think the police are gonna do next, ma'am? If the lieutenant can't find the missing book, will he still arrest your brother-in-law, and maybe your father-in-law, too?"

"I don't know. I only know that I want to do all I can to keep it from getting to that point."

Ruby leaned closer to Concordia and dropped her voice to a conspiratorial murmur. "Does that mean you're gonna to be investigatin' again?"

Did Concordia detect a gleam in the matron's eye? For all of Ruby's disapproving sniffs over female snooping in the past, she'd been of enormous help when certain, er, subterfuges had been necessary.

"Ooh, Mrs. Bradley!" Maisie exclaimed, her eyes widening in excitement. "You're so good at investigating! What are you going to do first? Search for clues, like they do in those detective stories?"

Concordia snorted. "I will hardly be crawling along the gallery floor with a magnifying glass, hunting for bits of torn clothing." Although another look at the gallery would be a good idea. All she could recall amid the shock of discovery was Symond's body sprawled on the floor and an empty exhibit case.

Assuming the police were finished, perhaps Dorothy Phillips could let her in. The history professor might think it a rather ghoulish request. And was it even productive? Surely Capshaw had seen everything of importance. And had taken it away with him.

"What can we do to help?" Maisie asked.

Concordia noticed Ruby wince at the "we." *Lord save us from overeager girls.* She could almost hear the matron's oft-repeated sentiment spoken aloud.

She patted Ruby's hand. "Don't worry. All we'll need from you is to keep the tea coming, if you would." She turned to Maisie. "Do you have time to talk?"

"My Renaissance Art class is canceled today, so I'm free. Professor Benson's been asked to take over Mr. Richardson's economics class. They don't have a replacement for ours yet. That's all right—we're a bit ahead of the syllabus, anyway."

Richardson not teaching? Concordia frowned. She would have to ask the lady principal what was going on. Was he a suspect? If so, Capshaw was holding that information mighty close to the vest.

She felt her hopes lift a bit at the prospect. As pleasant a man as Richardson was, she'd much prefer the murderer be someone she barely knew—perhaps a man with shady dealings? One never knew about lawyers.

But now was not the time to entertain such fancies. "All right, then. Let's talk about Madeline Farraday."

The girl brightened. "Ah, yes. You said we'd get back to that."

Ruby stood. "I gotta start on my work. The kettle's refilled and back on the stove. Lemme know if you need anything else."

"Thanks, Ruby," Concordia said.

Once the matron had left the kitchen, Concordia asked, "How much has Madeline confided in you regarding her...circumstances?"

"She's very private about her past. I didn't want to intrude,"

Maisie said. "I know she's an orphan and has had to work for her living. I also know she's here on scholarship, just as I am."

"Nothing about her parentage?"

Maisie shook her head.

So she didn't know about Symond's relationship to Madeline. Concordia tried another tack. "Has she confided in you about Lawrence?"

"Somewhat. She was quite voluble about him in the beginning —waxing rhapsodic about his smile, his eyes, his—" She blushed.

Better to let that go. "In the beginning? Then what?"

"It was an on-again, off-again sort of romance," Maisie said. "They would quarrel about silly things. Then he'd send a note of apology, and all was well again. You saw her on Founder's Day— she was excessively put out by Lawrence's late arrival at the picnic. But this time, it must have been the last straw. She told me yesterday she'd broken it off for good."

That was before Madeline had a secret meeting with someone late last night. Now it seemed less likely to have been Lawrence.

"Did she say why?" Concordia asked.

"No." Maisie shifted impatiently. "Mrs. Bradley, what's going on with that girl? She's so temperamental."

"Well, she's facing additional difficulties of a personal nature. I can't say more. I will, however, encourage her to confide in you directly. You've been a good friend."

Maisie waved off the compliment, though Concordia noted the tinge of pink in her cheeks. "So when Lieutenant Capshaw came to your house and questioned her, it was because of her relationship with Lawrence?"

"In part."

"But Capshaw searched your home—" Maisie sucked in a breath. "He thinks *she* killed Mr. Symond and took the *Catalogue*? That's absurd." She was quiet for a moment, lost in thought. "Or perhaps...he thinks she helped Lawrence?"

"The lieutenant has considered both possibilities," Concordia said, "though now he believes it's less likely she's involved." That was what he'd said, at least, but who knew with Capshaw?

"Is it because he didn't find the *Catalogue* at the farmhouse?"

"I believe so."

Maisie narrowed her eyes. "I have a feeling you're holding back something. Madeline being involved with Lawrence doesn't seem enough of a reason for the police to suspect her."

Concordia blew out a breath. "You're right about that. There *is* more. One of the reasons Capshaw first suspected Madeline Farraday is because she is listed as a beneficiary in one of Isaiah Symond's wills. And he was a very rich man."

"But you said that Lawrence Bradley and his father were the beneficiaries."

"According to the *legal* will. There is another—more recent but unsigned. If Symond *had* signed it, Madeline would have inherited everything. Millions of dollars."

"Millions," Maisie echoed. "Mercy, she would have been an heiress."

"Yes."

"But why would he have left everything to her? What is she to him?"

Concordia blew out a breath. "I can't tell you that."

Maisie was quiet for a while. "I see," she said at last. "Wouldn't Madeline have waited for the will to be signed before killing him?"

"I'm not sure she knew it had yet to be signed. She might have assumed it was already final."

"For all her faults, I don't believe she would do such a thing," Maisie said.

"There's another reason Capshaw suspected her. It's something I wanted to ask you about." Concordia explained Madeline's middle-of-the-night trip to campus, ostensibly in search of a notebook, and the subsequent time she could not—would not—account for.

Maisie clucked her tongue. "That girl's going to get herself expelled at this rate."

She sounded like Ruby. Concordia suppressed a smile. Maisie Lovelace had certainly outgrown many of her own harum-scarum ways. "The bigger problem at the moment is that Mr. Symond was killed during that time. Madeline refuses to name who she was with. She says she doesn't want to get a friend in trouble. Capshaw can't confirm her whereabouts." She hesitated. "It wasn't you, was it?"

"I told you—I was up in my room, working late on a paper. Miss Crandall gave me permission to stay up past lights-out to finish. You can ask her, if you'd like."

Concordia waved a hand. "That isn't necessary. Do you have any idea who it could be?"

"Before their relationship ended, there was Lawrence, of course."

Concordia nodded. "But you said yourself she'd already broken it off with him by then."

"I wonder...what if it isn't a student? What about a teacher?"

"A teacher?"

"She's close to Miss Jenkins and Miss Cowles."

"It couldn't have been Miss Jenkins—they parted ways after Madeline found her notebook. And as for Miss Cowles"—Concordia made a face—"the idea of the librarian being sociable with a student in the middle of the night staggers the imagination."

Maisie snorted. "True. What about Miss Pomeroy? She keeps odd hours."

"Even if it was one of them, why keep silent about it? Madeline claimed she didn't want to get a friend into trouble. Both the lady principal and the librarian have every right to be out of bed at any hour. The ten o'clock rule doesn't apply to them."

"I'm out of ideas, then," Maisie said. "Madeline and I have very few classes in common since she's two years behind me. She might have formed a recent acquaintance."

Concordia sighed. "We may never know."

After making arrangements with Maisie for the next outing of the Bicycle Club, Concordia turned back to the Hall. Perhaps Sam had received a reply to her telegram. She could check on her way to the gallery to see Miss Phillips.

He seems rather sweet on the lady, Maisie had said.

Concordia tugged at the mailroom door. A far-fetched notion. Miss Phillips and George Lovelace were of completely different backgrounds—she a scholar and world traveler, he a clock-maker and general handyman. Perhaps the feeling was one-sided. She remembered Lovelace bringing Miss Phillips her favorite tea. Was it simply kindness, or was romantic feeling involved? Did Miss Phillips know?

"Mrs. Bradley!" Sam jumped off his stool. "I have something for ya." He thrust out a folded sheet of yellow paper.

DOCTOR SENT FOR. ON MY WAY. ~MOTHER

"Jimmy brought it 'round mebbe ten minutes ago," Sam said.

Knowing her mother, the carriage was probably pulling up to the farmhouse by now. "Thanks, Sam." She handed him another coin.

He grinned. "Any time, ma'am."

Concordia found Dorothy Phillips on her hands and knees, scrubbing the floor beneath a display table. "Miss Phillips! You shouldn't be doing that."

The curator sat back on her heels and pushed her graying hair from her brow. "Hello, dear."

Concordia's stomach clenched when she realized the cleaning rag she held was stained a reddish-brown and more of the same substance stuck to the floor. "You should not be the one cleaning this up," she repeated.

Miss Phillips shrugged. "I've dealt with worse in my travels, believe me. But you're right—I wouldn't have volunteered for this. The custodian couldn't take care of it until later. I cannot sit by without at least starting to put things to rights."

Concordia stood back to survey the scene. Most of the floor was hardwood except for a wide Persian carpet runner down the middle of the room, between the rows of exhibit tables on each side. The space had been immaculate during the exhibit opening the night before, but innumerable pairs of feet had tracked in damp leaves and dirt since then. On a small side table, someone— Capshaw, no doubt—had pulled out all of Lovelace's tools and arranged them neatly, the empty leather case beside them. Concordia knew they had not been that way when they'd found Symond. She would have noticed that. Where had the tool case been? She wished she could remember.

She drew closer to the Blake exhibit. An easel holding one of the lithographs had been knocked over, though the art piece itself had only a corner of its backing bent. The table sign announcing the Blake lectures had landed beneath an opposite display. She approached the table, which still stood at an angle, one end having been shoved back. Her stomach clenched. Symond's body, gone now, had been sprawled beneath this end of the table. It must have pushed out from under him as he fell.

She took a breath. "I assume the police are finished here?"

"Finally." Miss Phillips resumed her scrubbing.

Concordia leaned closer to the empty exhibit case. The door hung open. Several deep scoring marks were visible in the wood that framed the lock. The case otherwise looked perfectly intact, no cracks or chips in the glass, and the velvet-lined stand within was undisturbed. She experimentally tried to close the door, but it wouldn't stay shut. "Can the case be repaired?"

"I'd say so. George can smooth over the scratch marks and

replace the lock." Dorothy Phillips made a face. "Not that it seems much of a deterrent."

Concordia looked around at the disarray. "I'd like to help."

"Actually, it's propitious that you've come. As the exhibit was given in your honor, I wanted your opinion as to what we should do now."

"Do now? Oh—you mean, with the *Descriptive Catalogue* still missing, we have to decide whether or not to leave the rest of the exhibit on display?"

"Exactly. What's left are only support pieces. It was the *Catalogue* that tied it all together."

"I see your point. Leaving everything else in place only emphasizes the theft of the Blake piece. I'd say the best course is to take down the remainder and store it for now." And hope that the *Catalogue* was found.

"I agree," Miss Phillips said, "but I was concerned you'd be offended by the suggestion."

"Not at all. I'll help you put it all away. I heard about Mr. Lovelace having to go to the police station."

A pained expression crossed the history professor's face. "More questions. Poor George. He's a good man. He doesn't deserve such trouble."

Miss Phillips unlocked the storeroom as Concordia loaded the glass case on the wheeled cart. Despite her earlier jest about looking for torn bits of clothing and other such clues, she carefully examined the interior and bottom of the case before Miss Phillips came back in the room. She saw nothing unusual.

It took several trips with the cart before they were done.

"It looks so empty now," Concordia said ruefully.

Dorothy Phillips made a face. "That it does. Once George is back, I'll ask him to shift the tables to space everything better."

"He's quite devoted in his work, isn't he?" Concordia said.

Miss Phillips didn't meet her eye, but the flush at her neck as she leaned over to swipe a speck of lint from a table made it clear. *Ah. She knows he's in love with her. But does she return the feeling?*

Not wanting to embarrass the lady, she changed the subject. "I've wondered how Isaiah Symond came to own a Blake *Catalogue*. The reporter couldn't pin him down to any specific details. I grant you, his collection is eclectic—I've been to his house—but I saw no other items there of a literary nature."

The flush quickly receded from Dorothy Phillips's cheeks. "He was an opportunistic man. If someone else valued it, he wanted it."

That had been Concordia's impression of him as well, especially after speaking to Mr. Richardson at Symond's dinner party—

Wait a minute.

She stared at Miss Phillips. "You speak quite definitively about him. How would you know? Your acquaintance was quite recent, was it not? The two of you only would have spoken a few times."

"I should have said, 'It is my impression that he was an opportunistic man.'" The history professor didn't meet her eye. "I simply misspoke."

Concordia remembered Symond's behavior at the reception, the inordinate attention he paid to the lady, his insistence upon accompanying Miss Phillips to the gallery last night, and the woman's relief when Concordia had volunteered to come along. She also recalled Miss Phillips's words when Capshaw interviewed her about Symond's behavior: *Once a notion was fixed in his mind, there was no budging him.*

"Miss Phillips, you knew Isaiah Symond before." It was a statement, not a question.

The lady hesitated, then blew out a breath. "Sadly, yes."

"Why did you pretend—why did you *both* pretend—you had not?"

"Let us talk in my office."

CHAPTER 9

Cherish pity, lest you drive an angel from your door.

— WILLIAM BLAKE

"It was about fifteen years ago," Dorothy Phillips began, keeping her eyes fixed upon the pencil she gripped. "We were on board a riverboat steamer taking us up the Nile to Luxor. Symond was on holiday in the company of another man. I was returning from a dig with a dear friend of mine, Marie." Her eyes flicked over to Concordia. "She once owned the *Descriptive Catalogue.*"

Concordia felt a chill. She had a sense of where this was going.

"Although Marie is a Blake scholar, she'd listened to me going on about ancient tombs often enough that she wanted to experience a dig for herself. We had a marvelous time."

She grew quiet and went back to staring at her pencil.

"But something happened," Concordia said.

"You'll excuse my glossing over the painful specifics. I must protect Marie's privacy. Let us just say that, during our time on board, Isaiah Symond found himself in the position to blackmail her."

"She gave him the *Catalogue?*"

"It was the only thing of value she had with her. She'd wisely left her other valuables behind, as one cannot avoid unscrupulous guides and pickpockets in the tourist areas."

"How did she come to bring the *Catalogue* with her?"

A pained expression crossed Miss Phillips's face. "She planned to give it to me as a gift for bringing her on the excursion. An exchange of academic interests, if you will. I also gave Symond what money I had."

Anger settled in Concordia's chest like a stone. "That's despicable. I'm so sorry."

"You see why I did not wish to acknowledge the man. Even though he kept silent on the subject, he privately needled me about it this week, speculating aloud as to whether he should go to the police with Marie's secret."

Concordia's gaze strayed to the array of figurines and artifacts on the windowsill behind Dorothy Phillips's desk. "Did he demand the cat statuette for his continued silence?"

"I'm afraid so." The pencil snapped in her hands, and she tossed the pieces on the desk in disgust. "What worries me is if the lieutenant finds the figurine among Symond's belongings. He would trace it back to me. I would then come under suspicion."

"How would Capshaw identify the figurine as yours? Plenty of people own such little trinkets. Symond traveled to Egypt, too, and could have picked it up himself."

The lady shook her head. "Remember a few years ago, when the heart scarab went missing and Colonel Adams was killed? Capshaw interviewed me in my office. The statuette was on display. He remarked upon it, as you have. I'm sure he'll remember if he sees it elsewhere."

"But you can say you gave it to Symond in appreciation for his donation," Concordia protested. She didn't want to encourage her to lie to the policeman—Capshaw's warning to John Bradley was fresh in her mind—but Miss Phillips couldn't possibly be guilty of murder. She bit her lip. Her inquiry was netting more than she'd bargained for. She'd hoped to find something to clear her brother-in-law, and now Miss Phillips was looking like an equally promising suspect.

Miss Phillips squared her shoulders. "We shall see."

Concordia was more than ready to go home and change out of her cycling outfit when she ran into the lady principal as she emerged from the mail room.

"Ah, Concordia dear, I was just coming to look for you," Miss Pomeroy said, blue eyes widening behind her spectacles. "Sam said you might still be around here somewhere. I have a favor to ask."

"Of course."

"Would you mind taking over Miss Crandall's rhetoric class? Only for a few weeks."

"What's wrong with Charlotte?" Concordia asked. "Is she ill?"

"No, no, nothing of the kind," Miss Pomeroy said quickly. "Mr. Richardson has to step away from teaching his economics class for a few weeks while he takes care of the extra workload at his law practice." Her expression grew troubled, and her voice dropped of its own accord. "Because of the man who died, you know. He must manage the necessary final affairs."

"Ah. I'd heard Professor Benson was taking over the economics class but didn't know why," Concordia said.

"Yes, she has qualifications in that field as well as in history, thank goodness. We've arranged for Miss Crandall to teach Miss Benson's Renaissance art class, and so we need you to—"

"Teach Charlotte's rhetoric course. Now, I see."

"It's a dreadful muddle, to be sure," the lady principal said, "but it's the only way to fill the gaps."

"Of course. I'm happy to help."

Gertrude Pomeroy's forehead smoothed in relief. "Thank you, dear."

"You're sure the school is willing to engage me in that capacity?" Concordia asked, remembering the heated debate at the reception.

"It seems we have little choice in the matter" came a gruff voice from behind them. Randolph Maynard had emerged from the mail room with a stack of letters. Eyebrow raised, his gaze swept over Concordia's cycling costume. She flushed but tried to assume a nonchalant air.

"We shall expect you to dress more appropriately, Mrs. Bradley, if you are to be a constant presence on campus over the next few weeks." He muttered, "Bradley has his hands full.... Modern women...Heaven help us if a trustee catches sight of her...." Without another word, he turned on his heel and headed for the stairwell.

Miss Pomeroy pushed up her spectacles as they watched him go.

"That was mild, for him," Concordia observed.

"Indeed," Miss Pomeroy murmured. "Oh! I nearly forgot." She dug into her skirt pocket and extracted a key. "You may use Mr. Richardson's office while he's gone. Miss Crandall's class meets tomorrow at ten. She says she has notes for you."

This was happening so quickly. Concordia took a breath and curled her hand around the key. "I'll check with her later. Thank you, Miss Pomeroy."

The lady principal smiled. "It's good to have you back."

At the sight of her mother's carriage and what she assumed was the doctor's buggy in front of the house, Concordia left her bicycle beside the porch and hurried inside. "Mother!" she called.

Letitia Wells came down the stairs, carrying Mrs. Houston's suitcase and valise. "Hello, dear."

Concordia took the cases and put them by the front door. "How is she? What does the doctor say?"

"He's re-wrapping her ankle now. Don't worry—it's just a sprain, as Miss Jenkins said. But we think it's best if she recuperates back home."

Concordia nodded. She'd expected that.

Letitia's lips twitched as she looked her up and down. "I see you're well enough to ride."

Concordia felt a brief twinge of guilt, though she didn't quite know why. She still grieved the lost child, but her own body was prodding her to move on. She blew out a breath. "I feel much better."

"You can manage without Mrs. Houston, then?"

"Absolutely. Thank you for lending her to us."

"Don't wait too long to hire someone," her mother warned.

"I'm sure Sophia will contact me soon about a suitable prospect. Besides, I'll be teaching for the next few weeks, so it will be easier for David and me to get meals in the school dining room."

Letitia narrowed her eyes. "Teaching? Is someone ill?"

That's right—she didn't know about Isaiah Symond's death. Concordia gave her a condensed account of what happened.

"How terrible." Her mother fixed her with a sharp eye. "Promise me that you won't get involved in another murder investigation."

"But this one involves David's family."

Letitia's eyebrow lifted. "All the more reason to stay out of it, I'd say. You're new to the Bradley family. You have no way of navigating whatever long-standing grudges, secrets, or fears these people may harbor. Emotions will be running high right now."

Concordia was quiet for a moment. "I see your point. I cannot *promise*, but I imagine I'll be too busy to...meddle."

Letitia gave a wan smile. "We shall see."

"Has Miss Farraday gone already?" Concordia asked.

"Yes...oh! I almost forgot. She left you a note." She fished it out of her pocket. "A very composed and mature lady, this Miss Farraday. She reminds me of Sophia in many respects."

Concordia smiled as she scanned the young lady's note of thanks. "Mrs. Houston wasn't over-fond of her."

Letitia shrugged. "Mrs. Houston is a dear woman but a product of a different time."

"And what about you, Mother?" Concordia asked.

"While I am fond of bygone days, one must try to live in the present." She gave a wry smile. "Not always an easy task."

David returned a few hours after Concordia's mother and Mrs. Houston had gone.

Over a quick dinner of cold chicken and cornbread left for them by the housekeeper, Concordia caught him up on the woman's mishap.

"She tripped over the cat?" David scowled. "The beast is lucky I don't make a fur collar out of him."

"He's kept out of the way since then. But we're still in need of hired help. I'm going to check with Sophia at my first opportunity. How was your symposium?"

He shook his head. "Complicated. I'll tell you later. Right now, I want to know more about Great-Uncle Isaiah's death. Papa's telegram wasn't exactly forthcoming."

As succinctly as she could, she recounted what had happened last night, what she knew of Capshaw's investigation so far, and the shocking news of Madeline Farraday's true parentage.

Their plates had long stood empty by the time she was done.

She was too tired to tell him about Miss Phillips and her previous sad acquaintance with Isaiah. That could wait.

David helped her carry the dishes to the sink, washing them while she dried and put them away. "I'm sorry I wasn't here. Mrs. Houston's accident...finding my great-uncle dead...the police searching the house...what an upheaval!"

She smiled. "Well, I lived to tell the tale."

He kissed the top of her head. "I'm very lucky to have such a self-sufficient wife."

Concordia smiled, privately vowing to remember he said that. She had a feeling she might need to remind him later.

He rolled down his sleeves. "Shall we go and pay the family a visit? I'm sure Papa is most anxious to talk to me."

The Bradley family had gathered in their spacious parlor when David and Concordia arrived. Georgeanna sat in a rocking chair, doing needlepoint beneath the light of an electric wall sconce. John was perusing a newspaper. Drusilla had a small book open in her lap—one of her favorite self-improvement guides, Concordia guessed. The woman's beloved little pug dog, Bandit, lay at her feet, snoring softly, his belly in the air, in case anyone charitable enough to give him a rub might pass by.

Where was Lawrence? Concordia felt a brief moment of panic. Had the police taken him away?

No, surely not. She would not be witnessing this tranquil domestic scene if that were the case.

The maid who escorted them bobbed a curtsy towards Georgeanna. "Mr. David and his wife, ma'am."

Georgeanna stood as David crossed the room. "David, dear!" she exclaimed, embracing him. "Oh, it has been a *dreadful* day. I'm so glad you've come."

"Of course," he said, shaking hands with his father and nodding toward Drusilla. "Where's Lawrence?"

"Working late, poor dear," Georgeanna said. "Isaiah's lawyer is busy getting the estate settled, so he needs Lawrence to take care of other matters."

"It's probably just as well," David said. "Easier to have a frank conversation about Lawrence without him here." He helped Concordia into a chair before settling himself.

John Bradley's brow furrowed. "There is no 'frank conversation' to be had about Lawrence. He had nothing to do with Isaiah's death. That's all."

"Then why did Capshaw search your house?" David asked.

Drusilla let out a groan. "I've never been so humiliated in all my days. Strange men poking into my armoire, pawing through my petticoats! I do not care to be treated like a common thief."

Georgeanna met Concordia's eye. "As it happens, we discovered a thief of another stripe—the aptly named Bandit. Their search turned up two mismatched slippers behind the armoire—chewed to bits, of course—and a pipe that John has been missing for days. We have to watch the little beast every minute."

The dog's ears twitched at the sound of his name, but he didn't bother opening his eyes.

"The police search turned up nothing else, I assume?" David asked.

"Of course not," John snapped. "They're grasping at straws."

"Their suspicion is only natural, you must admit," David said. "You and Lawrence are the co-heirs. Capshaw has to pursue that line of inquiry."

John rubbed the back of his neck, setting his collar slightly askew. "I know. But plenty of people had a motive to kill the old man. His lawyer, for instance. According to Lawrence, Isaiah and Richardson argued constantly. Just last week, he overheard a particularly loud dispute through the door of Richardson's inner office."

Concordia remembered Symond's antagonism towards Richardson the night of the dinner party. Was it possible? Ernest

Richardson had stayed behind at the reception at Sycamore House when she'd left with Symond and Miss Phillips. What had happened after that? Surely Lieutenant Capshaw would establish everyone's whereabouts that night, including the lawyer's. She wished she could get Capshaw to tell her what he knew.

She suppressed a sigh. She may as well plan a trip to the moon.

"Isaiah argued with nearly everyone," David said. "I recall some heated discussions between the two of you, Papa."

John flushed. "Not recently." His voice was gruff. "I've avoided his company since his return."

David tapped his finger to his lips thoughtfully. "That you have. You've shown great restraint. I suppose the lawyer *is* a possibility. We know very little about him. But Isaiah trusted him all these years. For all his faults, he was no fool."

"Did Lawrence tell the police about Isaiah's arguments with Richardson?" Concordia asked.

"Naturally," John said. "All we got was the usual tripe about looking into everyone." He shifted restlessly. "Once that lieutenant has fixed upon Lawrence, why would he bother looking elsewhere? He'll take the easy way out."

"Not Capshaw," Concordia said. "I know him. He cares about the truth."

Drusilla glared at her. Too late, Concordia realized a genteel woman shouldn't claim a close acquaintance with a policeman. She saw another of Drusilla's self-improvement books looming in her near future.

"*You* certainly haven't helped allay his suspicions," David said to his father. "I understand Capshaw took you to task for not being entirely forthcoming about Lawrence's whereabouts. What's this I hear about my brother showing up drunk at Isaiah's house late last night?"

"I had no idea," John said. "We'd retired by then."

"Has Lawrence returned to his old habit of drinking to excess?" David asked.

"Absolutely not," John declared. "But he's a grown man—of course he's going to enjoy a glass of wine with dinner or port with his cigar afterward. Nothing wrong with that."

David didn't offer a rejoinder.

The room was quiet for a few minutes.

"Did Capshaw say what was going to happen next?" Concordia finally asked. "I'd hoped he would look into whether the responsible party was a thief. If one thinks about it," she added, recalling Ruby's words, "why would a family member attack Isaiah at the college, rather than in his home or out on the street at night?"

Out of the corner of her eye, she saw Georgeanna wince. Perhaps she had put things a bit too bluntly for genteel conversation. But there was nothing genteel about these circumstances.

Drusilla, on the other hand, didn't seem distressed in the least. She leaned forward. "Perhaps. But I think it's more likely to be an unbalanced young woman at that school of yours, Concordia."

Concordia blinked. "You suggest one of the college students came into the gallery, hit Isaiah from behind, and stole the Blake *Catalogue*?" She didn't bother to conceal her skepticism.

Drusilla wagged a finger. "Rigorous study is deleterious to the female brain and nervous system. Dr. Clarke has written extensively on the subject." She looked over at David. "Thank heaven your wife is no longer part of that institution, though it may explain certain...other things." She gave Concordia a pointed look.

Concordia flushed. Drusilla must have guessed that she had been with child and then lost the babe the night of the dinner party. Could academic work truly cause such a malady? In a brief moment of panic, she considered it.

No. The doctor had reassured her she'd done nothing wrong. She blew out a breath. She shouldn't let Drusilla's old-fashioned notions get the better of her. Here they were, on the brink of the twentieth century. It was time to let go of ill-formed ideas.

David covered his wife's hand protectively. "To what *other things* do you refer, Aunt?" he challenged.

Georgeanna Bradley glared at her sister-in-law, who plucked at her skirts and fell silent.

Concordia was grateful for the staunch defense, although she realized she hadn't told David yet about teaching Charlotte's rhetoric class. She certainly wasn't going to say anything about it here.

Her lips twitched. *Hmm*, could her mind hold up under such rigor? She turned her chuckle into a cough as David leaned closer.

"Speaking of the female brain," he said to her, keeping his voice low, "has Capshaw *absolutely* cleared Miss Farraday?"

Drusilla was watching them, so Concordia whispered back. "Yes. He told me so when he left this morning, after searching the house."

But Drusilla had the ears of a bat. "Miss Farraday? You mean, the woman Lawrence has been seeing?"

"They are no longer seeing one another," John Bradley interjected, "for good reason." He explained the recent discovery of Madeline Farraday's paternity.

Drusilla's eyes widened. "Why had you not told me so before?" she demanded.

John raised an eyebrow in surprise. "It seemed unnecessary."

Drusilla gave a snort. "Well, I always knew Isaiah would get himself into trouble. But was he sure? I know an adventuress when I see one. She could have said anything he wanted to hear, in order to gain access to his fortune."

"It was the other way around, Drusilla," John said grimly. "Isaiah told the girl. She had not a clue as to her paternity. Besides, she does not inherit."

"Lawrence still refuses to believe she is Isaiah's daughter," Concordia said.

"One can hardly blame him," Georgeanna said. "Poor boy. He was fond of her."

"Poor Miss Farraday, as well," Concordia retorted. "Here she has a family at last, after being orphaned most of her life, but she is not welcomed because *Lawrence's* feelings take precedence."

David put a hand on hers. Whether in warning or entreaty, she did not know. No matter. She trusted her point was made.

Drusilla sat back with a sharp hiss. Georgeanna flushed scarlet.

John Bradley finally broke the ensuing silence. "I'm sorry to say you're right, Concordia. We have not yet reached out to the girl. But we must have a care for Lawrence and not put the two of them together precipitously."

Drusilla gave a snort. "I'm sure she is no better than she should be."

Concordia got up and stood by the window, pulling the curtain aside. She focused on a streetlamp at the corner, taking slow, deep breaths. Perhaps she should plead a headache and ask David to take her home. Any longer with these people, and she would certainly develop one.

David came up behind her and touched her elbow. "I apologize for Drusilla," he murmured. "For my entire family, actually. They're terribly worried about Lawrence and what might happen next."

Concordia turned to face him, briefly looking over his shoulder at her in-laws. They were no longer paying attention to her, thank goodness, and were arguing among themselves.

"I don't think Lawrence is Capshaw's only suspect," she murmured back.

"Oh? What makes you say that?"

"I spoke to Maisie today—Sergeant Maloney came to question her and search her belongings, can you believe it? And they took her uncle to the station for more questions. I also had a chat with Miss Phillips, and—"

"I hope you aren't planning to become involved in the investigation," David interrupted. "Capshaw is more than equal to it."

"I know that," she retorted. At least he hadn't used the word *meddle*, but it still rankled. And here she was going to tell David about Dorothy Phillips's past acquaintance with Isaiah. Where was the husband who appreciated his *self-sufficient* wife?

All conversation ceased as Lawrence entered the parlor. The fatigue of the day was evident in his slumped shoulders and shadowed cheeks.

"Sorry to be late." He stood by the hearth, warming his hands. "I had quite a stack of papers to take care of before tomorrow."

"Have you eaten?" Georgeanna asked, reaching for the bell pull.

Lawrence shook his head. "I'm too tired to be hungry, Mama." He reached for the decanter of brandy on the sideboard.

Concordia and David still stood beside the window, so they were the only ones to see Lawrence slip a flask from his pocket, fill it, and tuck it away before pouring himself a glass for immediate consumption.

Concordia met David's eye in an uneasy look.

Upon returning home at last, they found a tan envelope wedged behind the screen door.

"What's this?" David asked. *Concordia* was sprawled across the front. He passed it over.

Even in the dim light, Concordia recognized the hand. "Ah! It's from Charlotte." Bless the girl for bringing it to the house. In the commotion of David's arrival and the visit to her relatives, she'd completely forgotten. *Mercy*, was it running a household, being embroiled in a murder investigation, or having married into the family of Capshaw's prime suspects that was disrupting her life so?

They headed for the sitting room, an alcove tucked beside the much larger common room and sharing its three-sided deep stone fireplace. It was a cozy spot, with its worn upholstered chairs, antique rocker, knitted throws, and a low bookcase of favorite reading material. David's beloved duck decoys adorned the deep mantel, along with the brass candlesticks belonging to Concordia's grandmother and a cut-glass bowl of fragrant chrysanthemums. Even if things were a trifle dusty at the moment, it was a soothing space she turned to again and again.

David soon had the fire blazing brightly and settled into his favorite chair. "So what did Charlotte leave for you?"

"Notes for her rhetoric class." She passed them over. "Miss Pomeroy has asked me to take it over for a few weeks, until Mr. Richardson is able to return to campus. I start tomorrow."

He frowned in confusion. "What has Richardson to do with Miss Crandall?"

She explained the shuffling of instructors.

He grinned. "That's quite the Round Robin of teaching staff. I'm thankful to be in the Chemistry Department, where all is quiet."

"Quiet in the Chemistry Department?" She raised an eyebrow. "Were you informed of the explosion in Professor Grundy's laboratory last week while you were at the symposium?"

He rolled his eyes. "Just a small—well, not an 'explosion,' exactly. A student simply combined a couple of chemicals she should not have. The result was a sudden release of gas, with a thermal component."

She snorted. "In other words, an explosion."

"Semantics." He waved a dismissive hand. "Speaking of a release of gas, I assume our dean has an opinion on the subject of the newly minted Mrs. Bradley teaching one of the school's esteemed classes?" His eyes twinkled in mischief.

Concordia wrinkled her nose at him. "Indeed, Mr. Maynard is delighted *no end* by the prospect, particularly when confronted by the sight of me in my bicycle attire today."

He laughed outright at that. "My dear," he murmured, pulling her onto his lap, "I am coming to appreciate what an unusual woman I have for a wife."

CHAPTER 10

WEEK 5, INSTRUCTOR CALENDAR, OCTOBER 1899

Without contraries is no progression.

— WILLIAM BLAKE

---

oncordia had to admit to a ripple of excitement as she dressed in her best pleated eggshell shirtwaist and navy wool skirt and took the path from the farmhouse to campus that morning. David walked with her, heading for his own morning class.

Before they came within sight of the quadrangle, he kissed her forehead lightly beneath her hat. "Good luck, my dear. Enjoy yourself."

She smiled and gave a little wave as she hurried to Moss Hall.

As with all the classrooms in Moss Hall, Room 208 was a blend of tradition and progress. The dark paneling, stained-glass atrium windows, and raised dais with the instructor's mahogany podium were reminders of the college's seminary days, whereas the retro-fitted electric wall sconces, steam heating, and new student desks represented a look ahead, a suggestion of the best that could be offered to the young women looking to improve their prospects in life.

Concordia recognized a few faces that turned up expectantly toward her, though most were unfamiliar. She took a breath. "Good morning, class." She wrote upon the chalkboard, "Elements of Rhetoric," and then her name, "Mrs. Bradley." Behind her, she could hear students stirring in their seats and whispering among themselves.

She knew what that was about. Best to tackle this issue head on.

She turned to face them. "It sounds as if someone has a question." A hand was raised. She checked the seating chart Charlotte had provided. "Yes, Miss...VanDrake."

Miss VanDrake, a freshman with a mop-head of excitable blond curls—judging by the manner in which they bobbed as she spoke—said, "You are a married lady, ma'am? I thought married women were not allowed to teach here."

"Stand up and ask your question, if you please, Miss VanDrake," Concordia said sternly. "You should be aware of the protocol by now."

The young lady flushed. She stood, smoothed her skirt, and repeated the question.

Before Concordia could answer, another student—one she knew from last year who was now a sophomore—jumped to Concordia's defense. "But Miss Wells—I mean, Mrs. Bradley—has been a professor here *forever*. She's the best literature teacher I've ever had! It shouldn't matter whether she's married or—"

"*Miss Caron.*" Concordia cut across what was sure to be a speech that would have the girl swearing a blood-oath to her before she was done. "You are out of order."

"I'm sorry, miss—*uh*, ma'am."

"You should stand up as well," Concordia said.

The young lady complied, clenching her gloved hands nervously.

Concordia regarded the two young ladies. An idea was beginning to form. "If I am to read the mood of the classroom correctly, we may have a debate on our hands." She wrote upon the board: "Should married women be permitted to teach?" She was wildly straying from Charlotte's lesson plan. She hoped she wouldn't mind.

The students read the proposed question, eyes alight, and began whispering excitedly among themselves. Concordia gave them a moment. The two young ladies also waited, still respectfully standing.

"Now then," Concordia began, "I propose that we divide the class into teams. Miss VanDrake shall lead the opposition to married women teaching at a women's college. Is that acceptable to you, miss?"

The girl shifted uneasily. "I don't know if I necessarily believe that. I was only asking the question—"

"And an excellent question it was, Miss VanDrake," Concordia cut in. "That is why I have confidence in you acting as the lead. Do not worry about whether you hold this conviction personally. We are engaging in an exercise to formulate inductively and deductively reasoned arguments." Her expression softened. "One must, from time to time, employ such adversarial forms in order to achieve this." She turned to Miss Caron. "Are you prepared to lead the team arguing in favor of married women teaching at a women's college?"

She grinned. "Yes, ma'am."

"Very good. The rest of the class, group yourselves beside these young ladies according to your preference. If one side has too many, I will randomly select students for the other team."

All in all, Concordia reflected, as she headed to her borrowed office with a stack of themes to be graded, the debate was a success. The students had offered cogent arguments for their positions, which was the point. The issue of their teacher being a married woman had been thoroughly hashed out without her having to contribute any personal details in her own defense. An added benefit was their increased confidence in her ability to teach them.

Richardson's office was in the east wing of the second floor, near the sophomore and junior study rooms and above the gallery. Shifting the stack of papers to the crook of her elbow, she got the door open and hurriedly plunked them on the desk as they slid out of her arms. Grading these would take some time. *Mercy*, she'd been a veritable lady of leisure up to this point.

The air had the stuffy, stale quality of disuse. She opened the window.

Ernest Richardson had thoughtfully cleaned out most of his personal effects from the desk, but she laughed out loud when she rummaged for a red pencil and found a bottle of hair tonic in the bottom drawer. "Madam Leroy's Hair Restorer: soothes all irritation of the scalp, makes the hair grow thick and lustrous." She twisted the cap, took a sniff, and wrinkled her nose. Thank goodness David wasn't inclined to use such stuff. Of course, Richardson seemed a bit vain about his appearance. She recalled the smoothly pomaded hair and the ornate gemstone cufflinks and signet ring.

She stuck it back where she found it.

Finally done with grading, she went over to shut the window. The sun had retreated behind the tree line, and long shadows stretched into the quadrangle.

Now that her mind was no longer occupied with student themes, she turned back to the puzzle of Symond's death. Miss

Phillips's past association with him troubled her. What if Capshaw discovered the lady's history? He would think it more than coincidence that the man was killed in the gallery.

Concordia wished she knew exactly what had happened between Miss Phillips and Isaiah Symond, so she could better judge if it was a valid concern now. What was the secret they shared? But Symond was dead, and the history professor was obviously not going to tell her anything more.

Perhaps Symond had left behind a personal journal or other correspondence that could provide a clue? Symond's lawyer might know something. She would have to tread carefully, however, so as not to give Miss Phillips away.

She went over to the bottom desk drawer, took out the tonic bottle, and stared at it thoughtfully. It was a poor excuse to see Mr. Richardson, but it would have to do. With David staying late to oversee a laboratory experiment—one hoped there would be no explosions this time—she was left to her own devices for the evening.

She got Richardson's address from Mr. Langdon's secretary using only a mild half-truth. After all, it would have been absurd to admit she was returning a gentleman's hair tonic.

Concordia headed for the trolley stop just beyond the campus grounds. Richardson lived not far from the Capshaws. Perhaps she'd have time to stop by to see Sophia. Could she wheedle information from her friend about the case?

Hope springs eternal, as they say.

Concordia waved to the gatekeeper on her way out.

"Yer not coming back after ten, are ya?" he called out.

"Don't worry." Bless the man, he kept forgetting she didn't live on campus anymore. She could make her way home without

137

traversing the school grounds, if need be. It was a longer walk, to be sure, but a locked gate didn't affect her at all.

"Mrs. Bradley!" a young lady called. It was Madeline Farraday, hurrying to catch up. "Are you taking the trolley, too?"

"I'll be glad for the company." Concordia slowed her pace. "Have you been able to settle back into a routine?"

"I'm managing."

Concordia waited, but no further answer was forthcoming. "How are things at the boarding house?"

"Fine, except for the mutton stew Mrs. Carr serves nearly *every* night." She grimaced.

Concordia had a sudden idea. It would mean waiting until another time to see Richardson, but she was feeling ambivalent about using a grooming product as an excuse to talk to him anyway. She would much rather spend her free time with Sophia. "I'm going to visit friends. Would you like to join me there and stay for dinner?"

"You're not going home to have dinner with your husband?"

Concordia explained David's commitment and her sad lack of cookery.

Madeline smiled for the first time. "I didn't think there was anything you couldn't do. You seem so perfect."

Concordia rolled her eyes. "I doubt you'd find a single soul to agree with you on that score."

"Where are we going? Will they mind if I come along?"

The streetcar glided to a stop in front of them, and Concordia paid both their fares and secured their transfer tickets. "The Capshaws. I have a standing invitation there."

Miss Farraday's eyes widened. "Capshaw? The policeman? You're friends with *him*?"

"Actually, I'm best friends with his wife, Sophia, and over the course of several years"—and several murders, but she didn't offer that bit of information—"I've developed a friendship of sorts with the lieutenant, too."

"Extraordinary." Madeline hesitated. "This isn't some sort of trap to get me to talk to him again, is it? He's already interviewed me twice."

"Miss Farraday!" Concordia exclaimed. "Do you really think I'd stoop to such subterfuge? It's not at all conducive to one's digestion."

The girl chuckled. "I suppose not. You know"—she dropped her voice as more passengers boarded at the next stop—"he's not such a bad sort. It's just his job that's disagreeable."

Amen to that, Concordia thought.

"Won't he—or his wife—find it odd that a former murder suspect is dining in their home? Doesn't it break some sort of fraternization rule?"

Concordia snorted. "Not that I am aware."

"I suppose the awkwardness is worth it, to avoid another night of mutton," the girl declared.

Sophia, baby on her hip, answered the door herself. "Concordia! What a nice surprise. You're staying for dinner, I hope?" Her gaze turned to Madeline. "And who is this?" She opened the door wider and welcomed them in as Concordia made the introductions.

If Sophia recognized the name—Concordia often wondered how much Capshaw shared of his cases at home—she didn't let on. "A pleasure to meet you, Miss Farraday. You must stay for dinner as well. We're having"—Concordia could see Madeline holding her breath—"chicken pot pie."

The girl exhaled. "Sounds wonderful."

"Oh yes, Mrs. Tonner's pastry is light as a feather. It will be a shame to lose her."

"Lose her? Why?" Concordia asked.

"We've been training her to work for you." Sophia shifted the restless infant to her shoulder and patted his back. "I'd say she needs another week or so and she'll be ready. We're expecting someone new to replace her by then."

"That's so kind," Concordia said. "We'll be glad to have her." If Mrs. Tonner's pastry was as good as Sophia claimed, she would have to spend much more time riding her bicycle to fit into her shirtwaists.

"Training her?" Madeline echoed. "I don't think I understand."

Sophia led them down the narrow hallway toward the parlor. Concordia noticed two pairs of black policemen's boots, of two different sizes, aligned neatly beside the coat rack.

Soon, the ladies had settled themselves comfortably upon the overstuffed chairs grouped beside the fire.

"We don't have the funds to hire experienced staff," Sophia explained, "but I work at the settlement house, where women are in need of work experience in order to gain employment and support their children. Many have fled abusive husbands, you see. So, some of them work for us here. They learn additional skills, and we provide them with references when they're ready." She shifted the child again, who was fussing in earnest now.

"May I see him?" Madeline asked, reaching for the baby.

Sophia hesitated and glanced at Concordia, who nodded. "She's had plenty of experience."

Madeline took the infant. She cooed softly and held him belly-down across the crook of her arm as she rubbed his back and rocked him gently. He let out a loud *burp* and promptly nodded off, his cheek resting contentedly upon the girl's forearm.

Sophia's eyes widened. "You'll have to teach me that."

Madeline smiled.

"Is the lieutenant dining with us tonight?" Concordia asked.

"Yes. He's talking with someone in the study. He should be finished soon."

"Where's Eli?" Last year, the Capshaws had formally adopted the orphaned boy, now fourteen years old.

"He's apprenticing with a carpenter after school. He'll be home late." Sophia turned to Madeline. "Our house is riddled with all sorts of comings and goings."

140

Madeline smiled. "All the more interesting, I'd say."

Concordia stood. "I'd like to meet Mrs. Tonner, if it won't disrupt her work."

"That should be fine. She wants to meet you, too. You know the way to the kitchen."

Once Concordia was in the hallway, however, she didn't head for the kitchen but turned toward the corridor that led to the study. She was thinking about the second pair of policemen's boots...Sergeant Maloney's, perhaps? If so, she'd dearly love to hear what he and Capshaw were discussing.

She stopped short. Her objective, the door of the study, was still several yards down the hall. However, a difficulty presented itself. Oh, not in terms of any sort of ethical quandary—she'd made peace with herself long ago about listening at doors, though she wasn't sure if David had. Of course, he didn't have to know.

The real difficulty was how to approach the keyhole without getting *caught*. She was about to sneak up on two very perceptive policemen while traversing creaky floorboards. She bit her lip and looked around.

Ah. The door immediately at hand led into the sitting room. She remembered from previous visits that it shared a fireplace with the study just beyond. If the flue was open, she should be able to hear.

She turned the knob. It opened easily—God bless the woman Sophia was training—and she slipped inside.

The sitting room had no fire at the moment, so she was able to crouch right beside the opening, taking care to keep her skirts from catching upon the andirons. She quieted her breath as she cocked her head to listen.

"—didn't really expect there to be anything suspicious in Richardson's safe."

Though the flue lent a muffled-yet-echoed quality, she knew the voice was Capshaw's.

After a brief moment of silence, he went on. "So—this is everything from Symond's desk?"

"Yes, sir." That voice had a brusque, rough-at-the-edges tone. Definitely Maloney. "Didn' really look it over carefully. Just made sure that was all of it. Wi' him being a rich guy, I figured it'd be better for you to go through it. 'Sides, that lawyer was looking over my shoulder the whole time, as if 'xpecting I'd make off with something."

Concordia would dearly love to see the contents of Symond's desk for herself. Could Miss Pomeroy's cat statuette be among the items?

She heard Capshaw chuckle. "Richardson's a protective one. His alibi check out?"

"As much as any o' them do. Says he got back home 'bout midnight, then went t'bed. His manservant backs him up."

Capshaw growled. "I wish the doc could give us a better time frame for Symond's death. Between eleven and one in the morning doesn't help us much."

"Anything else, sir?"

She heard Capshaw sigh. "That's it for now. Thanks, Sergeant. I'll go through it all later. I'm sure you're wanting to get home to your supper."

Concordia barely heard the last words as she got to her feet.

Drat! The contents of her reticule spilled out on the rug. She groped quickly in the dark for the items, jammed them back in, and quietly skittered to the door.

All was clear. She blew out a breath. After closing the door behind her, she hurried to the kitchen to make the acquaintance of her soon-to-be servant.

A short woman of slight build was vigorously mashing potatoes, her back to the door. Pale strands of hair escaped her topknot. She was wearing one of Sophia's checked aprons, which on her diminutive frame nearly touched the floor.

This was Mrs. Tonner? She looked not much older than a child.

Concordia cleared her throat. "Excuse me."

With a stifled shriek, the woman spun around, masher tool raised above her shoulder in a defensive posture. A blob of potato barely missed her and dropped on the counter.

"Oh dear, I am sorry," Concordia said, as the woman's shoulders relaxed and she set down her tool. "Are you Mrs. Tonner?"

"Most folks jes' call me Trixie." She wiped her hands on her apron.

Upon closer inspection, Concordia could see faded remnants of a bruise above her cheekbone. "I'm Mrs. Bradley."

Her eyes widened. "Oh! So you're the lady—" She gave an awkward bob. "Pleas'd to meet you, ma'am." She reached up with slender, work-roughened fingers to self-consciously smooth the hair from her forehead. "I'm happy to be coming to service for you and your husband."

"As are we." Concordia smiled. After a glance at the pot bubbling on the stove, she added, "We'll have plenty of time later to become better acquainted. I'll let you get back to your work."

She gave another bob. "Thank you, ma'am."

Capshaw was already in the parlor chatting with his wife and Madeline when Concordia returned. He stood politely, but she waved him back into his seat. "Thank you for having us on short notice."

"You're welcome, any time." He gestured toward Madeline, still holding the sleeping baby. "And you as well, young lady."

Sophia smiled as she regarded her infant son. "Indeed, I'm often looking for company, with Aaron's long hours away from the house. And I imagine meals other than boarding house fare would be welcome."

Madeline blushed. "Thank you, ma'am."

"Oh, do call me Sophia. Everyone else does."

Madeline smiled her thanks.

"Sophia tells me you met Mrs. Tonner." Capshaw stretched his feet toward the fire. "What do you think of her?"

"We didn't talk long, as she had both burners going at once," Concordia said. "I'd say she seems capable. But she looks quite...young."

"She's older than she appears," Sophia said. "Twenty-three."

Madeline brightened. "Ah, we're the same age. She must have married quite young. Is she widowed?"

"Not exactly," Capshaw said.

Concordia waited for more. When none was forthcoming, she said, "She's rather skittish. Jumped a mile and waved a potato masher at me before she recollected herself."

Madeline's eyes widened. "Really?"

Sophia and Capshaw exchanged a look.

Concordia shifted impatiently. "Would either of you care to tell me more about this woman? David and I deserve to know whether our future maid will make a habit of brandishing kitchen implements, should we catch her unawares." Heaven only knew how she would react to the cat darting across her path.

"Trixie showed up at the settlement house one day," Sophia said, "with a black eye and a sprained wrist, courtesy of her husband. By her account, he's always had a temper. That particular time, he was angry that dinner wasn't on the table as soon as he wanted it. Her tale, sadly, is not uncommon. We tended to her injuries and took her in."

"Are there any children?" Concordia asked.

"No," Sophia said. "The marriage is a recent one."

"What happened to her husband?" Madeline asked.

Capshaw's jaw tensed. "Tonner came looking for his wife at the settlement house, tried to drag her out by the hair. Sophia ran for help. Tonner got one good shot at the patrolman before he was subdued. Now he's cooling his heels in jail."

No wonder the poor woman flinched. While Concordia

admired Trixie's pluck to defend herself so avidly, she hoped the reflex would soon abate.

Everyone had second helpings of the pot pie and lingered over coffee after dinner. Concordia was surprised it was such a congenial gathering, as the addition of Madeline Farraday could have made things awkward. But the Capshaws' ready hospitality had put the girl at her ease. When she showed particular interest in Hartford Settlement House, Sophia, of course, was more than happy to talk about a project that had been her passion for the past ten years.

"The need is greater than ever before, as the city's population continues to grow," Sophia said, dropping a lump of sugar in her coffee. "We want to expand the school program for the primary grades, but we first need funds for a new building."

Madeline leaned forward, eyes bright with interest. "Our economics class is going to visit your institution next week. I hope we can see what you already have in place." She waved a hand toward Concordia. "In fact, Mrs. Bradley is to be one of our chaperones on the trip."

Capshaw raised an eyebrow. "One would think the Atheneum a better choice for a class excursion."

"Our professor thinks it's an excellent opportunity to learn about the funding of a charitable organization and the day-to-day use of its money," Madeline explained. "And we've been sewing clothes and stuffed animals to give to the children."

Sophia smiled. "I'm sure they'll be happy to see you all."

Concordia stood and set aside her napkin. "If you will excuse me a moment."

Capshaw stood politely, then re-seated himself as she left the room.

She didn't have much time. She hurried into the study and closed the door behind her.

Sitting atop Capshaw's desk was a large box. That had to be it. With one last glance over her shoulder, she started rummaging through it. If Symond kept the statuette displayed on his desk, it would be here.

Yes—there it was, tucked near the bottom, among papers, writing implements, keys, and a letter opener.

She examined the black stone figurine, a slim cat that sat regally upon a small, throne-like block with hieroglyphic writing etched into its base. At a scarce six inches, it should fit in her pocket.…

She blew out a breath. Was she really going to take it away with her?

But it wasn't evidence. And it was only fair that Miss Phillips should have it back, as it should never have been extorted from her in the first place. The only thing lost by its removal was proof of Isaiah Symond's mean, petty nature.

Even so, Capshaw would be furious with her if he found out. She shivered.

Well, then, he wasn't going to find out.

She tucked it in her pocket and made sure the box was exactly back in its place.

CHAPTER 11

WEEK 7, INSTRUCTOR CALENDAR, OCTOBER 1899

He who desires, but acts not, breeds pestilence.

— WILLIAM BLAKE

---

*C*oncordia had just put on her stout walking boots when Charlotte Crandall stepped onto the front porch of the Bradley house, a large, empty basket under each arm.

"Do we need that many chestnuts for next week?" Concordia asked, buttoning her jacket against the autumnal chill. The frost would be on the pumpkins in earnest by All Hallow's Eve.

Charlotte rolled her eyes. "If you remember last year's nut-burning, we went through an entire basket. You know how enthusiastic the students are about the superstition."

Charlotte was right about that. The burning of the nuts—or *nits*, as they were referred to in Scotland, where the tradition originated—was the most popular of the activities offered at the Halloween Ball. Each girl took a turn throwing a pair of nuts into the fire and watching them burn while naming a particular young man she favored. If the nuts popped or jumped apart, the union would not last. But if they burned brightly, a romance might be in the offing. Concordia recalled the Robert Burns verse:

Some kindle couthie side by side,
And burn thegither trimly;
Some start awa wi' saucy pride,
An' jump out owre the chimlie....

The activity was not without its hazards, however—over-eager young ladies crowding in front of the fire in voluminous ball gowns, nuts burning and popping, occasionally jumping clean out of the fire. It took a firm hand to maintain control of the proceedings.

Naturally, that firm hand was Randolph Maynard, though he was none too thrilled at the prospect.

Concordia led the way to the barn to retrieve the long-handled hook. "I wonder if our dean has enough patience to supervise the burning of *two* baskets' worth of chestnuts."

Charlotte smiled. "We won't burn them all. Ruby asked us to gather extra. The girls have been clamoring for her chestnut soup, and she's also making candied chestnuts for the ball's buffet. You said there should be plenty on your property?"

"Indeed." Concordia tugged at the barn door. "I took a walk through the grove last week, and the ground was thick with them. We'll bring the pole in case we need to knock down more."

"Caesar!" Charlotte exclaimed, as the large orange tabby sauntered out of the barn and twined among her skirts. "I haven't seen you in ages."

"Ah, he remembers you."

Charlotte allowed him to sniff her hand before he rubbed his head against it. "He's doing well—more energetic than I've seen him."

Concordia remembered the housekeeper's tumble down the stairs because of the *energetic* beast. And now they were about to get a new maid who might take a spatula to the poor thing if he gave her a fright. "We try to keep him mostly out-of-doors these days. He finally stopped terrorizing the chickens and has turned his attentions to the field mice." She passed over the hook. "It's working out well."

Charlotte met her eye. "I still miss Margaret Banning," she said quietly. "This will be our first Halloween Ball without her."

"It seems strange, doesn't it?" Concordia said. As cantankerous as the old lady had been, she missed her, too. But best to steer clear of the subject. Miss Banning's passing had been under less-than-ideal circumstances. "Did I hear correctly—the administration is permitting the students to bring male guests to the ball?" That had never been the case in the history of the school.

"Oh, yes," Charlotte said. "The girls are quite excited."

No surprise there. "Why the change in policy?"

"The college is scaling back the dance next spring—where the girls were permitted escorts—to save money. That will be a seniors-only occasion. The Halloween Ball seemed the best option to compensate. Not every girl will have an escort, of course, but one cannot completely deprive the students of male attention." Charlotte winked.

Concordia shook her head. Halloween, pranks, and boys? It was a mischievous combination. "It seems I've missed quite a bit, now that I no longer attend faculty meetings. There have been no other drastic changes, I trust? We're not hosting the ball in the Tower of London, for instance?"

Charlotte chuckled. "It's at Sycamore House, as usual. But we'll need every available chaperone, with the added male presence."

Concordia suppressed a smile at the memory of Charlotte Crandall at the last ball the young lady had attended as a student. She—and her gentleman companion—had most definitely required a chaperone back then.

"What's so funny?" Charlotte asked.

"Oh? Nothing. David and I will be happy to chaperone."

"I hoped you would. Besides the regular staff, President Langdon has recruited several faculty members from Trinity."

The cat trotted behind them as they made their way to the stand of chestnut trees just beyond the pasture.

"Does Caesar follow you around like this regularly?" Charlotte asked.

"Only when it's mealtime. He's practically dog-like then."

If cats were capable of scornful looks—and many claim that to be the case—Caesar most certainly cast one her way before veering off to the pasture.

"My students tell me they're enjoying the rhetoric class," Charlotte said. "Thank you for stepping in."

"My pleasure. And we're finally getting back to your lesson plan. How much longer will Richardson be out, do you know?"

Charlotte shrugged. "Perhaps until Thanksgiving. At least, that's what the administration is planning for." She looked at Concordia anxiously. "I hope this isn't a disruption to your... personal life."

Concordia could think of several aspects of her life right now that were far more disruptive. "Not terribly so. How are you progressing with the senior play?"

Charlotte grimaced. "Time-consuming doesn't begin to describe it. At least we're nearly finished with the auditions, but hurt feelings are running high at the moment. I don't know how you did it these past years."

Concordia smiled to herself. That was one aspect of her former life she didn't miss in the least.

The afternoon, though chill, was pleasant enough, with the sun peeking through the clouds from time to time. The breeze died down considerably as Concordia and Charlotte entered the grove and began gathering the partly open, spiny pods that littered the ground, picking carefully among them for intact sets of chestnuts within.

"I think we're going to need that hook," Concordia said. "Many of these have been gnawed by animals already."

As Charlotte was much taller than Concordia, she took charge of the pole and wielded it with enthusiasm. When they had enough to fill their baskets, they headed back to the porch to sort through their bounty.

"It seems you have a visitor." Charlotte pointed to a young man in a dark woolen coat with a high, light-brown fur collar. He lingered uncertainly by Concordia's front door.

"Why, that looks like Miss Farraday's beau, Lawrence Bradley," Charlotte said.

His face smoothed in relief when he caught sight of them. He waved and hurried down the stone walk.

"Um, well"—Concordia dropped her voice—"they are no longer romantically involved."

"Really? They seemed profoundly attached to each other. What has happened?"

"It's a long story," Concordia murmured. "But don't mention Miss Farraday in his presence. It's a painful subject."

Charlotte gave a quick nod as he came up to greet them.

"Ladies, how nice to see you." He tipped his cap deferentially. "Here, let me take those," he added, reaching for their baskets.

"Thank you," Concordia said. "Were you looking for David?" Though Lawrence and David were not exactly confidants, she couldn't imagine what else would have brought him here.

"Actually, I wanted to speak to you...alone?" He shot a quick look at Charlotte.

Charlotte took the hint. "I should be going."

"What about the chestnuts?" Concordia asked.

"If you don't mind keeping them for now," Charlotte said, "I'll bring a couple of girls back with me tomorrow after dinner. They should be doing some of the work, after all. We can shuck the pods then." She inclined her head toward Lawrence. "Goodbye, Mr. Bradley."

But he had already turned back to the house without another word. By the time Concordia had said goodbye to Charlotte, he was through the front door with the baskets.

She sniffed at his rudeness. He could have at least waited for her. She was mistress of this house. And he had not taken proper leave of the woman who had graciously allowed him the private conversation he sought.

She followed him in and hung up her jacket. He'd stowed the baskets out of the way in the vestibule and stood politely now, waiting for her to precede him into the parlor. She honestly didn't know how to address this impulsive-one-moment, decorous-the-next duality of the man's nature. It was unsettling.

She didn't bother to take his coat—perhaps he would leave more quickly that way. She poked the fire and put on a fresh log before seating herself and gesturing toward the rocking chair beside the hearth. "I'm surprised to see you here in the middle of the workday. I would have expected you to be in Mr. Richardson's office."

He sat at its edge, as if reluctant to make himself too comfortable. "I was out already, delivering documents to some of Mr. Richardson's clients. I thought I'd stop by."

"Oh? Can I be of some assistance?" she asked politely.

He seemed to struggle with ordering his thoughts. She waited.

"It's regarding Madeline," he said finally. "She has sent back every note and refuses to communicate with me."

"I imagine she's upset by the situation as a whole. This is naturally most difficult for her. Try not to take it personally. You are not to blame for your great-uncle's past."

He blew out an exasperated breath. "But I *am* to blame. I made things far worse. I could have ended the relationship weeks before she found out from Mr. Richardson."

"How could you have possibly known—oh, I see. Your great-uncle had already told you?"

He gave a miserable nod, looking down at his feet. "Just before the semester began. I'd introduced her to him by then, at the Atheneum. It's the first time he'd laid eyes on her. He told me later that he recognized the resemblance to her mother right away. He had Richardson ask some discreet questions about Miss Farraday, to check his hunch. Then he told me."

She couldn't believe what she was hearing. "You continued to court the poor girl for two more weeks—allowing her to form a deeper attachment—*after* you learned she is in actuality your"—she nearly choked upon the word—"aunt?"

He flinched. "You must understand, Concordia—at the time, I didn't *believe* him! I thought he was lying, playing another cruel joke."

"Cruel joke? What do you mean?"

"You don't know what he was like—giving with one hand and taking away with the other. He'd promised me part ownership of the ranch…he knew I loved it there…then he sold it to his foreman instead. After the three years of service I'd given him." He blew out a breath. "He could see how much I cared for Madeline, so when he told me…I thought he was toying with me again."

She could see how it might have been. Isaiah Symond had cried wolf one too many times, and Lawrence, already motivated by self-interest, had not believed his claim about Madeline Farraday. Then Symond, alarmed by Lawrence continuing the relationship with the young lady, had sent his lawyer to break the news to her.

"It's a wonder, really, that I'm a co-heir in his will," Lawrence went on. "For years he would promise to leave me money, then take offense at something I'd done and change it again. And now we know he was going to take me out of will again but was killed before he had the chance."

"Mercy, don't let the police hear you talk like that," she said. "You're one of Capshaw's best suspects."

He flushed and looked down at his hands.

She watched him in silence. *One of Capshaw's best suspects.* That might be why Madeline refused to engage in a correspondence with Lawrence—maybe she feared he'd killed his great-uncle in a rage over their doomed love affair. Or in a fit of greed.

She refrained from voicing the thought aloud. "You believe she refuses to communicate with you because you delayed telling her?" she asked instead.

"I'm sure of it."

"How did she find out?"

Lawrence scowled. "That policeman told her."

"Capshaw? He found out from Mr. Richardson, I suppose?"

"I think so."

"I'm exceedingly sorry to hear it," she said, "but the young lady was bound to learn about it eventually. Why are you telling *me*?"

"Madeline values your opinion. Even when she wanted to quit school, she stayed because she didn't want to disappoint you."

Concordia sat back in surprise. "She wanted to quit?"

"But she didn't," he said, "because you had gone to such trouble to get her admitted to Hartford Women's College."

Concordia smiled. "It wasn't as much trouble as some might imply." Dean Maynard in particular came to mind.

"But why go to such lengths for a stranger?" he asked. "I've wondered about that."

She hesitated. Would Lawrence understand how important it was for a young woman to have an education, to choose a path in life that suited her?

She decided on the simple explanation. "I thought it was a shame that her intellect was languishing in a menial job." She fell silent, watching the flames in the fireplace dance and curl around the logs, the light reflecting off the brass andirons. Memories of the summer flooded back. "She also reminded me of someone," she added, half to herself.

"Oh? Who?"

"Victoria Lester." She waved a dismissive hand. "You wouldn't have known her. She was a former student who had to drop out for financial reasons. She'd planned to return as soon as she'd saved enough."

"Oh? What happened to her?"

She was murdered. Concordia didn't want to say it aloud, because in all honesty she would also have to add: *I should have stopped it.*

She clenched her hands until they ached. Had she *pushed* Madeline Farraday into attending Hartford Women's College? Had she advocated for her, made her an exception, coaxed and mentored, all to live out a dead girl's dream of going back to school? Was Concordia using Miss Farraday to atone for Miss Lester being robbed of her future?

"Concordia? Concordia, are you all right?"

She looked up to see Lawrence crouched next to her, holding out his handkerchief.

She smiled her thanks, dabbed at her eyes, and passed it back. "I will be."

He hesitated, with the caution bred into every male at the sight of a woman's tears. "Do you want to...talk about it?" he asked politely, as he resumed his seat.

Obviously, neither of them wanted *that.* "Never mind," she said. "What were you saying before?"

"I was hoping you could speak with her."

"Who?" Certainly, no one could speak to Miss Lester, ever again. Concordia took a breath, shifting her attention firmly to the here and now.

"Madeline, of course." He raked a hand through his hair. "To explain why I acted as I did."

"To what end, Lawrence?" she asked quietly. "Is it not better for the two of you to remain apart and give the ardent feeling between you time to subside?"

"I fully intend to keep my distance, believe me. I only want to know she's forgiven me. Then I can rest easy."

Concordia did not bother to mask her skeptical expression.

"You place too much confidence in my influence."

"She'll listen to you, I know it. And there's something else I want you to tell her. I've made a new will. If something happens to me, she'll get my share of Uncle Isaiah's inheritance."

"There's no cause to be worrying about that sort of thing," Concordia protested. "You're young and in good health."

"One never knows," he said gloomily. "Will you talk to her?"

She sighed. "Very well."

Lawrence smiled his thanks and stood.

Concordia held up a hand. "Before you go, I want to ask you something." She took a breath for courage, wondering what David would think of her broaching the subject when the rest of the Bradley clan seemed to be avoiding it.

He waited.

"Why have you gone back to drinking spirits? You know how much trouble that caused years ago."

He raised a self-conscious hand to his breast-coat pocket, almost defensively. "How can you ask me that? Do you not know what I've endured? The only woman I've ever loved turns out to be a close relation and therefore unattainable. My father doesn't trust me, my brother barely speaks to me, and the police suspect me of murdering my great-uncle." He gave a bitter laugh. "Would *you* not turn to brandy for a bit of comfort?"

"No, I would not," she retorted. Her tone sounded harsh and domineering, even to her own ear. Like Aunt Drusilla. *Mercy.*

He winced.

"I'm sorry, Lawrence." She softened her tone. "I know you have troubles, but surely you can see that brandy is not the solution. And consider all that you have. You will soon become a millionaire. You have youth, intelligence, and pleasing looks. You may direct your own course in life. You will meet any number of women, one of whom is bound to help you fall in love again."

His lips grew pale. "You will *never* understand," he hissed.

She watched him slam the parlor door on his way out.

CHAPTER 12

WEEKS 7-8, INSTRUCTOR CALENDAR, OCTOBER 1899

He who would do good to another must do it in Minute Particulars;
General Good is the plea of the scoundrel, hypocrite and flatterer.

— WILLIAM BLAKE

*H*artford Women's College did not often organize in-town excursions, preferring to build a sense of student community through on-campus activities, where errant young men do not pose a distraction to the young ladies.

But today's visit to Hartford Settlement House by the economics class was to be a happy exception to that rule, and the young ladies chattered excitedly as they clutched bags filled with their handmade gifts for the children and walked to the trolley stop.

The petite, soft-spoken Professor Benson flashed Concordia a grateful look as they followed behind. "Thank heaven you could come, Mrs. Bradley. I would have found the prospect of monitoring fifteen young ladies on a streetcar back and forth to the settlement house especially daunting."

Concordia smiled. "They're a high-spirited bunch, I grant you that. I'm happy to. I'll have the chance to see my friend Sophia Capshaw again. She's in charge of the school program."

Professor Benson nodded. "I'd heard you two were acquainted."

Concordia also hoped to find a quiet moment to speak with Madeline Farraday about Lawrence. Her promise to her brother-in-law weighed heavily.

For the first leg of the trolley ride, they had the car completely to themselves. Concordia smiled as she noticed Madeline had moved to a bench in the back, accompanied by a trio of young ladies who shared a bag of sweets among them. It was nice to see her making more friends.

The private conversation about Lawrence could wait for now. The girl deserved to simply be a student for a little while at least, without the cares of a courtship gone wrong. Or a murder inquiry.

Once they reached the post office stop in the downtown district, their streetcar became crowded with stiff-collared men in pinstripe business suits. Some were taken aback at the sight of so many young ladies aboard on a weekday morning. Others attempted to engage the girls in conversation. A pointed look from Concordia usually was sufficient to discourage the latter.

This part of the ride was mercifully short, and soon they were pulling up to the Hartford Hospital stop, only a block from the settlement house.

Sophia was there to greet them and usher the group into a large meeting room. Concordia marveled at her friend's ceaseless energy. How she managed the care of her policeman husband, two children, and a household of her own, all while running the primary school program, was a marvel.

"Concordia, it's rare we get to do this so often," Sophia said, giving her a quick embrace.

Remorse squeezed Concordia's chest as she remembered the last time she had been in Sophia's home.

The figurine from Capshaw's evidence box was safely back in Miss Phillips's hands—and that lady had been effusive in her thanks—but now Concordia wasn't sure she'd done the right thing. She hadn't even told David about it.

"Trixie's ready to start her service whenever you want her," Sophia went on.

Concordia firmly tamped down her guilt. "That's wonderful! Is tomorrow too soon?" A home-cooked meal would be welcome, after successive weeks of dining-hall fare. And she'd noticed the bookshelves, sadly, did not dust themselves.

"Well, then, tomorrow it is," Sophia said.

Concordia pressed her hand briefly in gratitude as the young ladies found their chairs. All turned their attention to the director of the settlement house, Martha Newcombe.

Concordia stifled a yawn after an hour of Miss Newcombe expounding upon bookkeeping, fund-raising, and the challenges of applying for city permits. It all sounded terribly complicated—and terribly boring. Important work, to be sure, but she was glad there were others willing to devote their intellect and energy to such a cause.

"And now," Miss Newcombe was saying, "let us visit the play-room, where you can meet the children and distribute your gifts."

Concordia stood in the doorway of the sun-filled playroom, well away from the tumult of shrieking youngsters and energetic college girls. Toys and books littered the space. The young ladies knelt on the floor right along with the children, playing with spinning tops, wooden blocks, and brightly painted pull toys.

She found herself paying attention to the little ones, as they reached chubby fingers for a hand to hold or a lap to climb into. Her heart clenched with a now-familiar ache of loss.

Turning away, she noticed Madeline Farraday was comfortably ensconced in a window seat with a four-year-old girl on her lap, holding a large picture book in front of them. The child reached up to pat her cheek, and Madeline hugged her close.

Concordia navigated the chaos to join them at the window seat. "You seem to have a way with children," she murmured. First Sophia's baby, and now this child. "When I met you last summer, I didn't think you liked your job very much."

Madeline chuckled. "Oh, I like *children* fine. I don't care for their rich, uppity parents, who insist upon their progeny being spotless and well-behaved at all times." She turned the last page and started to close the book when the girl reached out and tapped it. "Again!" she demanded.

"Again? Well, all right then." Madeline smiled over the girl's head at Concordia, who left them to it.

The class arrived back to campus in time for the midday meal.

"Miss Farraday," Concordia called, as the girl started to follow the others into the dining hall, "could I have a word?"

Madeline waved her friends on and joined Concordia on a bench overlooking the quadrangle.

"I won't keep you long," Concordia began in apology, "but I wanted to speak with you about Lawrence."

Madeline stiffened.

"He regrets his role in complicating the situation," Concordia said quickly, before she could storm off.

Her eyes widened. "He told you?"

"Yes, he's quite distressed about it. But he promises to keep his distance."

Madeline snorted. "Sending me notes of supplication on a daily basis does not constitute *keeping one's distance.*"

Concordia winced. The man's impulsivity obviously warred with his common sense. "May I at least convey to him that you do not blame him for what has occurred? That might ease his mind somewhat."

The girl was silent.

"Then he would not feel compelled to write to you daily," Concordia added, "seeking reassurances to that effect."

Madeline's lips twitched. "Your logic is inescapable, Mrs. Bradley. You may tell him what you wish."

"I'd prefer to tell him what is *true*," Concordia retorted.

"The truth? I want nothing to do with him, or any of the Bradley family."

"Are you that bitter about your father abandoning you?"

"Bitter enough." Madeline smoothed her skirts. "Though Mr. Richardson tells me Symond never knew I existed until he first laid eyes on me last month. If true, then I should not lay the blame at his door. I don't know why my mother would not have told him. But it's possible—she was a proud woman."

"Why, then, do you want nothing to do with the family? Once the Bradleys come to accept you, they could be of help, and you wouldn't have to struggle so."

Madeline tilted her chin. "I got along well enough in the world before I knew of their existence, and I will continue to do so."

Pride ran in the family, it seemed.

Concordia was about to remonstrate with the girl when she noticed the tears on her downcast lashes. Then it hit her. "You suspect Lawrence *killed* his great-uncle?"

"I *know* he did. And that policeman knows it, too." Abruptly, she stood and ran off, leaving Concordia gaping after her.

"But the police haven't arrested Lawrence," David said. "It's been several weeks since Isaiah died. Multiple searches have turned up nothing. I doubt there is anything to worry about, my dear."

They had just returned from the evening meal in the dining

hall and were settled before a welcome blaze in the deep stone fireplace.

Despite its warmth, Concordia shivered. "Madeline hurried away before I could inquire further. But for her to say *she knows...*"

"It's disquieting," he agreed. "Let us review what we know that might serve to incriminate Lawrence. Perhaps we can find a hole somewhere." He ticked off the list on his fingers. "First, there is his motive. He was exceedingly angry at Isaiah for breaking up his courtship with Madeline Farraday. And we have seen my brother's temper get the better of him in times past."

"And if he knew he stood to inherit your great-uncle's fortune," Concordia interrupted, "that would be another motive."

"Although Richardson said Isaiah's new will made Miss Farraday the sole beneficiary," David said. "If it had been signed, Lawrence would have gained nothing."

She felt a prickle of unease. "Wouldn't your brother likely know about that? He works in Richardson's office."

"Yes, that's a black mark against him. If money was the motive, he would have to kill Isaiah before the new will was signed." He brightened. "One thing in Lawrence's favor, however, is that he was with Father for most of the evening."

"But not all of the evening," she pointed out. "Besides, your father is co-heir. In Capshaw's eyes, at least, that contaminates his objectivity, as does the fact that Lawrence is his son."

David tapped his chin thoughtfully. "So it comes down to whether Lawrence went straight home after leaving Isaiah's house, as he asserts, or rushed over to campus to confront him."

"Well, he couldn't have gotten through the front gate," Concordia said. "The gatekeeper locked it at ten o'clock. There's the east gate, of course, but someone would have noticed a vehicle coming in at that hour."

"Capshaw would have been sure to check on that," David said.

"If Lawrence's vehicle had been seen, we wouldn't be having this conversation. He'd be in jail. Could he have gotten in on foot?"

Concordia knew first-hand of a particular spot along the hedge where that was possible. "Well, the campus isn't *impenetrable*."

He shot her a look but didn't press further. Instead, he asked, "So what's happened to the Blake *Catalogue*? Are we to assume the murderer took it to create the illusion of a burglary gone wrong?"

The idea of a thief was looking quite remote now. Far too many people had disliked Isaiah Symond—Lawrence, John, Drusilla, Richardson, Miss Farraday...even Miss Phillips.

Feeling like a thief herself, Concordia was beginning to wish she'd never taken the figurine from Capshaw's desk.

She must have sighed aloud, as David's eyes softened in sympathy and he reached over to pat her hand. "It must be distressing to think the pamphlet could be gone forever."

"I fear that's the case. Whoever took it could have easily burned it. It isn't bulky." Even if the school never recovered it, she hoped it was still out there, somewhere, intact. She wasn't an expert in the field of literary collecting, but there probably weren't that many Blake *Catalogues* left. She met David's eye. "Would Lawrence have the wherewithal to think of taking the *Catalogue*? Symond's maid said he was obviously intoxicated. I don't have much experience with your brother in that condition."

"Thank heaven for that." He hunched forward, elbows resting on the chair arms, fingers steepled as he stared into the fire. "If he was intoxicated enough that he couldn't control his anger, I very much doubt he would think of such a misdirection."

She sucked in a breath. A terrible notion struck her.

"What is it?"

She bit her lip.

"Concordia?" he said sharply. "Tell me."

"What if Madeline came upon Lawrence in the gallery, just

after the fact? Perhaps she wanted to protect him. It could have been her idea to take the pamphlet to fool the police."

It would account for why Miss Farraday refused to explain her whereabouts when she was gone in the middle of the night and why she was so sure that Lawrence was responsible for Isaiah's death. But what could she have done with the *Catalogue*? By all accounts Capshaw had been thorough, searching the campus, their house, John Bradley's house, and Richardson's house and office.

The most expedient course would have been to destroy it, but Concordia had difficulty believing that Madeline—someone with an abiding love of literature—would sacrifice an item of such significance.

"It always comes back to Lawrence," David mused.

"I'm sorry," she said quietly.

He blew out a breath. "Let us consider alternatives. My father thought that Richardson was likely."

Concordia sat up straighter. "That's right. Didn't Lawrence hear them argue?"

"On more than one occasion. The most recent was the day before Isaiah's death."

"Does he know what they argued about? Money, I imagine."

David narrowed his eyes. "Lawrence said he couldn't make out the words through the closed inner door."

"And Capshaw knows of this, correct?"

"Yes. But of course, we have no idea what he did with the information after that. So who does that leave?"

"The list becomes more improbable as we go," she said. "Your entire family despised the man. But the notion of your mother or Aunt Drusilla knocking him over the head and taking the *Catalogue* defies belief. I don't think either one has set foot in the gallery, ever." She gave him a steady look, with a hint of a smile. "And you aren't in contention, as you were out of town. Count yourself lucky."

He grimaced. "Which leaves my father. Highly unlikely, for the same reason as my mother and aunt."

"Not quite the *same*," she corrected. "He inherits a fortune."

"I've known him all my life, Concordia," he said quietly, meeting her eye. "He would not do such a thing, for hatred or money."

"Do you feel the same about your brother?" she asked.

"I *want* to say yes, but I cannot." He reached under his spectacles to rub the bridge of his nose. "He seems to have straightened out his life, and yet—I cannot trust him fully."

She understood his ambivalence. There seemed a sort of— well, perhaps one could call it a soft spot in the core of Lawrence's character. His motivations and behaviors sprung from the needs of the moment, rather than being guided by an unshakable center.

"So we are back to Lawrence," she said.

"Or someone at the college," David said. "What about George? You said he'd been questioned multiple times, correct? His wrench was used to attack Isaiah. He could get into the gallery easily."

"But he was never arrested. Probably because Capshaw couldn't discover a motive." Miss Phillips, of course, had an excellent motive. What was the secret Symond had known? Would she have killed to protect her friend—or herself—from possible ruin?

By the woman's own admission, she'd gone into the gallery with Symond that night. There was no one else to say he was still alive when she left. With Lovelace's tools at hand, did the lady have the strength to kill him?

It might be time to confess to Capshaw that she'd taken the cat statuette and tell him why.

All was ready for the Bicycle Club's final excursion of the season, before the cold weather established itself in earnest. Concordia arrived promptly at Willow Cottage in her bicycling outfit. She'd left her machine in the woodshed the night before next to Maisie's bicycle so the girl could oil the sticking gears.

"I got everything working smoothly," Maisie said, pulling her own bicycle from the shed first. She reached back inside. "Wait until you see—" She sucked in a breath.

"What is it?" Concordia peered over her shoulder. "Why, there's no seat." The stem where the saddle should be was sticking up, bare.

Maisie's expression was grim. "The saddle was perfectly intact when I finished with your machine last night."

"It looks as if the prankster has struck again," Concordia said. "You'd better check yours."

But Maisie was already looking it over. "It seems all right. I don't understand it." She turned to her with worried eyes. "Do you still want to go on with the ride? You can borrow Anna's machine. She won't be coming."

Concordia knew, as the club sponsor, there would be no excursion without her. "Of course we'll go. I'll get to the bottom of this later. Even if the saddle doesn't turn up, I still have the original one back at home." David had given her the newer, more comfortable seat only last month. She shook her head. It hadn't lasted long.

The ride was well attended, with five other girls besides Concordia and Maisie joining them today. Though it was late in the month and Halloween was only a few days away, the air was still and the sun had sufficiently warmed them by the time they'd reached the towpath beyond the campus grounds. They rode in companionable silence.

Concordia breathed in the sharp tang of dried hay bales from the nearby farms and struggled to clear her mind. The prank disturbed her. She wanted to believe her bicycle was randomly chosen to be sabotaged, but it was difficult not to take it personally.

Something of greater import vied for her attention, however—her conversation yesterday with Miss Phillips. The professor had adamantly refused to reveal the details of what had happened all those years ago. Their interchange had grown more heated after Dorothy Phillips realized Concordia wanted to go to Capshaw about the figurine.

"I did not ask you to take back the statuette," she'd said, standing abruptly in her agitation. "You did that on your own."

"I'm aware of that. I'll explain it to him."

"He won't believe you. He'll think I put you up to it. It will make things far worse."

The lady had a point.

"I'm sorry." Concordia swallowed. "I suppose...I can keep it to myself."

Miss Phillips's expression softened. "I did not kill Symond. Never fear about that. You believe me, don't you?"

How could she say no?

Now, as the scenery whizzed by them, Concordia knew she'd been wrong to put it off. As soon as they finished the ride, she would tell David everything. Then he could advise her as to what to do.

"Watch out for the rocks," Maisie called.

Concordia swerved just in time.

"Who's that up ahead?" one of the girls asked.

Concordia shaded her eyes for a better look. A tall, burly-chested man in a cap and buttoned tunic uniform stood in the middle of the path, waiting. Her heart sank.

At the Kinsley Street Station, she glimpsed Miss Phillips at the end of the hall. She tried to catch the lady's eye, but the history professor looked straight ahead and pretended not to see her.

She must think I went to Capshaw after all, Concordia thought gloomily, though she wished she had—long ago. How had he found out?

Maloney cleared his throat as she lingered. "This way, ma'am."

As police interrogation rooms go—Concordia deliberately avoided reckoning how many she'd sat in…well, none since San Francisco, mercifully—this one was as Spartan as one would expect. The bright light did little to warm the cold tile floor, and the few sticks of furniture in the space were worn and dilapidated. But at least the sergeant brought her tea. It was hot and strong, served in a mug with a chipped handle. Had she seen this one before? Surely not. If this was their best mug for visitors, heaven help the condition of the rest of them.

At last, her feet began to warm, and her shivering subsided. After a few more sips, she set the mug down, carefully maneuvering around the splinter in her chair arm.

"Am I under arrest?" she asked Maloney, who had been quietly observing her the entire time.

He unsuccessfully suppressed a snort. "Yer a cool one. Most college ladies would be in hysterics or fainting dead away."

She was tempted to ask how many *college ladies* he counted among his acquaintances but decided the question would be impertinent. "Well? Am I?"

"That's up to the lieuten'nt, ma'am."

He got up at the sound of a knock and stepped out.

All Concordia could catch were bits of a whispered conversation. Then she heard a familiar voice.

"David!"

He burst through the door, despite Maloney's attempt to hold him back. She fell into his arms and cried.

So much for a composed *college lady*.

"All right, Lieutenant, my wife has told you everything she knows." David assumed his sternest professorial voice as he addressed Capshaw, who didn't seem in the least intimidated. "It's time to let her go."

Capshaw glared at Concordia. "There is still the matter of tampering with evidence."

"I didn't consider it *evidence* at the time. I only sought to protect Dorothy Phillips from distress." She looked down at her hands. "She'd suffered enough because of Isaiah Symond."

"Which gave her a powerful motive for murdering the man. One that I never knew of before today," he retorted. "It was not your place to determine the importance of that." He leaned in closer. "But what bothers me most is that you were in *my* home, enjoying *my* hospitality. I trusted you to act accordingly. Instead, you took advantage of it."

He was right, of course. She felt the backs of her eyes prickle but kept a firm grip on her composure. It would not do to succumb to missish tears. "I regretted it almost as soon as I did it," she said quietly. "And I admit my courage failed me in confessing it to you right away. I'm deeply sorry. I promise"—she tried to keep the quaver out of her voice—"I shall never betray your trust again."

Capshaw held her gaze for a long moment before turning away. "Take her home."

One look from David as he escorted her from the room told her she would not get off so easily with her husband. She left feeling even worse than before. If Lawrence ceased to be a suspect in Capshaw's mind, it would be because Miss Phillips and her secret had come to his attention.

Concordia was convinced they both were innocent. But how could she prove it?

CHAPTER 13

SATURDAY, OCT 28, 1899 - HALLOWEEN MASQUERADE BALL

It is easier to forgive an enemy than to forgive a friend.

— WILLIAM BLAKE

*C*oncordia and David climbed the front steps of Sycamore House, lined with merry paper lanterns to dispel the gloom. The porch was decorated in high style, with charming arrangements of cornstalks, gourds, bittersweet vines, and pots of chrysanthemums. Each of the groupings was wrapped in a bow of bright vermillion. Concordia's lips twitched. How many yards of ribbon did the girls go through in a school year? Likely enough to keep the town milliners in business.

The students would be here within the hour, and the stone drive in front of the building would soon be full of conveyances from off-campus guests. There was still much to prepare.

Hannah Jenkins looked up from her clipboard as they entered the hall, her forehead smoothed in relief. "Ah, Mr. Bradley, just the gentleman I was hoping to see. Your help is needed to shift a particularly large banquette in the dining hall."

"Of course." David clasped his wife's hand briefly in goodbye and hurried away.

Miss Jenkins turned to her. "Concordia, I have you overseeing the apple dunking again this year, if you don't mind."

Concordia nodded. She'd fully expected to be recruited for that. She'd taken over for Gertrude Pomeroy the year before, as the apple dunking had quickly turned into a spectacles-dunking. The lady principal's glasses repeatedly slid down her nose and into the tub—and they discovered that silver spectacles are difficult to find in a galvanized barrel filled with water and apples.

"Do I have help?"

"Maisie Lovelace."

"Excellent. Who's reading the tea leaves?"

"That will fall to Miss Crandall and myself. And what a mess it is, I can tell you." She glanced at her clipboard. "I have another task for you right after dinner, if you're willing."

"Patrolling the gardens and terrace during the dance?" Concordia guessed.

"I've put Dean Maynard in charge of that."

Concordia stifled a laugh. Between Maynard's hair-trigger irascibility and suspicious nature, the virtue of every young lady at the dance was absolutely assured. Woe betide any offending college youth facing such wrath.

"The committee decided upon a round of parlor games after dinner, to keep the guests occupied while the dance floor is cleared," Miss Jenkins said. "You and I, along with Miss Phillips and Miss Pomeroy, will lead the games in separate parts of the house."

Concordia stiffened. *Miss Phillips.* Days had passed since the police had taken them to the station. She'd later learned the history professor had returned to campus by dinner time. Obviously, Capshaw hadn't arrested her. Thank heaven for that, but was she a suspect still? Concordia's feeble attempt to protect her from suspicion had made her look all the more guilty.

Well, tonight she would look for an opportunity to speak with the lady in private and offer fervent apologies for making such a mess of things.

"Everything all right, dear?" Miss Jenkins asked.

"Oh! Yes, but I'm afraid I don't know many parlor games." They'd been a small family growing up, her older sister and herself the only children. "What if we have a round of ghost stories instead?"

The traditional way to tell ghost stories on Halloween was to dim the lights and then light a dish of alcohol-soaked salt, which burned during the tale. The storyteller was obliged to finish before the flame died or else stop immediately, no matter how thrilling the story had become. It *did* encourage concision.

Miss Jenkins laughed. "I'm sure the girls know any number of tall tales."

"That's what I'm counting on." With a wave, she headed for the kitchen.

Maisie Lovelace arrived in time to help her carry the tubs and basket of apples to the screened porch out back. "You really should put on an apron first, Mrs. Bradley. It would be a shame to mar your charming supper frock."

It was a lovely dress, Concordia had to admit—a gift from her mother. Midnight blue wasn't a tint she would have chosen for herself, but the effect was softened by the short balloon sleeves and girdle drapery of cascading opalescent ribbon.

She pulled two aprons from the hook by the door and passed one to the girl, looking appreciatively at Maisie's floor-length, flowing white dress, deep sleeves, and simple gold sash. The girl's long, dark hair was completely brushed out, with a circlet of artificial pearls upon her head. "You appear to be a maid from…the court of Camelot?"

Maisie smiled. "I'm the Lady of Shalott, though she is typically painted as light-haired."

"No matter. You capture the spirit of the lady." Concordia quoted the Tennyson poem:

She look'd down to Camelot.
Out flew the web and floated wide;
The mirror crack'd from side to side;
'The curse is come upon me,' cried
  The Lady of Shalott.

Maisie chuckled. "Let's hope we fare better than she."

"Is there a Sir Lancelot to brighten your evening?" Concordia teased.

Maisie blushed. "Perhaps."

They made short work of filling the tubs.

"How is your uncle?" Concordia asked. "I haven't seen him since—well, in a while."

"You'll see him tonight. He's going to join us for the buffet meal. Miss Pomeroy wanted to show her gratitude—he was needed at the last minute to clean a bird's nest out of Sycamore House's chimney. The dean, of course, isn't happy about him coming."

Concordia smirked. "Mr. Maynard is a generally unhappy man, so I wouldn't put much stock in that."

"He's caught on that Uncle has a *tendre* for Miss Phillips."

"Oh? How did he learn of it?"

"The campus rumor mill, of course. Besides, May-Not's quite perceptive in his own right. With Uncle George spending most of his time in the gallery with Miss Phillips—well, people are bound to talk. I wouldn't mind the speculation if they kept their opinions to themselves." She scowled. "But the dean pointedly remarks upon Uncle being 'too interested by half' in Miss Phillips and wonders aloud why he spends so much time around her."

"He says these things in front of the two of them?" Concordia asked.

"Mostly in Miss Phillips's hearing. He seems to hold her responsible, which seems grossly unfair."

"I'd say so. Do you know if she...um, returns the feeling toward your uncle?"

Maisie blushed. "I didn't think it my place to ask him. I'm certainly not going to ask Miss Phillips."

"No, of course not."

"But he's very protective of her. He's not at all happy about her having been summoned to the police station." She glanced at Concordia, then looked away.

Concordia started. "Does he hold me responsible?"

"I'm afraid so. I'm sorry," she added quickly. "I hope you know that *I* don't feel that way at all."

Concordia wasn't surprised that some version of the story had circulated by now. "I don't know exactly what you heard, but you should know that I do believe Miss Phillips is innocent of Isaiah Symond's murder. I never indicated otherwise."

The sounds of laughter and footsteps along the hall brought them back to the task at hand. "We'd better grab some towels."

David joined them after the first round of students arrived, freeing Miss Lovelace to enjoy the activities.

Maisie passed back the apron, a twinkle in her eye. "I know just where I'll go first."

"The nut-burning? Good luck, dear."

The girl grinned. "I'll let you know."

"What was that about?" David asked after she'd left.

"I suspect Maisie has a new love interest."

He chuckled. "A great number of the All Hallow's Eve activities seem centered around predicting one's future mate."

"You're only now realizing that?"

"When I was a lad, I was more interested in egging or flour-ing the grown-ups." He grinned. "Especially the grumpy ones."

"I have difficulty imagining you as a prankster."

"You'd be surprised." He passed a towel to a student who'd been splashed.

"Well, then, you're in for an education." She surveyed the room. Several students who'd already secured an apple were standing around, waiting for their friends to finish. "Girls," she called, "we have apples to spare if you'd like to do a paring. But you have to be willing to eat the apple afterward. We don't want to waste them."

General squeals met this invitation.

"A pairing of what?" he asked.

"No, no—a *paring*, as in paring an apple peel. Watch." She passed a peeler to the girl closest to her.

The student carefully started at the top, going around and around until most of the fruit was peeled and she was left with one long strand of apple skin. She passed the peeler to her friend and waited for her to do the same. They nodded to each other. "Ready?" They threw the peels over their shoulders.

"What on earth?" he exclaimed.

The girls crouched to examine them. "Ooh, I see an *A*!" one called.

Other girls crowded around. "It looks like a *D* to me," another said skeptically.

He leaned close to Concordia. "Are you going to explain this?"

She chuckled and murmured back, "The shape of the peel as it lands is supposed to indicate the initial of the man you are to marry."

He clasped her hand while no one was looking, pressing it briefly before letting go. "I must say—I'm relieved to be married already and spared such shenanigans."

"You are instead saddled with other *shenanigans*." She looked up at him, her eyes clouded with regret. "I bring all sorts of unwelcome trouble to your life, I fear."

His eyes softened. "It's all part of the deal, my dear. Besides, it's my side of the family that started it this time. Don't worry. This will all come out right. You'll see."

Eventually the groups coming for the apple dunking grew sparse. Concordia checked her watch. "We should clean up. Dinner will be soon."

David dumped out the tubs of water while Concordia dried the leftover apples and put them back in the basket. They stopped in the kitchen to return them.

"Where do you want them?" Concordia asked the cook's assistant.

The girl swiped the back of her hand across her damp forehead. "Next to the—"

"Ellie!" the cook called, hands on ample hips, face red with annoyance. "Where on earth have you put the sack of flour? I can't find it."

"In the pantry, ma'am." She hurried over to help her look. "It was here just half an hour ago, honest."

"We should go," David said, lips twitching.

She was about to ask what he found so amusing when the bell rang for dinner.

Even the spacious dining room of Sycamore House had difficulty accommodating all of the tables needed for guests. As it was, the dessert buffet had to be set up in the vestibule. But that was all right—few guests were at risk of overlooking the delicious offerings at the end of their meal. As they passed by, Concordia cast a longing glance at the pumpkin crème brûlée, the apple galette, and a plate piled with meringues.

"Dinner first, *then* dessert," David said, drawing her arm through his.

She leaned in a little, savoring the warmth of him and the faint scent of his bay rum aftershave. "Naturally."

They were seated with Lady Principal Pomeroy, Dean Maynard, Miss Cowles, Miss Jenkins, Professor Benson, and to Concordia's surprise, Mr. Richardson.

As with most of the male guests, the lawyer was not in costume, instead wearing black evening tails. His hair was smoothly slicked back, though suspiciously blacker than she remembered. She smiled to herself. And people said *women* were vain.

"Does this mean you'll resume teaching your economics class next week?" she asked, her heart sinking a little. She'd be giving up Charlotte Crandall's class sooner than she thought.

He brushed a crumb from his lapel. "Perhaps. I've finished with the disposition of Isaiah's estate, but I want to catch up on what my clerk has been doing with the other accounts. Oh, not that Lawrence isn't perfectly capable," he added hastily, catching David's eye, "but one can't leave sensitive matters entirely to someone so young."

As the conversation appeared to be moving in a tedious direction, Concordia occupied herself with surveying the room. The college boys had joined the festivities now, and it seemed about half the young ladies had an escort. Most of the young men were in evening attire, though a few sported costumes. One enterprising young man was dressed as Blackbeard the pirate, complete with tricorn hat, knee-length boots, and a wig and long beard that covered most of his face. Another college youth was dressed as a knight. A helmet concealed his head completely.

She felt a prickle of unease. She did not like that she couldn't see their faces. Over the years, she'd come to know a fair number of the boys who attended Trinity, as they often visited the young ladies or escorted them to social functions. But here, tonight, she had no way to identify these men, much less read their facial expressions to determine their intentions.

"Excuse me," she interrupted. She nodded toward Randolph Maynard. "May I speak with you in private, Dean?"

With a puzzled frown, he got up as she stepped away from the table.

"What is it, Mrs. Bradley?" he asked impatiently, lowering his heavy brows. "Another mystery to solve?"

"Only the mystery of the young men over there." She inclined her head discreetly in the direction of the two, who were now leaning close to a group of smiling young ladies.

"I beg your pardon?"

Concordia sighed. How to explain her unease? "I don't like to seem overly suspicious"—Maynard snorted at that—"but their costumes border on disguises, don't you think? Should the intentions of either be less than honorable, he would be impossible to identify once he's shed the costume."

Maynard regarded the group, his scowl deepening. "I see your point," he said at last. "All right, I'll take care of it."

She returned to the table.

David raised an eyebrow as he pulled out her chair.

"I'll explain later," she whispered.

As the soup plates were removed and the guests returned to the buffet for the entrée, Concordia sought out Dorothy Phillips. There she was, standing beside the attentive George Lovelace, who was spooning a portion of duck a l'orange onto the lady's plate. Miss Phillips looked quite festive in a turquoise satin that suited her tanned complexion, dark hair, and light eyes. Lovelace was dressed in a dark suit which, judging by the odd creases and a hint of dust on the shoulders, appeared to spend most of its time in a closet.

Concordia approached them. "Miss Phillips, hello! Are you enjoying the evening?"

Lovelace glanced at Miss Phillips in a panic, but the lady was perfectly composed. She lifted her chin and met Concordia's eye. "Why, yes. This is far more enjoyable than certain other activities —a police interrogation comes to mind."

Concordia heard a snort of suppressed laughter behind her

and whipped around. Miss Cowles was reaching for the serving spoon, helping herself to the aspic with the concentration of a woman who wasn't eavesdropping in the least. Or perhaps she was simply being careful not to drop anything on her elbow-length, gray-silk opera gloves. Concordia turned back to Miss Phillips, but she and Lovelace were gone.

David was at her side in a moment. "Are you all right, dear?"

She blew out a breath. "Yes, of course. Let's return to the table."

Several girls from Richardson's economics class were standing beside their table, regaling the man with an account of their excursion to Hartford Settlement House.

"They do such good work there!" one girl exclaimed. "The children are so sweet."

"But they need to expand the school," another said. "Finding sufficient funds for the project has been a challenge."

Concordia had to look twice to realize the latter comment had been made by Madeline Farraday. She looked radiant this evening, dressed as the sprite Ariel from *The Tempest*. Gone was the troubled frown and hunched shoulders of a young lady with a burden. She stood straight, head lifted, blue eyes sparkling with animation, a crown of flowers atop her blond hair. She looked as if she could indeed summon the powers of nature to do her bidding.

Richardson looked over at Miss Benson. "Settlement house?"

Professor Benson explained the deviation from the original course plan. "But never fear," she added, "the students are on pace to finish the unit as planned."

Richardson smiled. "I wish I had someone with your sense of rigor running my office, dear lady. We would get far more done."

Concordia felt David shift in his seat beside her. As often as they privately wondered about Lawrence's faults, it did not sit well to hear a stranger make such references to the general company. Criticism was the express domain of *family*.

Soon, it was time to clear the dining hall so the staff could ready the room for dancing.

"Where will your group be gathering, dear?" Lady Principal Pomeroy asked Concordia, as they pulled their chairs out of the way.

"We will be telling ghost stories in"—she checked the slip Miss Jenkins had given her—"the library."

Miss Pomeroy shivered. "I've never enjoyed ghost stories, but you have fun."

David stepped closer in mock gallantry. "I shall be sure to keep the lady safe from specters, never fear."

"After you fetch the salt and other supplies we need," Concordia reminded him.

He bowed. "I live to serve."

The library was crammed with students, many with their escorts —two dozen, at least. Concordia wanted to create a spectral mood, so she didn't bother to turn up the lights as they filed in and waited while David borrowed extra chairs from nearby unoccupied rooms. Soon, everyone was settled, a small dish of alcohol-soaked salt in front of each volunteer storyteller.

Concordia went over to close the door. A sniffling girl rushed in.

"Miss Farraday?" Concordia whispered. "What's wrong?"

"Close the door, please!" she hissed. Her eyes were wide and red-rimmed, her crown of flowers askew.

Concordia looked out. The youth with the pirate beard lingered in the hallway, leaning casually against the wall. As soon as he caught sight of her, he hurried away. Apparently, the dean had not been sufficiently intimidating.

"Are you all right?" Concordia murmured to the girl as she shut the door.

Madeline gave a short nod.

Concordia had no choice but to let it go for the moment. Even quietly explaining the situation to David so he could go track down the young man would take time and draw unwanted attention. She ushered Madeline to the back of the room where she could lean against the credenza—all the chairs were taken.

The guests had quieted, looking at her expectantly.

Concordia struck a match and touched it to the salt in front of the first storyteller. A tall, yellow flame sprung up. "Let us begin."

All in all, she reflected, the session had gone well. The overriding theme of most of the stories was that of lovers who'd died tragically, lingering to haunt the other if he or she proved unfaithful. David paced the back of the room during the stories, clearing his throat strategically as certain heads drew too close together. Given the tension in the room during some of the tales, even that bit of noise caused several girls to jump in fright. She chuckled to herself and turned up the lights as the last of them left.

Except for Madeline—she'd remained behind, ostensibly to help Concordia and David, but Concordia knew the young man in the pirate costume was on her mind.

Suddenly, Madeline let out an exclamation. "Mrs. Bradley! Your dress!"

"What? What is it?" Concordia couldn't see where Madeline was pointing, and there was no mirror to hand. She reached behind her and felt something sticky. *Oh no.*

David came over for a closer look. "Molasses or honey, I'd say. But how did—?" He turned back to the chairs with a grunt. "The seats over here are smeared with it." He continued his examination. "And back here, other seats are dusted with flour."

"The missing flour!" Concordia exclaimed. If only that had been the worst of it.

David met Concordia's eye. "I missed this in the dim light. I'm so sorry."

She shook her head. "It's not your fault. I should have turned up the lights to begin with. The girls can be a mischievous lot, particularly when trying to impress male companions." The college boys might have had a hand in the stunt, too. Certainly more than a single student was involved. The affected chairs had come from the study and music room as well as here in the library.

"I can help you clean up your dress," Madeline offered, "but someone will have to tend to these chairs before they're irrecoverable."

Concordia turned to David. "Will you inform the president or the dean? Oh, and keep an eye out for a certain young man, dressed in a pirate costume." She waved a hand toward Madeline, who shifted uneasily. "He's been bothering Miss Farraday. I last saw him in the hall, but then he ran off."

"Indeed?" David raised an eyebrow. "You are unharmed, I trust, Miss Farraday?"

The girl nodded, though to Concordia's eye she still looked pale.

"Do you know him?" he asked.

She hesitated.

Concordia leaned in. "Madeline? You know him? Who is he?"

The young lady threw herself on Concordia's shoulder and sobbed. "L—Lawrence."

CHAPTER 14

Can I see another's woe, and not be in sorrow too?

— WILLIAM BLAKE

---

avid went in search of his brother while Concordia calmed the girl.

"Don't worry, dear. Mr. Bradley will make sure he doesn't bother you anymore. I'm so sorry." She patted Madeline's shoulder and passed her a clean handkerchief. "Did you know he was coming here?"

She shook her head. "I didn't even recognize him when he first approached me. It was only when he spoke."

"When was this?"

"Just after talking to Mr. Richardson at your table. I went to fetch desserts for a couple of the girls, and he cornered me."

"What did he say?"

She dabbed her eyes. "He wanted me to forgive him, but—he wasn't making much sense after that. I think he was intoxicated."

This was worse than Concordia feared. "His speech was slurred?"

"Yes. And I could smell something on his breath. I assume it was spirits, but I don't have much experience with such things."

"What happened then?"

"I was able to slip away and rejoin my friends. He didn't dare pursue me then. I didn't see him after that, until I was on my way here. I pushed him away and ran. The rest you saw yourself." Madeline looked at her with troubled eyes. "You're sure your husband can keep him away from me?"

"I promise. The whole family will make sure of it."

Madeline rolled her eyes. "*The whole family.* Whenever I find a bit of happiness these days, someone in that family sabotages it. First Isaiah Symond, and now Lawrence." Her voice dropped to a throaty whisper. "I loved Lawrence once, you know. But now I'm...afraid of him."

"We'll have someone take you home," Concordia said. "You've had a trying night."

"What about your gown?"

She'd forgotten. *Mercy,* so many problems at once. "I'll worry about it later."

Strains of a waltz met their ears as Concordia walked Madeline to the cloakroom. In the distance, she spotted the white hair and brisk gait of the infirmarian, Miss Jenkins, who was coming down the corridor toward them.

"Concordia, I've been looking for you. Your husband is upstairs with Mr. Richardson, the dean, and—" She broke off at the sight of Miss Farraday. "Um, well, never mind that. But you should get up there right away. Second door on the right."

They must have found Lawrence. "Miss Farraday needs to get home. She's feeling—unwell."

"Oh?" Miss Jenkins put a hand to the girl's forehead. "No fever."

"It's a headache, miss," Madeline said. "I just need to lie down in peace and quiet."

"Don't we all," Miss Jenkins muttered darkly. "All right, Miss Farraday, go get your wrap, and I'll arrange it."

Concordia waited until Madeline was out of earshot. "Is Lawrence with them?" she murmured.

"He's in a bad way," Hannah Jenkins said. "Alcohol poisoning, I fear. He should go to the hospital or at least have a doctor tend to him here, but the gentlemen are dead set against either course. Perhaps you can persuade them."

"I'll do my best." She turned toward the stairs.

"Concordia!" She slipped a black silk shawl from her shoulders and held it out. "Better wrap this around your skirt or you'll be smearing whatever that is—molasses, I expect—everywhere."

Drat, she'd forgotten again.

The second door on the right turned out to be Randolph Maynard's living quarters. She took a breath as she stepped inside. Here she was again, traversing another inner sanctum belonging to the dean. At least this time, she wasn't wearing his trousers, but the night was young.

Lawrence was stretched out upon Maynard's Persian rug, David's rolled jacket beneath his head. The beard and wig had been removed. As she drew closer, she could see his eyes were closed, dark lashes brushing pale, clammy cheeks. His breathing was labored.

Richardson and David were crouched on the floor beside Lawrence, with Maynard standing, observing the whole. He raised an eyebrow as Concordia drew closer. "I once said you would cease to be trouble when you married, Mrs. Bradley," he murmured. "It appears I was mistaken."

Concordia refused to dignify the remark with a reply. "How is he?" she asked David.

"The worst I've seen him." He held up a pocket flask. "This was in his trouser pocket."

187

She hefted it. Nearly empty. She unscrewed the cap and gave a tentative sniff, then grimaced at the strongly medicinal but slightly sweet odor. "This doesn't smell like brandy."

"More like grain alcohol," David said, "though why he'd be drinking such rotgut I have no idea."

Maynard folded his arms. "The variety of spirits in which he chooses to pickle himself is immaterial. The sooner he is out of my study, the better."

Concordia bristled. "You were supposed to have been keeping an eye upon the young men in attendance tonight, Mr. Maynard. I even pointed him out to you, although I didn't know who he was because of the costume."

Maynard scowled. "I'd shown him the door soon after, believe me. He must have sneaked back in."

"Was he already intoxicated when you asked him to leave?"

He winced. "Yes." He glanced over at the prone man before turning to the door. "I'll see if the carriage has been brought 'round yet."

"Carriage?" Concordia asked as he left.

Lawrence started to wretch. David quickly turned his head toward a basin.

Richardson answered her question. "Your husband will be riding home with him while I fetch the family doctor."

"Miss Jenkins thinks he should go straight to the hospital," Concordia said.

David looked up from tending his brother. "The doctor may decide that's the best—"

"No," Lawrence's raspy voice interrupted. "I want to go *home* to die."

"You're not going to *die*, man!" David said in exasperation. "Stop talking like that."

"Madeline—won't forgive—me." Lawrence closed his eyes with a sigh. "I've made a mess—of things. I'm s-sorry."

After a quiet interval, Richardson whispered, "I think he's sleeping again."

Concordia drew the lawyer aside. "Were you aware of Lawrence's—um, problem?"

He shifted weight to his other foot. "Not exactly. I mean, *now* it makes sense. I noticed his productivity had dropped off. He'd leave things undone, fail to arrange a messenger for important documents, mis-file papers... He even went into my safe without permission."

But Lawrence wasn't sleeping, after all. "Safe," he said suddenly, opening his eyes and looking at Richardson.

Richardson cleared his throat as he looked over at the prone man. "Not to worry, not to worry, my dear fellow. All is forgiven."

Lawrence mumbled something and closed his eyes again.

Richardson shook his head. "Poor boy, I'm afraid I quite lost my temper when he went into my safe." He waved a hand. "But it's not important anymore."

"Why did you keep him on if he was making so many mistakes?" Concordia asked.

"He wasn't completely useless," the lawyer said. "There was too much work for me to handle alone. Besides, I knew the lad was under tremendous stress, between Symond's death and the police investigation. And to learn he would inherit millions on top of it all...who wouldn't be distracted? He would have quit once he came into the inheritance. No need to dismiss him on acrimonious terms."

Like thieves in the night, Richardson and David carried the semi-conscious Lawrence as Maynard led them down the back stairs, through the housekeeper's pantry, and out to the waiting carriage. Concordia followed.

With nary a fare-thee-well, Maynard returned to the dining hall.

David clasped her hand. "Will you be able to get home? I suspect I'll be with him all night."

"I'll be fine. Take care of your brother."

Richardson hurriedly buttoned his coat. "My vehicle's just down the drive. I'll fetch the doctor as quick as I can." He tipped his top hat in her direction. "Ma'am."

Concordia was dead tired by the time she unlocked the door of the farmhouse. She took off her shoes and tiptoed past Trixie's first-floor bedroom on her way to the laundry room to clean up her dress.

"Is that you, ma'am?" Trixie called out from behind the door. Concordia pictured the diminutive woman crouched and ready to pounce. What would she have in hand this time? A hairbrush? Or, heaven forbid, a fireplace poker?

"Yes. It's all right, Trixie," she said. "Go back to sleep."

The bedroom door opened instead. The maid was clad in a long nightdress that brushed the floor, pale hair in a straggling braid over her shoulder, feet bare. "I couldn't sleep anyways. Where's Mr. Bradley? I only heard *you* come in."

"He had a family emergency."

"You want me to heat up some milk for ya? An' mebbe some cookies to go with?"

Concordia smiled. Trixie had already caught on to her weakness for sweets. Well, she *was* rather hungry. The buffet supper was ages ago. "That would be lovely. I'll be down in a few minutes." She turned toward the stairs, and the girl sucked in a breath.

"What's happened to your dress?"

The maid *tsk*ed as Concordia explained the prank at the ball. "Here, turn 'round, an' I'll unhook you. Then you can change into your robe. Leave me the dress. I'll give it a good soak tonight. That stain'll come right out in the morning."

Concordia obligingly turned and felt the woman's nimble fingers along her back. "Bless you, Trixie."

"An' I'm still going to get you the milk and cookies, too!" she exclaimed. "There. You're done."

Concordia shrugged off her gown as Trixie hustled to the kitchen.

David didn't return to the farmhouse until the next afternoon. The hollows under his reddened eyes and his sagging shoulders bespoke a difficult night. Her heart clenched. This could not be good news.

"How is he, David?"

He reached out his arms to her, and she held him close. "Tell me," she murmured into his shoulder.

"He's dead."

After David had a chance to clean up, he returned to the kitchen. Trixie fussed over them both, bringing tea and sandwiches before leaving them alone.

Concordia waited until he'd eaten. By then, some of his color had returned. "How did it happen?" she asked finally.

He pushed away his plate. "He was unconscious the whole ride home, but at least he didn't seem worse. We got him into bed, and the doctor came. By then, he was gasping. His lips were bluish. Doc said his heart was fluttering and gave him an injection." He looked down at his clenched hands. "But Lawrence never woke up. After a time, he stopped breathing completely."

"Oh David. I'm so sorry." She clasped his hands.

"He had so much to live for. I don't understand why he did this."

She blinked in surprise. "You believe he killed himself?"

"The doctor thinks it likely. When Papa left the room, he told me confidentially that Lawrence's symptoms weren't consistent with alcohol poisoning. He thinks a toxic dose of a stimulant is to blame."

"What sort of stimulant?"

"When he checked the flask, he said there was an underlying sweet odor that suggests cocaine."

She'd noticed something, too. "Where would Lawrence have gotten the drug?"

"Any number of patent medicines in the house—Aunt Drusilla's toothache drops, for instance—have cocaine in them. I'm not sure I want to go looking." He rubbed his neck in a weary gesture. "It doesn't change the fact that he's dead. I'm hoping it was an accidental overindulgence in spirits, rather than deliberate self-destruction."

"But why would he do it?" she asked.

"You remember one of the last things he said, when he was semi-conscious? 'Madeline won't forgive me.' He could have been despondent over the girl."

"Even if that were the case, they could not have carried on as they had before."

"I know."

"We must keep this from her. The guilt would be a terrible burden."

He hesitated. "Speaking of guilt—and I'm reluctant to say this aloud—I've been wondering if Lawrence *did* kill Isaiah. Perhaps he couldn't live with the guilt any longer." He blew out a breath. "My mind is in a muddle, dear. I don't know what to think."

She bit her lip. It all felt wrong. "Killing himself in such a manner doesn't make sense."

He sat up straighter. "Go on."

"Why do it so publicly? Why carry a flask of poison—mixed with alcohol, I assume, as both Maynard and Madeline noted that he was intoxicated—and drink from it throughout the evening? Who commits suicide surrounded by strangers and dressed in that ridiculous costume? Did he leave a note?"

"I searched his room. Nothing there." He rubbed the back of his neck. "I didn't tell you the worst of it. Capshaw arrived within an hour of Lawrence's passing."

"He...how did he know?"

"I wonder if he's had someone watching the house."

"What happened then?"

"He searched Lawrence's room as well. And I thought *I'd* been thorough...but Capshaw didn't find anything, either. He asked to examine Lawrence's brandy flask and was very annoyed that I'd already given it to the doctor for his chemist to analyze."

"To analyze?" She sat back in surprise. "I thought you didn't want to know. You said it wouldn't change the fact that your brother is dead."

He winced. "Frankly, I'm conflicted. I suppose I *do* want to know—as long as it could be kept confidential. Now that the police are involved, I highly doubt it will turn out that way."

"What's Capshaw going to do?"

"Since he very carefully noted the doctor's name and address in that infernal pad of his, I assume he'll confiscate the flask and the police will have their own chemist do an analysis."

"Still, the doctor could be mistaken," she pointed out. "Alcohol poisoning might very well be the cause of your brother's death."

His expression brightened a bit, which made her heart feel heavy. How sad it was that this was the best outcome to be hoped for.

CHAPTER 15

WEEK 10, INSTRUCTOR CALENDAR, NOVEMBER 1899

A fool sees not the same tree that a wise man sees.

— WILLIAM BLAKE

---

*C*oncordia and David were relieved to finally return home for good one mid-November morning, two weeks after Lawrence's death. They'd been staying with John, Georgeanna, and Drusilla, helping with the tasks that fall to those left behind when a loved one dies—not only the funeral service but settling accounts, going through effects, and writing letters.

Concordia thought she'd never be so happy to see their homely farmhouse door—despite its weathered paint and listing hinges—as she was at this moment.

Trixie let them in. "Oh, I'm so glad you're back! It feels like ages you were gone." With a self-conscious curtsy, she passed David a stack of letters. "I was saving these for you."

"I hope you haven't been too lonely here in the house by yourself," Concordia said.

"Oh, no, ma'am. The lad comes to feed the chickens an' take care of the horse ev'ry day, an' I had Caesar for comp'ny."

"Caesar?" David said. "The cat never struck me as terribly...friendly."

"He seems to have taken to me," Trixie said. "I was lettin' him sleep in my room while you were gone. I hope you don't mind."

Concordia smiled. "Not at all."

"By the way, ma'am, a lady came to see you yesterday."

"Oh? Who?"

Trixie sucked her bottom lip as she thought. "Um, Crenshaw? No, that's not right—Randall? Um...."

"Crandall, perhaps?"

Her eyes lit up. "That's it! Miss Crandall." She held out a slip of paper. "She left a note. She's one of your teacher friends, right?"

"Yes." Concordia unfolded the page. "Thanks, Trixie." She followed David into the common room and settled into a chair to read.

After an interval, she leaned her head back and closed her eyes.

"Something wrong?" he asked.

"Hmm? Oh. Nothing you can do anything about, I'm afraid." She passed him the note.

"Can you speak with Miss Farraday? She hasn't attended classes since the Halloween Ball. She told Maisie today that she's dropping out. ~Charlotte"

"I suppose Lawrence's death has upset her greatly," he said.

"That's no reason for the girl to throw away her future."

He met her eye. "Perhaps that's not the future she wants for herself."

Concordia's first impulse was to bristle at such a notion—what young lady would not want the opportunity to go to school?—but she knew he was right. She also knew she'd been resisting that idea for quite some time. She blew out a breath. "I've been terribly unfair to Miss Farraday. I should not have pushed her so."

He raised an eyebrow. "Why have you? I've wondered."

She could say it now, out loud, to him. "Victoria Lester."

To her relief, he didn't require any more to understand what she meant. His eyes softened. "You realize, of course, that Miss Farraday is not Miss Lester."

She grimaced. "And nothing I do for Madeline will ever bring Victoria back." Had she been unconsciously clinging to such a notion? Perhaps.

She stood.

"What are you going to do?"

"Find out what's on Madeline's mind."

Mrs. Carr, the landlady at Madeline's boarding house, ushered Concordia into the small guest parlor reserved for her boarders. A brown terrier followed, yapping at the newcomer's heels.

"Down, Brutus!"

The dog quieted with a faint whine and a suspicious look in Concordia's direction.

"I'll let her know you're here."

Concordia stopped her before she left. "How has she been?"

The woman's eyes softened as she clucked her tongue. "Mighty weepy. The death of that young man hit her hard, it seems. She's hardly gotten out of bed for weeks now. Maybe your visit will cheer her. Wait here." The dog trotted after his mistress, with one last baleful look in Concordia's direction.

It took some time before Madeline came downstairs. She'd tidied herself, but Concordia could see her face held the unmistakable traces of tears and sleepless nights.

"Sit down, dear," Concordia said, patting the cushion beside her. "I'm so sorry I couldn't come sooner to see how you were faring."

Madeline gave a wan smile. "I understand. You were busy with the family."

"I didn't realize Lawrence's death had affected you so deeply. My recent impression was that you wished to distance yourself from him. You were quite frightened the night of the Halloween Ball."

"That's true. I'd never seen him like that." She drew a breath. "But I haven't been entirely honest with you, Mrs. Bradley."

"Oh?"

"There's a reason he sought me out at the ball. He wanted to continue our conversation of the day before."

Concordia blinked. "Conversation? What made you change your mind about speaking to him?"

She looked down at her hands. "I wondered...maybe I'd been too hasty in assuming his guilt. So I agreed to see him at Mr. Richardson's office."

"Why *did* you think him guilty in the first place?"

"Because he lied to Lieutenant Capshaw. He was there, on campus, the night Isaiah Symond died."

Concordia's eyes narrowed. "So the friend you were with, whom you refused to name—it was Lawrence, after all?"

She shook her head. "That was Miss Cowles."

"Wait—*Miss Cowles*? Why would you conceal that?"

"She asked me to," Madeline said simply.

Concordia weighed which angle to pursue first. What a muddle. "Where does Lawrence fit in? Start from the beginning, please. The night of the murder. You left with Miss Jenkins, and...."

"And I found my notebook by the quadrangle fountain. I said goodnight to Miss Jenkins and crossed the quadrangle on my way to the gatekeeper's cottage." She stopped abruptly.

"Yes? What then?"

"I saw him—Lawrence, I mean—walking away from the side door of Founder's Hall."

Ah, now they were getting somewhere. "Did you approach him?"

"No."

"But you're sure it was him?"

"I couldn't see his face from that distance, but I'm sure—the compact build, the wide shoulders...and of course, his coat."

"His coat?"

"Yes, it's rather distinctive—a dark wool overcoat with a high beaver fur collar and brass buttons in a double row."

Concordia pursed her lips. She'd seen Lawrence in the coat as well, when he'd paid her a visit at the farmhouse. Still, it was hardly proof. "I grant you, it's a distinctive feature, but I'm sure many men possess such a coat. He didn't see you, I take it?"

"No. After he was gone, I went over to the Hall to see what he might have been up to."

Concordia's spine tingled in apprehension. "What then?"

"I went in through the door he'd come out of—the side door that opens into the stairwell."

Concordia sat back in surprise. "It was unlocked? What time was this?" Dorothy Phillips had locked that door around eleven o'clock.

Madeline made a face. "I'm not sure. Not long after I got to campus and parted ways with Miss Jenkins. Twelve thirty?"

An hour and a half after Miss Phillips had gone. Who else could have—wait, Madeline had mentioned someone else. "You said you were with Miss Cowles. How does she come into this?"

"She heard the door and stepped into the stairwell from the library side just as I came through. I thought I was going to get into trouble for being out past curfew. Her look was black enough, at first. But she saw I was upset. She invited me in. We had tea and a lovely chat in her office."

"Really?" *Jane Cowles? A lovely chat?*

Madeline nodded. "I needed someone to talk to, and she was surprisingly receptive. I've become familiar with her ways, after helping in the library regularly. She's not as prickly as she generally seems."

"Did you tell her about Symond being your father and the problem of Lawrence?"

"Yes—and about whether I really wanted to...continue with college." She cleared her throat and looked at the floor.

"You couldn't tell *me* that?" Concordia tried to keep the hurt from her voice.

"I didn't want to disappoint you." Her voice was husky with regret.

"My dear, I'm sorry I placed such an unfair expectation upon you. I simply wanted you to have a chance to follow your dreams."

The girl's forehead cleared as she met Concordia's eye. "Dreams take many forms, Mrs. Bradley. I don't know if this is mine or not."

"I see." David had been right.

"I do plan to return to classes and finish out the semester. Then I'll decide what to do next."

"That's up to you, dear."

"Just so you know—that night, Miss Cowles was quite helpful. She told me she never gave up on her career, and I shouldn't, either. She said we ladies must be self-reliant. She'd had troubles with a suitor herself, long ago. She didn't provide details, only saying it ended badly."

Concordia felt as if her eyebrows couldn't raise themselves any higher. The notion of the acid-tongued librarian ever having a suitor defied belief. Even more of an enigma, however, was why Miss Cowles would want her tête-à-tête with the student kept secret. She put that question to Madeline.

"I was too tired—and worried about getting back so late when I realized the time—that I didn't ask," the girl said. "I assumed she preferred to keep her friendlier inclinations a secret. People are almost as afraid of her as they are of May-Not."

"Perhaps." Still, it seemed odd. Miss Cowles might have been up to something. But was that *something* as dastardly as striking

Isaiah Symond and taking the Blake *Catalogue?* What possible motive would she have for either one?

She was so preoccupied that she missed what Madeline said next. "What was that, dear?"

"I said, 'That's why I agreed to see Lawrence at the office.' I wanted to give him a chance to explain his presence at Founder's Hall that night."

Concordia sat up straighter. "Oh? And what did he say?"

"He absolutely denied being there—said I was mistaken."

They were quiet for a long while.

"Did you believe him?" Concordia asked finally.

She spread her hands in front of her in a gesture of indecision. "I wanted to. I told him I had to think it over."

"But Lawrence wasn't satisfied with that," Concordia guessed, "and tried to press you for something more definite at the Halloween Ball."

Madeline's expression clouded. "His behavior was abhorrent— dressing in that absurd costume, drinking to excess, harassing me in public. That was not the same gentleman with whom I'd had a calm, rational discussion only the day before. The man at the ball seemed capable of anything. So which man did I see at Founder's Hall, the night Symond died—the rational one or the angry, drunken one? What if Lawrence was so intoxicated then that he didn't *remember* killing his great-uncle?"

The rap of knuckles on the door jamb interrupted them.

It was the landlady. "Miss Farraday, a gentleman to see you." She stepped aside to allow Ernest Richardson to enter.

Richardson removed his hat and smoothed his hair. "Miss Farraday, I've been trying to reach you. As you have not responded to my letters, I decided to come in person."

Concordia frowned. Teachers didn't usually seek out truant college students.

The girl sighed. "I'm sorry, Mr. Richardson, for not coming to class. With all that has happened...I was not equal to it."

He waved a dismissive hand. "I'm not here in that capacity, though your absence has been worrisome. I've come to inform you of your legacy."

"My...what?"

"Lawrence Bradley left the entirety of his estate to you. As he inherited half of Isaiah Symond's wealth a few weeks ago, that makes you a very rich young lady now."

He was met with stunned silence.

"How much?" Concordia finally asked. When Lawrence had told her of the change to his will, she'd dismissed it as an extravagant gesture from a mercurial man who could change his mind at any moment. Much like his great-uncle.

Richardson pursed his lips. "It's an estimate at the moment, but I'd say roughly two and a half million dollars."

"Mercy," Madeline breathed. "I don't know if I should accept it. I was ready to walk away from Isaiah Symond's money, but now... oh, Mrs. Bradley, there *is* good I can do with such funds. Your friend Sophia's school program at the settlement house...but it seems wrong to benefit from Lawrence's death. I wasn't very nice to him the night he died."

Concordia clasped the girl's hand. "That was an unfortunate occurrence, to be sure, but not your fault. Lawrence was at his worst then. But when he was at his best, he cared for you deeply. He wanted to correct the injustice done to you long ago. I would accept the legacy, dear, and remember the good in Lawrence."

The lawyer cleared his throat. "There *is* an impediment. John Bradley is contesting his son's recent will, claiming that Lawrence was in a weak-minded state because of his alcoholic tendencies, and that you pressed your advantage to have him sign a will in your favor."

"That's absurd," Concordia said.

Richardson shrugged. "To my mind—and I'm sure the witnesses to his signature will attest to this as well—Lawrence was in perfect possession of his faculties when he signed the will.

I don't believe Bradley has a case. However, we must go through the process, which will take time."

"How much time?" Madeline asked.

"Bradley just filed his papers today. It depends on when the court can schedule a hearing. We're getting close to the holidays, and that may delay things."

"Are there any other 'impediments' Miss Farraday should know about?" Concordia asked.

"Only one" came a melancholic male voice.

Lieutenant Capshaw stood in the doorway, having pushed past the flustered landlady, who still hovered at his elbow.

Madeline paled but maintained her composure. "Thank you, Mrs. Carr. Could you close the door, please, on your way out?"

As the wide-eyed landlady reluctantly complied, Madeline gestured to the last chair in the tiny room. "I hope we're not expecting anyone else, Lieutenant. Please, sit down."

Concordia marveled at her calm. Perhaps the young lady had endured so many setbacks and shocks recently that she was numb to any more.

"What brings you here?" Madeline asked.

Capshaw drew out an envelope from his tunic pocket. "I'm afraid I have bad news about Lawrence Bradley's death. Here is our chemist's analysis of what remained in the young man's drinking flask."

Richardson leaned forward. "What does the analysis conclude, Lieutenant?"

"There was more than alcohol in the bottle. There was also cocaine, in a high enough concentration to kill a man drinking from a full flask."

Concordia drew a sharp breath. "Does anyone in the family know yet?"

He shook his head.

Richardson *tsked* in sympathy. "Poor lad. So he did kill himself.

I hope you will keep your discovery confidential. The family has been through enough."

"You forget," Capshaw said, "that the poison could have been put in the flask by a hand other than Lawrence's. I believe it to be murder."

Madeline blinked.

Concordia folded her hands in her lap and took a steadying breath. "So we have two murders, Isaiah and now Lawrence? Are they related?"

"Not necessarily," Capshaw said.

"What progress have you made in Isaiah's death?" Richardson asked. "It's been weeks now."

"My lead suspect is dead," Capshaw retorted.

"If you believe Lawrence was responsible for Isaiah's death," Richardson said, "wouldn't the lad taking his own life make sense? Both deaths are explained that way."

Capshaw didn't respond, instead regarding him thoughtfully. "Mr. Richardson, did I hear correctly that Miss Farraday is Lawrence Bradley's legatee?"

"Pending an unsuccessful challenge to the will, yes."

Capshaw glanced at Madeline. "I have some questions for you, miss."

The girl sighed. "I want to get to the bottom of all this as much as you do, sir."

"Would you like Mrs. Bradley to stay while we talk?"

She nodded.

"Is that agreeable to you?" Capshaw asked Concordia.

"Yes, of course."

"Very well." Capshaw waved a hand toward Richardson. "I won't keep you, sir. I'm sure you have a number of tasks to take care of."

Richardson hesitated, then got up from his chair. Concordia imagined he wanted to stay, but he obviously had no standing with either party.

After he'd excused himself and left, Capshaw leaned back in his chair. "Now then, Miss Farraday, let us talk frankly about Lawrence Bradley, shall we?"

Concordia left with Capshaw when he'd finished.

"I'll walk you to your stop," Capshaw said.

"Thank you." She knew it was out of his way, but no doubt he wanted to hash out what Madeline had recounted. The girl had been perfectly forthright about all of it—her visit to Richardson's office, her attempts to avoid him at the Halloween Ball because of his odd behavior—even going back to what she'd seen the night Isaiah Symond had died, and the time she'd spent with Jane Cowles. Concordia hoped such honesty would count in her favor.

"It sounds as if the Halloween Ball was quite the event," he began, steadying her by the elbow as they weaved through the press of people along the downtown sidewalk. At this hour, most of them were harried businessmen in search of their noontime meal.

"That's an understatement," she said. "But tell me, please—do you believe Madeline is innocent of putting poison in Lawrence's brandy flask?"

"You know what they say," he said lightly. "Poison is a woman's weapon."

"I don't see how she would have had the opportunity that night. There were too many people about. And how would she have taken it from his person without him knowing?"

"More likely she would have done so before the ball," Capshaw said. "By all accounts, Lawrence had already started showing the effects of the alcohol, and such an amount would have taken time to consume."

"But when—? Oh. You mean the day before, when she visited Lawrence at the office?"

"Exactly. If he kept the flask in an inner jacket pocket and hung the coat on a hook in the office, it would have been a simple enough task."

"Not so simple," she argued. "How could she have done it without his noticing? One would have to grope around to find the bottle and extricate it, then unscrew the cap, pour in the poison, replace the cap, and slip the bottle back in the pocket—all without being caught."

"She would only need another flask, prepared ahead of time," Capshaw said. "A simple switch out of the leather case, and it is done. The bottle itself was quite ordinary."

"But she would have to know he kept a flask of spirits *and* what it looked like in order to produce an identical one."

"They were on rather intimate terms with each other, at least until very recently," Capshaw said.

"Others close to Lawrence could have had the same information."

"I'm aware of that. Besides Miss Farraday, we have the members of the Bradley household and their servants, and possibly Ernest Richardson, though I doubt he would have kept Lawrence on in the first place if he'd caught the man nipping from a bottle during work hours."

"True. You'll have to add David and me to the list as well. We saw Lawrence surreptitiously refilling it one night at the Bradley house."

He snorted. "Which brings us to motive. *Why* would someone kill Lawrence Bradley? The most obvious reason, of course, is money."

"Which is why you questioned Miss Farraday."

"Yes. She has both a motive—Lawrence's millions—and the opportunity to carry it out."

"There's another possibility," Concordia said. "The person who killed Symond might have feared Lawrence had discovered his identity. Madeline told you she saw Lawrence there. Perhaps he observed something."

Capshaw's brow furrowed in skepticism. "Then why did he not say so before? I questioned him several times, and he never even admitted to going to the gallery that night, much less seeing something important."

"I imagine he didn't want to make himself more of a suspect in your eyes by admitting he was anywhere near the dead man. As to seeing something, he could have been so intoxicated that his memory was spotty. If recollection returned later, he might have confronted the murderer with what he knew."

Capshaw was silent for a long time. Finally, as they waited for a gap in traffic to cross to the trolley stop corner, he said, "You may have a point." His tone was grudging, but at least he wasn't single-mindedly pursuing the idea of Madeline Farraday as Lawrence's murderer.

And there was yet another murder to solve. "You told Mr. Richardson that Lawrence was your 'best suspect' in Symond's death," Concordia said. "Do you still believe that?"

He shook his head.

"Whom do you suspect now?" Concordia asked.

The trolley car came to a stop in front of them. He helped her up. "I'm not ready to share that yet. You'll know soon enough."

To her surprise, Capshaw stepped aboard as well.

"Where are you going?"

"To campus, to speak with Miss Cowles. I must corroborate what Miss Farraday has claimed about that night." With a twinkle in his eye, he added, "Want to come along? There should be another lady present to keep things proper."

She answered with a twinkle of her own. "Need you ask?"

CHAPTER 16

The man who never alters his opinions is like standing water, and breeds reptiles of the mind.

— WILLIAM BLAKE

---

*M*iss Cowles was not in the library. A student assistant suggested the staff lounge. Concordia and Capshaw dutifully trouped up to the third floor, only to find Miss Jenkins and Miss Phillips enjoying a quiet cup of tea. No sign of Jane Cowles.

Across the room, Concordia locked eyes with a neutral-expressioned Dorothy Phillips. Had the history professor forgiven her? Not likely, when she was standing next to the very policeman who'd interrogated the lady.

Concordia was about to follow Capshaw to the door when Miss Phillips stood. "Just a moment, dear."

Concordia glanced at Capshaw.

"I'll check for her at DeLacey House," he said. "You can catch up when you're free." He closed the door behind him.

Hannah Jenkins fetched a cup of tea. "We were just talking about you."

"Oh?"

Miss Jenkins gestured toward the history professor. "Dorothy has something she wants to say."

Miss Phillips leaned forward. "I regret my anger at the Halloween Ball. I was still stinging from my experience at the police station."

"That's understandable," Concordia said. "It is I who should apologize."

Miss Phillips fell silent.

Miss Jenkins prodded the middle-aged lady. "There's plenty of blame to go around. However, Dorothy's own pique had an unintended consequence—isn't that right?"

"All too true." Miss Phillips met Concordia's eye. "George was the one who sabotaged the chairs. I'm so sorry. He was upset by what I had undergone, and he was looking to exact a mild bit of revenge on you."

"Mild?" Concordia echoed, thinking of how Trixie had laboriously soaked and scrubbed at her best ball gown. "The molasses was difficult to remove."

Dorothy Phillips frowned. "George said they only spread flour on the seats."

"'They'?" Concordia repeated. "Who helped him?"

"He didn't name her," Miss Phillips said. "He would only say that she pulled him aside when he arrived at the ball and suggested the idea as a way of retaliating against you. She supplied him with flour from the kitchen."

"I would not have expected it of George Lovelace," Concordia said. "It's a juvenile stunt for a grown man to engage in."

Miss Jenkins snorted. "It certainly is. President Langdon has dismissed him."

Concordia had a brief thought for Maisie and how she was taking the news of her uncle's disgrace.

Miss Phillips's expression grew pained as the silence lengthened. "You must believe me, Concordia—I didn't know he was planning to do that. I sincerely wish he had not. He's become quite protective of me lately. Ever since—oh, it doesn't matter," she finished angrily, dashing tears from her eyes.

"Ever since Isaiah Symond came back into your life, you mean?" Concordia asked. "You told George about Symond's blackmail, I take it?"

Dorothy Phillips kept her gaze fixed upon the clenched, age-mottled hands in her lap. "Yes."

"Then he may have been responsible for Symond's murder." Concordia saw, from the corner of her eye, Miss Jenkins give a start of surprise.

"I'm sure that thought has occurred to you as well," she went on.

Miss Phillips shrugged, still not looking up.

Concordia exchanged a glance with Miss Jenkins before addressing the history professor once again. She kept her voice gentle. "Did you find Isaiah Symond's body before we did? Did you take the Blake *Catalogue* in order to protect George Lovelace and make it look like a theft gone wrong?"

Miss Phillips lifted her head then. "No, I did *not*. I never returned to the gallery after parting ways with Symond—until you came to DeLacey House with the news." She shifted restlessly. "I already told Capshaw all this."

Concordia suppressed a sigh, not sure she believed her. "Did you tell Capshaw why Symond was blackmailing you in the first place?"

Miss Phillips took off her spectacles and rubbed her eyes.

Miss Jenkins passed over a clean handkerchief. "There's no point in keeping it a secret any longer. It's in the past."

"So what happened?" Concordia asked. "All I know is that

something unpleasant took place on your riverboat trip up the Nile. When was that—fifteen years ago?"

"About that," Miss Phillips said. "The fact is, I—I killed a man."

So, *not* a misfortune that had befallen her friend, as the lady had first asserted. "Who? How did it happen?"

"Isaiah Symond was traveling with a friend of his, an archaeologist by the name of Samuel Bixby. I knew of Bixby's academic reputation—which was formidable—but had never met him before then." She made a face. "I wish it had stayed that way. He was merely an annoyance at first, boasting of his achievements, ingratiating himself with the women on board, standing a bit too close for comfort—that sort of thing. He often became intoxicated over dinner, which proved the case that night. We had dinner ashore at a local establishment, and then our group re-boarded the riverboat to retire. I lingered on the upper deck, enjoying the night air. It was rather late. Everyone else had gone to bed. I was the only one up—or so I thought. Bixby joined me at the railing. What started as a pleasant conversation about common interests quickly turned into an aggressive, unwanted advance. I tried to scream, but he covered my mouth. I fought him. In the struggle— I'm still not sure how it happened—I was able to push him away, but the force of it sent him over the railing and into the river."

"He drowned?" Concordia asked.

Miss Phillips shivered. "That part of the river was infested with crocodiles. They got to him too quickly for any help to make a difference."

A chill rippled up Concordia's spine. What a horrible way to die, villain or no. "How did Symond come to be involved?"

"He'd reached the upper deck in search of his friend and saw what happened. The man's cries from the river roused the crew. Symond whispered to me to let him handle it. When we were finally asked what we knew of it, he recounted a story of Bixby being so inebriated that when he'd leaned over the railing to be sick, he fell over the side."

"It's surprising he would help you in that way," Concordia said.

"I was touched at first by what I thought was a chivalrous, protective gesture," Miss Phillips said, "but was soon disabused of that notion the next morning when Symond demanded money for his silence. I gave him everything I had with me. He also wanted the Blake *Catalogue* as a 'souvenir,' he called it. We had shown it to him earlier, you see."

They were all quiet for a while. Finally, Concordia asked, "Does Capshaw know?"

"I had no choice but to tell him."

"What did he say?"

"That he was going to check into it. I told him he could certainly try, but the riverboat company had been taken over by a succession of others over the years. Who knows what records remain? He was also going to contact my friend, but she's currently in Toronto. I'd hoped to avoid telling her the *Catalogue* is gone forever."

Concordia grimaced. That was the least of the lady's worries now. Her story no doubt confirmed to Capshaw that, when desperate enough, Dorothy Phillips had a fierce, protective instinct that would not bode well for any man who threatened her.

The maid answering the door of DeLacey House had been expecting her. "They're in Miss Cowles's quarters. Excuse me, ma'am, I have to get back to my work."

After a quick tap on Miss Cowles's partly open door, Concordia let herself in.

The study was as orderly and regimented as the woman herself—book spines dust-free and arranged flush in tidy rows upon their shelves, sewing basket neatly organized by thread color and ready at hand beside the reading lamp, picture frames lined up side by side on the mantel.

Capshaw rose politely, but Concordia waved him back into his seat and sat upon the desk chair across from the two of them. At her elbow was Miss Cowles's desk, which sported a row of small drawers on top. One of them didn't close completely because the stained finger of a gray-silk glove stuck out. It was the single out-of-place element in the room, as if the woman had quickly shoved it in there at the last minute.

Miss Cowles's eyes flickered in her direction. "Why are *you* here?" Her upper lip curled. "Dabbling in amateur detection again, Mrs. Bradley? I hardly think your husband would approve."

Concordia smiled. "That is not your concern, Miss Cowles."

"Mrs. Bradley is here at my invitation." Capshaw already had a pencil and his customary wadded notepad propped on his knee. He shuffled back a page. "To catch you up, Mrs. Bradley, Miss Cowles has corroborated Miss Farraday's story that they were together in the library, talking and drinking tea, the night Symond was killed."

"Miss Farraday was hazy about exactly when you were together," Concordia said, inclining her head toward Miss Cowles. "Do you remember what time that was?"

"Of course I remember," the librarian snapped. "It was just after twelve thirty when I heard the stairwell door open. We parted ways at one thirty."

"How long had you been in the library before Miss Farraday showed up?" Capshaw asked.

"All evening. I attended the exhibit opening at the gallery, then went straight back to my work."

Capshaw was thumbing through pages of notes. "You didn't attend the reception, then?"

"We had a large shipment of books come in. It was a night's work to catalogue them all."

"How could that be?" Concordia asked. "I saw no light through the windows of the Hall when I accompanied Miss Phillips and Mr. Symond to check the locks."

"Most of my time was spent in the storeroom," she snapped. "There are no windows there."

Capshaw gave Concordia a quelling look. "And when did the exhibit opening conclude?"

"Nine o'clock," Miss Cowles said.

Concordia nodded to herself. That sounded about right.

"Did you hear anything unusual going on in Founder's Hall while you were in the library?" he asked.

"Unusual? How do you mean?"

"Footsteps, doors closing, voices—"

"Especially sounds you might have heard between eleven o'clock and the time you encountered Miss Farraday," Concordia interjected, which earned her a black look from the policeman.

"That's a very specific time frame," Miss Cowles said.

Capshaw crossed his legs, no doubt trying to get comfortable in the hard chair. "The police physician thinks the man had been dead two or three hours before he examined the body. He arrived on the scene at three that morning."

Miss Cowles shuddered. "To think that happened when I was alone...." She blew out a breath as she thought. "No, I'm sorry. I heard nothing. But as I said, I was in the storeroom most of the time, unpacking boxes."

Concordia wasn't sure whether to believe her. It was true the interior room used for library storage had no windows and was rather insulated, yet it seemed odd that Miss Cowles would not have heard anything in Founder's Hall, even though she'd heard Miss Farraday open the stairwell door. So many people, including the murderer, had come and gone that night. And something else didn't make sense....

"Did you unlock the stairwell door?" Concordia asked suddenly, remembering Miss Phillips's account.

Miss Cowles frowned. "No. It's rarely locked."

Concordia didn't answer but gave Capshaw a pointed look.

Had the murderer unlocked the side door? That would imply someone with a key.

The policeman grunted. "That could be very telling. I'll check again with Miss Phillips."

Miss Cowles looked back and forth between them, brows raised.

Concordia leaned back in her chair, glancing again at the desk. The gray glove protruding from the drawer annoyed her. She reached over to tuck it back in.

"Leave my property alone, if you please," Miss Cowles snapped. Her long, thin nose quivered with indignation.

Why was it so important? In a moment of inspiration, Concordia pulled it out instead. Yes, she'd seen it before, an elbow-length opera glove of fine, gray silk with pearl buttons. "You wore a pair like this at the Halloween Ball, did you not?"

Miss Cowles froze, suddenly wary.

Concordia plucked at the stained forefinger of the right-hand glove. Several things were making sense now.

"What a shame! There's a mark here." She held it up. "I see you have tried to remove it, without success."

Capshaw shifted restlessly, no doubt out of his element when it came to female accoutrements. But Concordia could tell he was watching the interchange closely. He must know she was on to something.

Miss Cowles leaned close and snatched it back. "Yes, most regrettable. It is my best pair."

Concordia met the lady's eye. "Molasses is notoriously difficult to remove. However, our new maid, Trixie, has had success with that particular substance quite recently. I'm sure she could help."

Capshaw's mouth dropped open as he watched the librarian collapse back into her chair and put her head in her hands.

"Did *he* tell you?" came the lady's muffled voice.

"George Lovelace, you mean?" Concordia asked. "No. I recognized the glove, and once I realized that several of the pranks this semester have been directed at me or something that involved me, the connection to you wasn't hard to make. No doubt you considered yourself safe from discovery each time. The seats at the ball could easily be attributed to the same prankster who smeared the chapel pews, had George not confessed to it. But other incidents were not so generalized and have made me wonder. The collapse of my chair in the study alcove but no other—oh, I know you *claimed* there'd been one before—my bicycle sabotaged, but not Maisie's machine—"

She had been about to ask her *why*. It was a tempting question. *Why* did the librarian harbor such hostility? Why was her kindliness only a thin veneer—worn away to reveal a caustic remark in the staff mailroom or a derisive snort in the buffet line?

A new idea, far more pressing, had taken hold. "Then there was the upside-down *Catalogue* inside the display case and the missing bulb." She glanced at Capshaw, who raised a quizzical eyebrow in her direction, as if to say: *And now, Mrs. Bradley?*

She took a breath. "Miss Cowles, won't you show us where you've hidden the Blake *Catalogue?*"

Miss Cowles had shelved it in the library, a perfect place to evade a search, as the police would have had to pull down every book in order to make a thorough examination of the space. And why would they?

As an additional precaution, the librarian had wedged it between a pair of obscure tomes by the philosopher Samuel von Pufendorf, which no one at the school ever consulted.

Capshaw stepped forward as the woman carefully pulled it out. "I'll take that, miss. It's evidence."

She handed it over with a sigh. "And the bulb is in my pencil drawer." She gestured half-heartedly toward the circulation desk. "That's that, I suppose. I'm finished here."

"Why would you do such a thing?" Concordia asked.

Miss Cowles stood straighter and gave her a cold, contemptuous stare. "I don't think I care to tell you, *Mrs. Bradley.*"

Concordia suppressed a shiver at the hatred in that gaze.

"Well, you are going to have to tell *me*, sooner or later," Capshaw said. "Of more immediate concern is how you managed it. Why didn't Symond stop you?"

Miss Cowles frowned. "He wasn't there. No one was."

Capshaw's eyes widened. "What do you mean? What time did you steal the *Catalogue*?"

"Shortly after everyone left for the reception, about nine thirty. I'd set out empty boxes beside the stairwell for the custodian to dispose of and noticed that all was quiet. On a whim, I checked the gallery doors and found that Miss Phillips had neglected to lock them. A simple letter-opener did the trick on the exhibit case."

Concordia looked at Capshaw. "But Miss Phillips said the *Catalogue* was there when she and Symond checked. That was ten thirty or eleven."

His expression was grim. "*Someone* is lying."

After impressing upon Miss Cowles the necessity of remaining available for further questions, Capshaw escorted Concordia out of Founder's Hall. "How did you figure it out?"

"Once I realized Miss Cowles was responsible for at least one of the pranks—the molasses-smeared chairs at the Halloween Ball—it occurred to me that the exhibit case had been broken with such care that repairing it would hardly be a problem at all. A staff member, especially one of Miss Cowles's orderly nature, would not wish to cause more damage than was necessary."

She flushed at Capshaw's look of grudging admiration. "Now what do we do?" she asked.

"There is no *we*," he said. "*You* will go home."

Concordia knew a protest would get her nowhere. "All right, then, what are *you* going to do?"

"Find Miss Phillips."

"So you believe Miss Cowles?"

He gave her a look of impatience under thick, reddish eyebrows, though his gray eyes were also tinged with sympathy. "You already know the answer to that."

She did. If the woman was indeed responsible for killing Symond, she would have had to lie about the *Catalogue* still being there, in order to explain Symond's presence in the gallery. Otherwise, why protect the henhouse after the fox has raided it?

Miss Cowles, on the other hand, had no reason to lie. She didn't have Miss Phillips's unpleasant history with Symond. She barely knew the man.

"Will you come to the farmhouse afterward?" Concordia met his eyes pleadingly. "Please. Dorothy Phillips is my friend. I must know what happens to her. And what about David? Doesn't he deserve to know everything, as it was his brother you suspected most of all?"

Capshaw's expression softened. "All right, then. It may be a long while."

"We'll wait."

Trixie kept Concordia and David well-supplied with coffee as they talked all evening and well into the night. Concordia hadn't realized how much she had to tell him. It seemed ages ago that they had hashed out the possibilities of Isaiah Symond's murder. Lawrence's recent death had eclipsed it.

David shook his head when she got to the part about Jane Cowles. "What a bitter, vindictive woman. I cannot believe she would stoop so low. And she refused to tell you why?"

"Holding back an explanation was one last act of bitterness, I suppose. But something Madeline told me gives me an idea of it. Apparently, Miss Cowles had a suitor long ago and the courtship 'ended badly,' as Madeline put it."

He leaned forward. "Does she know what happened?"

"No. But the librarian's advice to the girl was to never give up on her career."

"So Miss Cowles picked a career over love, but what has that to do with you? Your choice was the opposite."

"Not exactly. I did give up teaching, but I've had the good fortune to still be part of campus life, at least somewhat. I'd also been permitted to serve in a teaching capacity, temporary as it was. There's been a great deal of resistance, of course. But all those years ago, women such as Miss Cowles didn't have even that luxury." Concordia sighed. Perhaps the next generation of women wouldn't face such a difficult choice.

"You believe she acted out of jealousy?"

"That's my working theory. To be honest, I'm not sure I want to spend more time with her in an attempt to find out. Interaction with the woman is disagreeable."

"What's next? Do we keep it confidential or tell the administration about her behavior?"

"It isn't up to us," she said. "Capshaw has custody of the *Catalogue* now. It will be returned to the school eventually, and the entire story will come out."

"Not the *entire* story," he said. "We don't know who killed Isaiah. You say Capshaw's talking to Miss Phillips and George Lovelace now?"

"That was his intent," she said. "He promised to come tell us what he finds out."

David grimaced. "Meanwhile, we're no closer to answers about Lawrence's death. I care about that far more."

"I know."

Capshaw was as good as his word, though it wasn't until breakfast when he came over.

"Sit down, Lieutenant," David said, gesturing to a chair. "You must be tired."

Capshaw gratefully took a seat at the kitchen table. Trixie loaded a plate of toast and eggs and set it in front of him.

He nodded his thanks. "You seem to be settling in well, Trixie."

She smiled. "I'll leave you all to talk. Holler if you need anything."

Concordia barely waited until Capshaw had stopped chewing. "Well? What have you learned?"

"Miss Phillips and Mr. Lovelace have both been taken into custody."

Her heart sank. "They conspired to kill Symond?"

Capshaw set aside his fork. "Each has confessed to killing him. Their stories are incompatible. I had no choice but to arrest them both."

"Is there *any* common ground?" she asked.

"Other than the fact that the *Catalogue* was already gone before Symond died, none," Capshaw retorted. "Miss Phillips had no choice but to finally admit *that*."

"What did she say happened?" Concordia asked.

"Symond attacked her in a rage when they discovered the loss. She defended herself with the wrench that was at hand. A flimsy story, in my mind, as Symond's wound was in the back of his head. And what of the punch in the nose?"

"What about George?" David asked.

"His tale is hardly better, as he says he encountered Miss Phillips running out of the building in tears right when he got there with the keys. She would not tell him what was wrong, so he went in to investigate, saw Symond standing in front of the empty case, very much alive. He says he argued with Symond, struck him in anger, and then had to strike him again when he came after him. He fell down dead from the second blow."

"So Miss Phillips says Symond was already dead when she left, and Lovelace says he was still alive?" David asked.

"That's right, although Miss Phillips swears that Lovelace wasn't there at all."

"What time did they say it happened?" Concordia asked.

"Miss Phillips said it was close to eleven—shortly after you left them to tend to your housekeeper. We interviewed Lovelace separately. At first he said midnight, and then said it might have been earlier."

"What if each thinks the other killed Symond, and *neither* is guilty?" Concordia suggested. "They could be protecting each other."

David unsuccessfully smothered a snort.

Capshaw smiled at her indulgently. "This is not a convoluted piece of fiction, Concordia. One of them is the guilty party. I'll get to the bottom of it, don't you worry."

CHAPTER 17

WEEKS 12-13, INSTRUCTOR CALENDAR, DECEMBER 1899

I will not cease from mental fight, nor shall my sword sleep in my hand.

— WILLIAM BLAKE

---

*C*oncordia had difficulty sorting fact from speculation during the next two weeks, which was why, shortly after the Thanksgiving recess, she was startled to see Miss Phillips duck into her office behind the gallery, box in hand.

Why hadn't Capshaw told her?

It was mere happenstance Concordia was there at all, returning borrowed books to the now Cowles-free library. She had a feeling she would be recruited soon to help the staff here.

She hurried to catch up and tapped on the open door.

"Miss Phillips? It's—it's good to see you again."

The lady looked at her with shadowed eyes. "I would think you'd be glad to be rid of me. I've made quite a mess of things." She sighed. "Sit down, dear. Just shove that box aside."

Concordia sat. "I assume you told the police the truth and they let you go?"

"Last week, actually. I'm grateful the authorities didn't press charges against me for making false statements." Miss Phillips winced. "I've made a number of those."

"Has Langdon fired you?" Concordia asked.

"He had no choice. I would have resigned, of course, even if he hadn't taken that step. But I've only now worked up the nerve to return and pack."

They were quiet for a minute. Finally, Concordia asked, "What really happened that night?"

"Even I don't know the whole story, but I suppose you deserve to at least hear my part of it." She picked up the cat statuette and kept her gaze upon it as she spoke, as if reluctant to meet Concordia's eye. "Symond and I walked into the gallery to find the case broken open and the *Catalogue* gone. He threatened to have me fired for my lapse. He also threatened to tell everyone about the incident in Egypt, saying that I'd deliberately killed his friend...for spurning *me*. Can you believe it?"

"How horrible."

Miss Phillips grimaced. "George walked in on us. He was bringing back my keys. He flew at Symond in a fury. Punched him right in the nose, knocked him to the floor."

"What happened then?"

"Symond was out cold, which surprised me. The blow didn't seem that hard."

"Well, he was quite elderly," Concordia said. "Perhaps he suffered from an ailment we didn't know about." That might explain why he'd returned to Hartford for good.

"But he was *alive* then, Concordia. I saw him breathing. George told me to go home. He said he'd rouse Symond, make sure he was all right, and apologize...essentially, straighten things out and try to get him to leave me alone. Sort of a *man to man* appeal, I suppose."

"Did you believe him?"

"Of course, but I very much doubted the success of his plan. I returned to my quarters, but not to wait for George to fix things. I started packing. I knew I'd be dismissed, if not worse, depending on whatever Symond decided to say. I didn't make much progress before I needed to sit down." She made a face. "Then I must have fallen asleep."

"The valise—I remember seeing it out when I came in to rouse you," Concordia said.

"You can imagine my shock at the news of Isaiah Symond's death. And then to learn George's wrench was the weapon, from an additional blow—" She shook her head. "All I could think was to cover for George. He must have had to defend himself when Symond regained consciousness. If Symond lunged for him and George grabbed the wrench...? So I left out the part about the *Catalogue* already being gone and told that absurd story about leaving Symond in the gallery to get the keys and then locking him in. I was hoping the police would believe it was a thief who killed him."

"Did you know at the time that Miss Cowles was responsible for taking the *Catalogue*?" Concordia asked.

"No, and I still have trouble believing one of our own staff would do something like that. At the time, I thought our student pranksters were to blame. I wanted to confront the miscreants and quietly get it back. Symond was dead set against the idea."

Concordia winced at the unfortunate choice of words. "Then you knew the identity of the pranksters?"

"Well, at least the ones responsible for the stunt in the chapel. Miss Jenkins told me of two girls on her junior class basketball team who resented the sophomores being allowed to practice with them. They wanted to put the sophomores in their place— get them in trouble for the molasses in the freshmen pews and the upside-down hymnals. I couldn't figure out their motivation for taking the *Catalogue*, but you recall we did find it upside down and the light bulb missing the day before. It seemed part of a pattern."

"Miss Cowles was clever," Concordia said. "It threw us off the track. But there were other pranks she directed at me as well. You remember the one George helped with at the Halloween Ball."

Miss Phillips flushed. "How could I forget? She used George's outrage on my behalf to vent her own bitter feeling toward you."

"Do you know anything of Miss Cowles's history?" Concordia asked. "Miss Farraday mentioned a courtship gone awry."

"Miss Jenkins knows her history better than I, but yes, I'd heard she declined an offer of marriage in order to remain here as librarian. That was ages ago, of course. Why—? Ah. You think that's why she resented you?"

"I suppose."

"How sadly misplaced," Miss Phillips said. "It's difficult enough for professional women to have personal lives completely of our choosing. We should not direct our frustrations at one another."

She stood and reached for a box.

"Let me help you," Concordia offered.

They were quiet for a while, stacking books and wrapping the artifacts that lined the shelves.

"How is Maisie doing?" Miss Phillips asked.

"I haven't seen her lately," Concordia said, "but according to Charlotte, she's having a difficult time. Her teachers are allowing her to finish her work after the Christmas recess. She's been visiting her uncle in jail as often as they will allow. She refuses to believe in his guilt."

"I know how she feels," Miss Phillips murmured. "I still find it difficult to believe. He seemed genuinely remorseful after punching Symond. It makes no sense."

"I agree. I don't think he did it."

Miss Phillips's eyes widened. "But he confessed."

"To protect you. You know how devoted he is. Besides, there are other things that don't make sense. For instance, Symond was hit on the back of the head. Your first thought was George was defending himself, and George himself told Capshaw as much. If that was the case, wouldn't he have struck Symond from the front? Second, the tool bag was not near at hand. Someone had said—I think it was you—that George's tools were tucked in a corner out of sight during the exhibit opening. That's clear across the room. How could he have reached for the wrench in a panic? Third, if all this happened right after you reached the gallery, why did George return nearly three hours later, when I ran into him?"

Miss Phillips brushed the dust off her hands. "The lieutenant posed those very questions to me. I had no good answer to them, then or now."

Concordia wished she was privy to Capshaw's thinking in that regard, but those days were long over. She had to trust him to find the solution without her—dare she say it?—interference. "Where will you go?"

"I'll stay at a boardinghouse for now. Madeline recommends Mrs. Carr's establishment, if she'll have me. After George's trial, I sail for Morocco. I have friends there. I hope to find work soon after. Perhaps an expedition will take me on." Her eyes took on a wistful look. "It's been a long time."

"Where shall I send you the Blake *Catalogue* when the police are finished with it? It's yours, after all."

Dorothy Phillips scowled. "I want no part of it, and I'm sure Marie feels the same." Her expression softened. "You keep it, dear. That way I know it will be in good hands."

It was the night of the Christmas Revels, which marked the official end of the fall semester at Hartford Women's College. The week had been busy with parties, gift exchanges, and other celebrations, and most students were already packed to leave the next day.

Concordia was ready to be done with this particular semester, though glad the students were ending it on a positive note. Youth is ever resilient in that regard.

She smoothed her kelly-green plaid skirt and straightened the cuffs of her cream-tinted shirtwaist. "How do I look?" she asked David, who sat in the overstuffed chair by the fire.

He nodded in approval. "Lovely, as always," he croaked, then turned away to cough into his kerchief.

"You poor darling." She tucked the afghan more securely around him. "I'm sorry you have to miss it." She picked up the poker and prodded a log deeper into the flames. "Perhaps I should stay home with you."

"Nonsense!" Trixie said, walking in with a soup-and-toast-laden tray. "I'll take good care of the master while you're gone. Don't you worry."

The bell rang.

"That must be Mother's carriage." Concordia frowned at her husband. "Are you sure?"

"I'll be fine" came David's hoarse whisper. "You go...have fun."

Concordia stepped into the carriage to find that Sophia had come along, too. "Sophia!" she cried. "This is a surprise."

"For me as well," Sophia said. "It's all thanks to your mother." She gave Letitia Wells a grateful glance. "She asked Mrs. Houston to watch the baby tonight, to give me a night of leisure."

"How is Mrs. Houston?" Concordia asked. "Sufficiently recovered, I hope?"

"Oh, yes," Letitia said. "She's been up and around for the past few weeks."

"Thank heaven for that," Concordia murmured. Poor Mrs. Houston. She was no doubt grateful to be back at her mother's calm, orderly, cat-free household. "What about Eli and your husband—aren't they coming?" she asked Sophia, as the carriage turned onto the main road to campus.

"Eli and Aaron are in Boston. There's an apprenticeship

opportunity for the boy there, so they've gone to find out more. Oh, Concordia—I wanted to ask you about these." Sophia rummaged in her purse, pulling out a small bottle and a handkerchief. "Our new maid found them under a chair in the sitting room, which sadly hadn't been cleaned in weeks. Are they yours?" She passed them over. "I only ask because the handkerchief has your monogram, but I cannot account for the other."

Concordia's mouth dropped open. It was indeed her handkerchief, and the bottle read: "Madam Leroy's Hair Restorer."

Mercy, she'd forgotten all about Richardson's tonic bottle. She must have missed it in the dark, when she tried to recover the spilled contents of her reticule after her eavesdropping session.

She felt her cheeks flush. "Yes, those are mine."

She started to stuff them in her purse when her mother stopped her. "What's the bottle? I can't see it in the dim light."

Concordia reluctantly passed it over. Her mother held it up to the window and read aloud, "'Madam Leroy's Hair Restorer: soothes all irritation of the scalp, makes the hair grow thick and lustrous.'" She fixed her daughter with an inquiring look. "Would you care to explain how such a thing came into your possession in the first place, before making its way to Sophia's sitting room?"

Sophia leaned forward. Obviously, she was interested, too.

Concordia frantically tried to formulate an answer as her mother unscrewed the cap and wrinkled her nose. "Ugh, how horrid."

It *was* rather horrid-smelling. Concordia caught a whiff of it even sitting across from her.

Wait a minute. She reached for the bottle. "May I?" She tentatively held it under her nose. Yes, it was familiar.

This was in Lawrence's flask! A ripple of excitement shot through her. That would mean—

"Concordia?" Her mother pressed. "Are you going to answer my question?"

The carriage rattled to a stop.

"It looks like we're here. I'll explain later." She re-capped the bottle and surreptitiously glanced at the back side for an ingredient list, but all she saw were testimonials extolling the virtues of the product. No help there. She tucked it in her purse.

Were there any varieties of hair tonic that contained cocaine? She should ask David when she got home.

Her mother raised a skeptical eyebrow but seemed to concede the argument as hopeless as they climbed out of the carriage.

Bright red bows and clumps of mistletoe, gathered from the Bradley woods, created a welcome seasonal display. However, the mingling scents of pine boughs, burnt bulb filaments, and white heliotrope perfume—as essential to any matron's night-out ensemble as her wrap and opera gloves—was a bit overwhelming. She wished she'd brought a fan.

She caught sight of Madeline, who waved excitedly.

"You look wonderful, dear!" Concordia exclaimed, after she introduced her mother. "The burgundy velvet is quite becoming to your complexion."

Out of the corner of her eye, she saw Sophia's lips twitch. And no wonder. Complimenting the young lady on how well her attire suited her coloring was the domain of the established matron. *Mercy*, being a married woman was starting to creep up on her. Someone pass the white heliotrope.

"Miss Jenkins asked me to fetch more chairs from the storage closet," Madeline said. "Will you come with me, Mrs. Bradley?" She leaned in and dropped her voice. "There's something I want to tell you."

"Of course. I want to tell you something, too."

Once they were out of earshot, Madeline said, "I have news! John Bradley's petition has been denied. Soon, the legacy will come to me."

"How very exciting." She wondered how the Bradley household was handling this recent development. Drusilla must be more convinced than ever of Madeline's *adventuress* designs.

"Mr. Richardson told me today. He said I should hire someone to manage my business interests soon. I've been considering whether to engage him in that capacity, since I already know him."

Concordia grimaced. "You may want to find someone else." She drew her aside to a quiet corner and pulled out the bottle, recounting its provenance.

Madeline's eyes widened. "How dastardly! And here I was about to trust him even further."

"It's only a suspicion, mind you," Concordia warned.

"Why would he poison Lawrence?"

"Lawrence was a clerk in Richardson's office. Maybe he discovered evidence of something illegal going on." She sucked in a breath. Richardson's office…Richardson's safe. *He even went into my safe without permission*, the lawyer had said. *Poor boy, I'm afraid I quite lost my temper when he did that.*

Lawrence, in his semi-conscious state the night he died, had repeated it. *Safe….* Had he simply echoed what he'd heard, or was he trying to tell them something? It was the last thing she'd heard him say.

"Well, then, we must go to the police!" Madeline's voice rose in her excitement.

Concordia clasped her arm in a *shushing* gesture. "A bit more quietly, if you please. Is Richardson here tonight?"

Madeline nodded. "In the front row, alongside President Langdon and Dean Maynard. So, what about the police?"

"I prefer to discuss it with Lieutenant Capshaw directly, but he's out of town at the moment." Drat, she forgot to ask Sophia when he was getting back. "We'll bide our time, but Richardson mustn't know we suspect him."

"I don't want to wait," Madeline said, sticking out a stubborn chin.

"We don't have any kind of solid evidence. A scent is nothing to go by."

A pained expression flitted briefly across Madeline's face. "Poor Lawrence. He didn't deserve this."

"I know. Capshaw will find the evidence if it's there. I'm sure of it."

"But it's been weeks since Lawrence died. The proof might be long gone—" She broke off as the chimes rang for the performance to begin.

"We'd better get back," Concordia murmured, grabbing a chair.

The students' concluding performance was met by enthusiastic applause. Soon the crowd filled the lobby and reception room, thirsty patrons in search of lemonade and spiced punch, with homemade ginger babies to complete the offerings. Concordia couldn't find Sophia, Madeline, or her mother in the press of people. In resignation, she stood in line by herself for a cup of punch.

"Oh! I beg your pardon, dear." It was the lady principal, struggling to thread her way through the crowd. "I didn't mean to bump you."

Concordia smiled. "No bother. Would you like to wait with me in line?"

"No, thank you, dear. The dean reminded me of paperwork I've yet to finish. I hope to leave for my sister's by tomorrow's train, so it must be done tonight."

"How unfortunate," Concordia said. Maynard was quite skilled at pointing out the work everyone *else* had to do.

They were both jostled by a rotund gentleman who nearly stepped on Concordia's foot. "I beg your pardon," he murmured absently, then moved on.

On the other hand, she didn't think Miss Pomeroy was missing much in this crush. "I'll stop by your office with a glass of punch," she offered.

Miss Pomeroy brightened. "How kind! Thank you, dear."

. . .

The chatter of the crowd was still ringing in her ears when Concordia stepped out of the auditorium, balancing two cups and a napkin full of cookies. She breathed deeply. The cold air was refreshing after the close space, and the stars twinkled brightly as she traversed the quadrangle for the Hall. The side door was unlocked as usual—fortunate, as she no longer possessed a building key—and she successfully brought her offering to Miss Pomeroy's second-floor office with nary a spill or lost crumb.

Her mission accomplished and the punch consumed, she turned back to the stairwell, then hesitated. Was the door at the end of the hall—Mr. Richardson's door—cracked open, ever so slightly? No light shone through.

She slipped down the hall and cautiously put an eye to the opening. A tall, slim woman, her back to the door, was leaning over the desk, rummaging in a drawer. Concordia squinted in the dark. The lady was wearing what looked to be a burgundy dress.

"Miss Farraday!" Concordia hissed, pulling the door wide.

The girl whirled around, clutching her bosom. "Oh! Mrs. Bradley, you scared me to death!"

Concordia stepped inside and closed the door behind her, but didn't turn on the light. "What are you doing here?"

"Looking for evidence, of course," she said placidly.

"Looking for evidence." Concordia sighed. The cheek of the girl. "How did you get in?"

"The latch didn't connect fully with the strike plate. It happens quite often with these old doors. Maisie taught me a trick to push back the latch to get the door open."

Concordia rolled her eyes, wondering what else Maisie had taught her.

"It's a good thing, too," Madeline went on, "because Richardson would have locked his keys in here otherwise." She held them up. "We'll have to get out of here soon before he comes back looking for them."

"I wholeheartedly agree," Concordia said. "Let's go."

"Wait! That isn't the most interesting thing I found. Look at this!" she pointed at something white on the desk.

Concordia picked up what felt like a thin card and held it up to the light of the door's transom window. "A train ticket."

"That's right, and it's one-way. For tomorrow." Madeline raised an eyebrow. "What does that suggest to you?"

"There are several explanations. Not everyone buys a round-trip ticket, especially when they aren't sure of the rest of their itinerary. I assume you're trying to say that he's fleeing, never to return?" In other words, the melodramatic explanation.

"Exactly. And here's why I think that." Madeline reached for an envelope by the lamp.

It was addressed to Richardson at his law office on Main Street—he must have been carrying it around, then set it down here. She pulled out the single sheet and held it up to the light.

My darling Ernest,
I've booked our passage aboard the British King for Antwerp. We depart
eleven a.m. Saturday morning. I will await you there.
I cannot wait to start our new adventure, my love.
Yours, Aurora

"*Now* can we call the police?" Madeline asked.

"We have no more evidence than we did before," Concordia said. "The letter isn't incriminating in itself. There's no nefarious scheme put forward." Save for the scandalous behavior of an unmarried man going off alone with a woman, of course. But the police would run themselves ragged chasing after every cad who did that. "Did you find anything else?"

"No. But we know he killed Lawrence, and now he's going to

Belgium. If we do nothing to stop him, he'll never be brought to justice."

"I agree that a trip abroad suggests he may be trying to disappear," Concordia said, "but they do have police in Europe, you know. We must go about this methodically. There's no room for shortcuts if we're to find the truth." She blew out a breath. *Methodical? No shortcuts? Mercy*, was she hearing herself? Capshaw would get a chuckle out of that.

"But all that takes time," Madeline said impatiently.

Concordia held up a hand. "Let me finish. We're assuming a great deal that we have to be sure of. First, the tonic has to be tested to determine its ingredients. Those can be compared to what the chemist found in Lawrence's flask. If they match, then Capshaw is perfectly within his rights to delve into what motives Richardson might've had to kill Lawrence."

"Before the Revels, you said Lawrence may have discovered Richardson was engaged in something illegal."

"Right," Concordia said. "and if so, I suspect it would involve the diversion of funds. According to Lawrence, Symond and Richardson argued frequently about the management of Symond's business accounts."

"I've noticed Richardson wears expensive suits and shoes," Madeline said. "And tonight he had on a tie pin I could have sworn was a diamond. But how could the police prove he'd come by his money illegally? I'm sure he's clever enough to cover it up. If he stole from Symond, for example, wouldn't that have come to light when his estate was settled and his inheritors got the money?"

"Good point. I have a friend who's a private investigator," Concordia said. "She told me—"

"*She?*"

"That's a story for another time. Anyway, she said that criminals often keep two ledgers, one real and one false, in order to keep better track of complicated graft schemes."

Madeline sucked in a breath. "If we could find the real ledger... and maybe some of the stolen money, too? That would be proof that Richardson had reason to kill Lawrence. It would at least be enough for Capshaw to look into when he returns."

"And where would you suggest we find such evidence? You want to break into the man's house?"

Madeline dangled the keys. "It wouldn't be *breaking* in. But maybe his law office would be a better place to look. There wouldn't be a housekeeper or butler to worry about. And he'd be more likely to keep a ledger where he has all his other documents at hand."

Safe. Concordia couldn't get Lawrence's voice out of her head.

"What is it?" Madeline said. "You're awfully quiet."

"*If* there's something incriminating that Richardson hasn't yet destroyed," Concordia said, "it would be locked up in his office safe." She hesitated. "But no—that can't be right."

"Why not?"

"The police searched the safe."

"How do you know?" Madeline asked.

"*Um*, well—I heard Capshaw talking about it with someone." She wasn't about to tell the girl she'd eavesdropped upon Capshaw and Maloney.

"He might have taken out anything incriminating before the police searched the safe, then put it back again," Madeline said.

"Perhaps, but Richardson's keys aren't going to get you into a steel-walled box. And neither will one of Maisie's tricks. If we can convince Capshaw about Richardson, *he* can look."

"*Convincing*," the girl murmured. "Yes, it does come down to that."

Brisk footsteps sounded in the hall.

Concordia frantically gestured for Madeline to hide out of sight of the frosted glass. Thank goodness she'd shut the door completely behind her. The lights in the office were still out. She held her breath as she waited.

They heard footsteps approaching the door, then the knob being tested. Finally, the footsteps moved on.

Concordia exhaled.

After the sounds faded and they heard a door close in the distance, she peeked out. The corridor was clear. "That was close. Let's go."

Once they were safely in the stairwell, Concordia murmured, "Do you have a way to get home this time of night? The streetcars have stopped running."

"Miss Crandall already gave me permission to stay with Maisie at Willow Cottage tonight, because of the Revels."

"Good," Concordia said. "Go get some sleep. I'll send word once Capshaw returns. Try not to fret."

She returned to the reception hall to find Sophia.

Sophia and her mother were looking for her, too.

"Where have you been?" her mother demanded. "We were worried."

Sophia checked her watch. "I really should be getting back home. I don't like to leave the baby too long with someone else. He gets fussy late at night."

"I'm sorry," Concordia said, as they headed for their carriage on the circular drive in front of the auditorium. *Mercy*, it *was* getting late—only two other vehicles remained in front of the building. "I brought some refreshments to the lady principal. We had a chat in her office." She cleared her throat. "I—I suppose I lost track of the time."

Letitia Wells raised a skeptical brow as the driver handed her in.

"Sophia, when does your husband get back into town?" Concordia asked.

"Sometime tomorrow. Why?"

"There's something important I need to discuss with him."

"Oh? What's that?"

Concordia hesitated.

Letitia narrowed her eyes. "You were *not* chatting with Miss Pomeroy all this while, were you? You were snooping."

Though Concordia bristled at *snooping*, she knew there was no denying it. "How—"

"Your voice goes a bit higher when you lie, dear. You may want to work on that."

Sophia smothered a laugh. "It's true."

Well, *drat*.

"We'll take Sophia home first," Letitia said, "so you may tell us both what's going on." She patted her daughter's hand. "Then you and I shall have a cozy chat on the drive back to your house."

CHAPTER 18

*N*ot even her mother's cautions could dampen Concordia's eagerness to tell David what she'd discovered. She wanted to learn his thoughts on the possibility of cocaine being in the hair tonic. This was one of those rare occasions when having a chemistry professor for a husband actually had a practical use.

As she stepped into the sitting room, she realized their conversation would have to wait. David was fast asleep in his chair, face mashed against one of the many embroidered pillows Aunt Drusilla insisted upon making for them. He looked comfortable enough, though. Trixie must have covered him with the second afghan before she'd gone to bed.

No point in waking him. She turned down the lamp and left him to sleep.

She should retire for the night as well, but the thought of Ernest Richardson leaving town for good was not conducive to rest.

Footsteps echoed on the wood slats of the porch, followed by a brisk knock. She glanced at the clock. Who on earth would come to call at eleven at night?

Trixie had heard it, too, and burst out of her room, clutching a hearth brush. She looked at Concordia, her eyes wide. "Who is it?" she asked, in a high-pitched stage whisper.

"It's Charlotte," a muffled voice said through the door.

Concordia opened it.

"I'm sorry to trouble you at this hour." Worry lines creased the young woman's forehead, and the muscles in her square jaw clenched.

"That's all right. Come in, please. What's wrong?"

"Have you seen Maisie and Madeline?"

"They're missing?" Concordia felt a sinking sensation. "I did see Madeline—earlier. When we parted, she said was staying the night with Maisie."

"That's right," Charlotte said. "But when I made my rounds to look in on everyone after lights out, the girls were gone. I threw on a wrap"—she looked down ruefully at her thin shawl, not at all suited to the cold December night—"and checked the usual places on campus. No sign of them."

"Does anyone else know?"

"Only Ruby. I don't want to say anything to the administration if I can help it. With Maisie's uncle in jail, she has trouble enough. But where could they be?"

Concordia bit her lip as she thought. For both of them to be gone was highly suggestive.

Richardson's keys aren't going to get you into a steel-walled box. And neither will one of Maisie's tricks. Knowing those two, it wouldn't surprise her if they planned to make the attempt anyway. Getting into the lawyer's office wouldn't be difficult, if Madeline had sneaked back upstairs and retrieved Richardson's keys. But he must have gone back for them by now. Once he realized they were missing, what would he do next?

"Concordia?" Charlotte prompted. "You know something."

"I think I do." Concordia met her eye. "You're not going to like it."

David wasn't going to like it, either.

"David! David, wake up." Concordia rubbed his hands.

His eyes fluttered, and he mumbled.

"David! Charlotte's hitching Domino to the cart. Miss Lovelace and Miss Farraday are missing. They might have gone to Richardson's office in town. We have to go see."

He sighed in his sleep.

Concordia frowned. Why was he so difficult to awaken? "Trixie!" she called.

The maid hurried in. "What is it, ma'am?"

"I can't seem to rouse Mr. Bradley. Do you know what's wrong with him?"

"The doc gave him some medicine," Trixie said. "I 'spect that's why he's so sleepy."

Doctor? "Wait, what?"

"Mr. Bradley didn' want to worry you, ma'am, but we sent for the doctor while you were out, 'cause the coughing got real bad. The master had trouble getting a full breath." Her expression brightened. "But he ain't coughing no more, so the medicine worked."

"I wish someone had told me that before," Concordia said.

David's eyes fluttered open, and he smiled at her wanly. "Con-Concordia...hello, dear."

"David," Concordia leaned closer, "I fear Madeline and Maisie might be getting themselves into trouble. Charlotte and I need to go *now*. I know you'd want to come under normal circumstances, but you're in no condition to travel."

She wasn't sure how much he understood. His eyelids kept drifting closed until he struggled to open them again.

"Of course, dear...go ahead," he said finally. "I'll wait...here..." He leaned his head back against the cushion and closed his eyes once more.

Well, she'd tried. She turned to Trixie, regarding her thoughtfully. "I think we can leave Mr. Bradley alone for a while. Can you come with us to help?"

The maid's eyes widened. "Me? Help with what?"

"Why, one of Lieutenant Capshaw's cases. You said you owed him a debt, did you not?"

She nodded.

"We think two of the college girls in our care have taken it upon themselves to do a little sleuthing," Concordia went on. "We need to go get them before they come to harm."

The woman swallowed. "How can I help?"

Concordia didn't have much experience driving the old pony cart, but they made it to campus in good time to drop off Charlotte, who would explain the situation to President Langdon and have him call the police.

"Make sure they understand they're needed at Richardson's downtown office, regarding a case Capshaw is working on," Concordia said, as they passed through the front gate, still open even at this hour to accommodate the late Christmas Revels guests and their carriages.

"How can we be sure the girls are headed there?"

"It's the only explanation that makes sense. If it had been one girl or the other, maybe there'd be another possibility. But both?"

"I wish we could keep the administration out of this," Charlotte said, "and especially the police. Is there no way we can discreetly intercept the girls and bring them back?"

"There's no time for that. We have no idea when Richardson might have left. The young ladies would face trouble far more dire than a school reprimand if he catches them first."

"You're absolutely convinced Mr. Richardson murdered your brother-in-law?"

"I am. But I don't have any proof." That job would fall to Capshaw.

Charlotte stepped down from the cart and looked up at her and Trixie with troubled eyes. "You two, be careful."

Concordia flicked the reins and, after a few awkward stops and starts to turn them around, headed for the address she'd glimpsed on Richardson's letter. *338 Main Street.*

Trixie pulled her jacket tighter around her thin frame. "Shouldn't we wait for the police? After all, this Mr. Richardson you spoke of may just go home. It's awful late for him to go back to his office."

"I hope that's the case," Concordia said, "but we must assume he'd be alarmed that his keys are missing, especially right before he's leaving town. He may go to his office to make sure all is secure." She looked over at the woman and smiled. "Don't worry. You won't be anywhere near him. I'll want you to wait with the cart and keep a lookout."

Trixie blinked. "I feel like an accomplice on a sneak thief job."

Concordia sighed. She'd often had that feeling herself. "You'll get used to it."

Main Street was empty of traffic at this hour, and they made good time.

Richardson's office was the end building of a two-story, brick-fronted row of businesses along this stretch, just before the intersection of Charter Oak Avenue.

All of the windows were dark. Concordia felt a flicker of uncertainty. Were the girls here at all?

They must be. They might have taken the precaution of not showing a light. Maisie no doubt remembered, after last year's search of the engineering laboratory, that such a step was wise.

Concordia made a face. *Land sakes*, she was not exactly a beneficial influence upon the young lady. She seemed to have taught her more about subterfuge than anything else.

She felt a lurch as the horse stumbled, regained his footing, then stopped.

"Oh no," Trixie said. She hopped down and checked while the horse patiently waited.

"Is he all right?" Concordia whispered.

"It's hard to tell in this light. His shoe feels loose. He may have a pebble underneath. I can't reach in far enough to feel."

"At least we're here," Concordia said, "but we can't stand in the middle of Main. That would attract far too much attention." She climbed down as well.

Trixie shrugged. "I wouldn't know. *You're* the expert at all this...skullduggery. Ma'am." A hint of a smile played along her lips.

Concordia gave her a sideways look. Was the maid actually teasing her? It was the first time she'd seen a spark of humor in the woman.

They led the limping horse slowly, turning left onto Charter Oak.

A narrow alley opened to the left. Concordia coaxed the horse along, going carefully so as not to scrape the buildings close by on either side.

Soon they were tucked out of sight.

"What now?" Trixie asked nervously. "How are you going to get in?"

"I don't know yet." Concordia pointed to a second-story window that opened onto the alley. "I'm guessing this is one of Richardson's. If you see a man coming who isn't a policeman, throw a pebble or something up there to alert me, okay?"

"Yes, ma'am," Trixie said.

Concordia pressed her cold hands briefly in thanks and slipped away.

The back door seemed the most promising option, but it was locked tight. She put an ear to it and tried to quiet the thumping in her chest.

Yes, there was something. The sounds were faint. Possibly boot heels on the inner stairs. She waited for more.

A lady's murmur.

Taking a breath, Concordia tapped lightly. She winced as the sound, even subdued as it was, echoed in the alley. Then, silence. She put her ear to the door again.

The boot heels were on the move. She closed her eyes to better focus on them and to determine their direction. Having no idea where the night patrolman might be in his rounds of this block, she didn't dare knock again.

The sounds were coming closer to the other side of the door. *Thank heaven.*

She put her mouth to the keyhole. "Madeline? Maisie?" she whispered. "Let me in."

She heard a smothered exclamation. The sound of a bolt thrown back was followed by the door opening only wide enough for a hand to reach out and yank her inside.

A clock's chime roused David. After fighting his way through a number of afghans and embroidered pillows wedged every which way, he glanced up at the mantel clock. Could it really be midnight?

Concordia told him she had to go somewhere...or had he dreamt it?

After a search of the house turned up nothing in the way of wife, maid, or explanatory note, he went out to the barn. No horse or cart, either.

What had she gotten herself into this time? More of what she'd told him was coming back to him now, and none of it was reassuring. *I fear Madeline and Maisie might be getting themselves into trouble.*

He rolled his eyes. *Of course* his wife would feel obligated to rescue the girls.

He should have seen this coming. He'd told her so himself.

Step one—you are interested in a young lady's welfare. Step two— that young lady finds herself in trouble. Step three—you intervene. Then...boom!

There was no time to waste. His quickest option was to take Concordia's bicycle and ride to campus. Most likely the answers lay there. He ran for the shed to fetch her machine. It had been far too long since he'd ridden. He hoped he could get down Rook's Hill in the dark without breaking his neck.

CHAPTER 19

Prudence is a rich, ugly, old maid courted by incapacity.

— WILLIAM BLAKE

"Ow," Concordia murmured, rubbing her arm.

Madeline Farraday, her widened gray eyes briefly visible in the dim light of the street lamp outside, swiftly closed the door and locked it again. "Why are *you* here?" she hissed.

"Fetching you two before you come to harm or are arrested for trespass. Or both. Where's Maisie?"

"Upstairs, looking for the second safe. How did you know where we were?"

"Wait—what? A second safe? What makes you think he has a second safe?"

"I thought of it later. My former employer, Mr. Gemmer, had a second safe installed for private papers he didn't want his clerks prying into."

His clerks prying into. Perhaps that was the safe Lawrence had

247

stumbled onto, rather than the office safe the police had searched. If so, it would make sense that Richardson had found it upsetting —and perhaps a threat to his plans. "Have you found it yet?"

"No, and we've been here twenty minutes at least. Maisie's checking his private office upstairs, which is the most likely place. Just to be thorough, I've been searching down here. No luck. I was about to join Maisie upstairs when I heard you outside."

"We should get Maisie and go." Concordia peered cautiously through the window beside the back door. There was no sign of anyone except Trixie, thank goodness, but she didn't care to press their luck.

"But it's our only opportunity to find the evidence we need," Madeline protested, as they groped their way up the stairs.

"What if Richardson comes and finds us here? Have you considered that? If he's guilty of murder, he has nothing to lose by killing us. He's fleeing as it is."

"But he can't get in. We have his keys."

"He may have a spare set at home," Concordia pointed out. "Once his maid lets him into the house, he can retrieve them and come right over to reassure himself that everything is in order."

She heard Madeline's sharp intake of breath. "I hadn't thought of that." Madeline hurried up the stairs. "Maisie!" she called softly. "We have to go."

"Wait, Maddy—I found something!" came Maisie Lovelace's excited voice.

They followed the dim glow of a shuttered lantern.

Maisie hurried toward them. She stopped short. "Mrs. Bradley! How did—"

"We need to get out of here," Madeline said. "Richardson might have a spare key at home and could return here."

Maisie winced. "Good point. But first, come see!"

They followed her to a section of the lower wall, where the lantern and a tool pouch sat on the floor. A bead-board panel had been pried away and set aside, revealing a dark metal surface.

"It was well concealed," Maisie said.

"Can you get it open?" Madeline asked excitedly, as Maisie crouched on the floor.

"Maybe. It's a dial lock."

"No," Concordia said briskly, "we are not going to waste precious time in trying. You are no lock-picker, Miss Lovelace. We shall leave it to the police. Miss Crandall is even now having Mr. Langdon fetch them."

Madeline groaned. "We're in trouble."

"Don't worry, Mrs. Bradley." Maisie swept aside a dark lock of hair and put her ear to the safe. "I'll soon know if I can get it open. We'll be out of here in no time."

Concordia went over to the window behind Richardson's desk and looked down into the alley. Trixie was now standing beside the horse—probably for extra warmth, poor dear. When the woman glanced up, Concordia fluttered her hand. Trixie tiptoed around the corner, came back, and shook her head in her direction. At least no one was coming.

"Well…just a minute or two more," Concordia said grudgingly, crossing the room to rejoin Maisie. Despite herself, she was curious.

Maisie Lovelace unsuccessfully hid a smile.

"I'll keep a lookout downstairs," Madeline offered.

Concordia watched as Maisie fingered the combination dial. "How did you two get here from the school?"

"Hired a hansom. We had to walk quite a ways to find one this time of night. The cabbie dropped us off a couple of blocks down, in front of the hospital." Maisie chuckled. "Maddy made groaning sounds in the back of the cab from time to time. We told him it was lady trouble. He wanted no part of that." She put her ear to the door. "I'll need quiet now, to listen to the tumblers and focus on any resistance I can feel in the knob."

Concordia dearly wanted to ask how on earth Maisie became knowledgeable about dial locks, but that would have to wait. The sooner they were gone, the better. She checked her watch. She'd been here nearly five minutes already. Perhaps she should have Trixie move the cart farther away—

"Ha! Got it." Maisie triumphantly swung open the steel door. "I'm surprised he had such a cheap lock put in."

"See if there's a ledger book." Concordia held up the lantern. Piled within were stacks of neatly bound bills. "Mercy, so much money!"

Maisie craned her head to look. "How much do you think is there?"

Concordia shook her head. "We've no time to count it."

Maisie pulled out a cloth pouch perched atop one of the stacks and peeked inside. "Looks like a bunch of small rocks. It's hard to tell in the dim light. They look greenish, don't you think?" She passed it over.

"Odd." Concordia felt the bottom of the bag. There was something else, flat and rigid. Too small for a ledger. She pulled it out and held it up to the light. "It's a bank book."

"Now what?" Maisie asked.

Concordia restored the bank book and bag. "We put everything back the way we found it and close up the safe. We can't afford to stay any longer. We'll tell Capshaw where to find the safe when he returns." Though how she was going to explain their midnight foray, she had no idea.

Just then they heard a light pattering sound of gravel hitting the window. *Uh-oh.* Trixie's signal.

Concordia ran to the stairs. Madeline was racing up towards her. "He's outside the front door!" she hissed.

Concordia waved her off. "Don't come up *here.* Go out the back. Trixie's waiting in the alley with the cart. You two get help."

"But what about you and Maisie?"

They heard the door open. Concordia gestured to the girl to go.

With a last, frantic look over her shoulder, Madeline flew

down the stairs and headed for the back door. Concordia quietly crept back upstairs to rejoin Maisie. She locked the inner door, for all the good it would do. At most it would slow him down. They were trapped.

Maisie's dark eyes were wide with fear. "What do we do?"

Concordia flung the window wide open and stuck her head out. Trixie looked up, startled.

"Where's Madeline?" she called.

"She hasn't come out, ma'am," Trixie said.

Oh no. What happened to Madeline? She hadn't heard a scuffle or a cry downstairs.

There was a heavy tread on the stairs, then Richardson's voice at the door. "Whoever you are—unlock the door, right now!" They heard the fumbling of a keyring.

"You'll have to run for a patrolman," Concordia said to Trixie. "Leave the horse since he's lame. Oh, wait." She turned to Maisie, who'd come to the window. She pointed to the hay-filled cart. "Could you manage the drop? There should be enough hay to cushion your fall."

They heard the key in the lock.

Maisie blew out a breath and nodded. Concordia steadied her on the sill as the girl quickly gathered her skirts to free her feet.

Behind them, the unmistakable sounds of the door being flung open and swift steps crossing the room set Concordia's heart pounding.

Maisie let go.

Concordia watched her land atop the tarp that covered the hay. Trixie ran over to help her climb down.

The girl's thumbs-up signal was the last thing Concordia saw before Richardson was upon her. After a brief flash behind her eyes, everything went black.

~

A scowling Randolph Maynard opened the door of Sycamore House at David's persistent knock.

"I'm sorry to disturb you at this hour," David began. "Have you seen my—"

"Wife?" Maynard's lip curled. "No." He jerked a thumb over his shoulder. "But Edward's in the study, telephoning the police on her behalf."

David hurried down the hall. President Langdon had his ear to the receiver and waved him in as Charlotte Crandall paced the floor.

She stopped. "Mr. Bradley! Are you feeling better, sir?"

"Well enough. Where's Concordia?"

"She and Trixie headed to Richardson's office in town. They're trying to intercept Miss Lovelace and Miss Farraday."

"Why on earth would they go there?" David asked.

Charlotte explained Concordia's and Madeline's recent discoveries regarding Ernest Richardson.

David looked over at Langdon. "Are the police on their way?"

He shook his head. "I've been trying to reach the station for the past half an hour. The main trunk line is out, and the operator's having trouble re-routing the call to another station." He sighed. "So much for modern conveniences."

"May I borrow your buggy?" David asked. "I cannot abide simply sitting here."

"We should let the police handle it."

"My wife, my responsibility," David retorted.

Langdon blew out a breath. "All right. Have Randolph help you hitch up Chestnut."

"Thanks. What's the address?"

"338 Main Street."

~

"That was mighty daring, miss," Trixie whispered, helping Maisie clamber out of the cart.

Maisie winced as she hopped down. "It wasn't as graceful as I'd hoped. I've wrenched my ankle."

Trixie tucked Maisie's arm over her shoulder as they limped into the shadows.

"Mrs. Bradley and Miss Farraday are still in there."

"I know." Maisie blew out a breath. "Maybe we should go back in. After all, there are two of us and only one of him."

"I dunno," Trixie said nervously. "Mrs. Bradley said we should fetch a patrolman. It's not like we have a weapon or anything."

"We can improvise. And he wouldn't expect us to be back so soon. You check the front door, see if it's unlocked. I'll check the back."

Alas, the office was locked up tight. "I guess we go for help, then," Maisie said. "Let's hope we find a patrolman soon."

"Amen to that, miss. Can you make it with your ankle?"

Maisie nodded, the image of Mrs. Bradley crumpling at the hands of Richardson fresh in her mind. "I'll manage."

The back of Concordia's head radiated a pain that sent waves of nausea coursing through her when she moved. She very much wanted to move, as she was currently sprawled on her stomach, one cheek pressed against a wood floor that smelled of dust and old wax. Her skirts had bunched under her knees, allowing the chill of the room to pluck at her calves.

Where was she? Then she remembered. Richardson's office.

In the dark, she heard a grunt. She lifted her head gingerly. Richardson had shed his jacket and was perspiring in his shirtsleeves and vest as he positioned the inert form of Madeline Farraday upon a Turkish rug.

Concordia's heart froze with fear. "Madeline?" she called out.

The girl groaned but didn't wake.

At least she was alive.

Richardson muttered an oath and hurried over to Concordia. "You will stay silent and not attempt to escape, Mrs. Bradley," he growled. "I'll get to you in a minute. Any such action in the meantime, and I shall kill your friend."

She didn't doubt it. Not that she could get to her feet at the moment, much less outrun the man. "You are abominable," she croaked. "What did you do to her?"

"I had to keep her from getting out the door. I knocked her out with the butt of the gun I'd taken the precaution of bringing along. I had a feeling something was wrong when my keys went missing." He turned back to the young lady. "I don't wish to kill anyone. I simply want to leave without hindrance."

Concordia carefully sat up, wincing as a fresh jolt rippled through her skull. "The more precise phrase would be—you don't wish to kill anyone *else*. If that can be believed. After all, what's another murder to you? You're already responsible for Lawrence Bradley's death."

Richardson had finished clumsily rolling Madeline into the rug. Concordia dearly hoped the girl could breathe in there.

"Oh, you figured that out, did you?" He narrowed his eyes. "What gave me away?"

"His flask smelled like your hair tonic. I didn't realize it until recently."

He looked sufficiently startled by the notion of a lady knowing what his hair tonic smelled like but didn't ask the obvious question. Instead, he shrugged. "I liked the young man, but I had no choice. He caught on to what I'd done."

"When he discovered your second safe and saw the money?"

He scowled. "I passed off an explanation that seemed to satisfy him on that score."

"So why kill him?" She was silent for a long moment before it came to her. "Ah. Did he suspect you'd murdered his great-uncle?"

Her instincts had been right—neither Dorothy Phillips nor George Lovelace was to blame.

He raised an eyebrow in surprise. "Well now, aren't you the perceptive one."

"What made Lawrence suspicious of you?"

He pointed to the form in the rolled-up rug. "This one. She came to the office to see Lawrence. I overheard her, insisting she'd seen him come out of Founder's Hall that night."

Concordia frowned. What had misled Madeline? It was true the two men possessed a similar height and build, but—*the beaver collar.* "You were wearing Lawrence's overcoat? Why?"

"I discovered my own had a stain. I was on my way to the exhibit opening, and there was no time. We swapped coats."

"So Lawrence realized Miss Farraday had mistaken you for him, and he put it all together. Did he confront you with his suspicions?"

"No, but I could tell...the way he acted after that. He knew."

"Why kill Symond at our college?" She put an exploratory hand to the back of her head. Her hair was sticky, and a lump was forming. "For that matter, why kill him at all?"

"Getting rid of Isaiah was the plan ever since he returned from Brazil." Richardson kept a wary eye on her as he carried a battered-leather valise over to the safe and started to transfer its contents. "You no doubt concluded, when you saw the cash and the gems, that I'd been helping myself a bit here and there from Isaiah's accounts over the years."

Gems? "You mean the rocks in that bag are *gems?*" She asked.

He chuckled as he shook the pouch. "Uncut emeralds, actually. Symond not only oversaw the operation of the ranch during his years in Brazil, he also had a tidy little gem-smuggling scheme going on. He'd organized a network of men who worked in the local mines to bring him not only emeralds, but amethysts, topazes, and aquamarines."

"He told you of his smuggling?"

"Hardly. But he wasn't terribly subtle about it. Each year, when he'd return to Hartford to check on his home affairs, he'd also make a side trip to visit someone—a friend, he claimed—in New York City. But why bring along the same locked case on trips to see a friend? Highly suggestive. It wasn't hard to find out that the *friend* in New York was a gem-cutter who cut and sold the stones for him."

"So you started blackmailing Symond."

He smiled. "For a modest percentage of cash and gems."

"Then why kill him and end a lucrative arrangement?"

Richardson crouched low to reach into the deepest recess of the safe. "Isaiah's smuggling days were obviously over once he left Brazil for good. It also meant he now had more time to concentrate upon his affairs here at home. Since he'd returned earlier than I'd counted on, I had no time to tidy the books. He became suspicious of discrepancies in the accounts. I'd grown a bit sloppy in his absence, I must admit." He glanced at her over his shoulder. "One gets complacent, I suppose."

The dizziness and nausea were subsiding, but the pain had taken on a steady, throbbing quality. What she wouldn't give for a cool compress on the back of her head right now.

Without that luxury, she gritted her teeth and focused on the puzzle at hand. "You haven't answered my original question—why kill him at Hartford Women's College? Why not poison him quietly, as you did with Lawrence?"

Richardson sat back on his heels and regarded her thoughtfully. "My, my, you're a cool one. Must be what comes of giving women a college education."

"It must be," she sneered.

"It would have gone something like that, but I decided to accelerate my plans after Isaiah's altercation with the handyman."

"You came upon them arguing?" Neither George nor Dorothy had said anything about Richardson being nearby.

"No, Isaiah himself told me. I'd wondered where he'd gotten to and decided to check the gallery first before heading home myself. I saw a man runing out, but I wasn't close enough to see who it was. I'm sure he didn't see me—he was in too much of a hurry. I went in and found Isaiah in the gallery applying a handkerchief to his bloody nose. He told me what Lovelace had done. That was quite a punch. Needless to say, Isaiah was fit to be tied. Apparently he'd ordered the man out, threatening him with ruin, and Miss Phillips as well."

Concordia nodded to herself. That explained a great deal.

"But he wasn't done yet," Richardson went on. "Next he turned on *me*. Said he was tired of my thieving ways, and he'd order an audit of all his accounts in the morning. I had to act. There would never be a better opportunity to get rid of a big problem."

"And place the blame on someone else," she retorted. Despicable man.

"I saw the handyman's tool bag tucked away in the corner. The plan practically arranged itself."

She shuddered. "You cannot expect to get away with this."

He snapped the valise shut and regarded her thoughtfully. "My success depends upon what I do with you, my dear."

CHAPTER 20

The tigers of wrath are wiser than the horses of instruction.

— WILLIAM BLAKE

---

*E*ven with Trixie to support her, Maisie wasn't able to walk for very long. And they'd already covered two blocks of Main Street without a patrolman to be found. Maisie was beginning to wonder if she would need to stop yet again to rest her throbbing ankle.

Then, on the far side of the street, she spotted a man walking briskly along the sidewalk, holding a baton that swung in time as he moved. He crossed beneath a streetlamp, which picked up the brass buttons of his tunic and the shiny brim of his cap.

"Thank heavens," she breathed.

Concordia watched in dismay as Richardson yanked the telephone cord out of the wall and stripped it from the device.

"You won't be able to escape," she said, as he pulled her hands behind her back and began to tie them. "The police will be hunting for you, watching every train station and port in the area."

"Well, I'm certainly not going to show up at Union Depot for the 9:10 to New York City tomorrow morning." His breath was warm as he murmured in her ear. She shuddered.

"I know you and Miss Farraday saw the ticket and letter," he went on, "so I have to assume the information will be passed along to the authorities as well. But we should make it to Middletown before they catch on. I can get on a train there and proceed with an alternate plan."

"We?" Concordia repeated. They were standing beside Madeline, still wrapped in the rug. Could she hear them? In the gloom, Concordia gave the lump a discreet nudge with her foot. She thought she felt a twitch, but it was difficult to tell with Richardson tugging on her wrists.

"Of course. You, madam, are my insurance policy. If the police do intercept me before I get away, we will bargain for your safe return." She heard him expel a sigh of satisfaction. "There. Now, one more thing."

She gave a startled squeak of protest as he abruptly stuffed a handkerchief in her mouth. As she coughed and tried to spit it out, a length of cloth—a cravat, perhaps—quickly followed. He tied it all in place as she glared at him.

"Sorry, my dear, but I can't have you screaming for a patrolman once we head outside to my carriage." He pulled up her hood to better conceal the gag, then gripped her elbow in one hand, the valise and extra cord in the other. "Let's go."

With a mixture of trepidation and relief at leaving Madeline behind—at least the girl would be spared being taken hostage—she left the office with Richardson. She prayed

Trixie and Maisie would bring help soon to tend to the young lady.

Of course, it would be too late to help *her*. She was on her own.

Richardson's carriage was parked halfway down the block and around the corner on South Prospect Street. He steered her by the elbow. With her hands tied behind her, it was a struggle to keep her balance. The streets were still empty at this hour—not that she was in position to call out for aid, anyway—but in the distance, she thought she heard a buggy proceeding along Main Street at a rapid pace. Her hopes lifted, and she slowed, trying to listen, but Richardson pushed her along.

Finally, they reached his brougham.

He shoved her in, awkwardly propping her upon the bench, then climbing in and closing the door behind them.

It was pitch black. Not a bit of light from the street lamps penetrated the tightly closed, heavy window curtains. She heard him breathing heavily from his exertions, then felt him grasping at her ankles to tie them.

But she had no intention of meeting the same unseemly fate as his other victims. Now was her chance to fight back.

David left Langdon's buggy farther down Main Street, out of sight, and approached Richardson's office building with caution. He looked over his shoulder first before trying the front door. *Lord*, he felt like a house burglar.

The door was locked tight, and no light shone in the windows. All was quiet. He should check the back door to be sure.

He'd just started down the alley to circle to the back of the building when he came upon the horse and cart.

The animal whinnied softly at his approach.

David reached up to stroke the animal's nose. "Domino," he murmured, "I wish you could tell me where everyone is."

The horse shifted uneasily.

"Hmm, you're not putting much weight on that leg. What's wrong, old fellow?" He ran his hands down Domino's right fore-leg. No wound that he could determine, and the horse didn't flinch. He picked up the hoof. Ah, here was the problem. That dratted shoe had come loose again. Something must be stuck underneath.

He probed the gap with long fingers. Sure enough, there was a stone chip wedged in between. He pried it out. Domino put his hoof down with what David could have sworn was a relieved sigh.

David smiled. "You're welcome."

The sound of a quickly suppressed *yowl* stopped him in his tracks. It was coming from a side street half a block away, off Charter Oak. He ran toward it.

As he got closer, he saw a man hastily exiting the interior of a brougham, clutching the side of his face with one hand and a trailing cord with the other. The sound of kicking came from within.

In the light of the streetlamp, David recognized Ernest Richardson.

"Stop!" David yelled, charging across the street toward them.

Startled, Richardson dropped the cord, scrambled into the driver's seat, and grabbed the reins. The horse surged forward.

David continued to give foot chase down Charter Oak Avenue, though he knew he was woefully mismatched.

The unsecured side door flew open as the brougham picked up speed.

The last thing David saw as they turned the corner was his wife's feet—one unshod—sticking out of the opening.

Concordia certainly wanted to escape the brougham, but not like this. With her hands still tied behind her, she pushed and wriggled until she was entirely back inside, sitting up on the floor of the vehicle, torso propped and feet braced against the open door edges. They took a curve, and the door swung wildly. The wind whistled in, whipping her hair into her eyes.

There was nothing she could do about the door in her current circumstance. It was all she could do to keep from being flung through it with each reckless turn.

Richardson had to slow down some time. She would have to be prepared to jump. But she would need her hands free to manage it. She shifted her wrists, trying to stretch the bonds, wincing as the cord held firm and bit into her flesh.

If she couldn't loosen it, maybe there was a way to cut it.

Carefully, so as not to unseat herself as the floor jolted beneath her, she felt around, groping the metal bracket that anchored the bench behind her. She needed something rough. Anything.

At least he'd not been able to tie her ankles. She smiled in grim satisfaction at the memory of landing a few solid kicks to Richardson's face. Then she'd heard David's shout—what a welcome sound that was!—and Richardson had abandoned his task.

Where was David now? Could he follow?

David, chest tight with exertion and a fit of coughing, had to choose quickly—run two blocks back to where he'd left Langdon's buggy or half a block to Domino and the farm cart? The cart was slower, and the horse's shoe was already loose, but he didn't think he had it in him to run those extra blocks.

Then, between the gap in the buildings across the street, he spotted the brougham making the sharp turn onto Wyllys. So, Richardson was doubling back. That would mean he was heading to Wethersfield Avenue. It was the quickest way south out of town.

Decision made, David hurried back to Domino and climbed into the cart. "Here's hoping your shoe holds," he muttered. With a smart slap of the reins, they were off.

Over the clatter of the wheels, David heard the piercing sound of a policeman's whistle. He kept going.

～

"Must you do that?" Maisie said wearily, as the patrolman blew his whistle again. Trixie winced.

"Sorry, miss." The young man tucked it back in his vest. "I need someone to take you ladies back to the station. You'll be safe there."

"We want to go with you!" Maisie protested. "Our friends are in there."

He shook his head. "Too dangerous. You'd only be in the way. As it is, I'll want another man to come with me to check this out. By your account, this fellow—Richardson?—sounds desperate. Holding two women captive? Caution is warranted."

Maisie sniffed. He looked annoyingly young to be bossing people around, she thought, noting his prominent Adam's apple above the collar of his tunic and the light fuzz that brushed his cheek.

He stepped out to the middle of Main Street as a black wagon briskly approached, two uniformed men sitting on the front bench. The wagon slowed, and one hopped down. "What's the problem?"

"Come with me," the patrolman said. "I'll explain on the way." He waved up to the driver. "Take the two ladies back to the station so they can give their statements. One of them's hurt, though not too badly. See if Doc's available to fix her up."

～

Fully awake now, Madeline Farraday fought the rising panic of her confinement in the rug. She was all too aware of the dust and fibers that caught in her nose and throat as she breathed. It was maddening not to be able to move her arms, pinned as they were, or flex her limbs. All she could do was wriggle and shift herself by inches.

It was deadly quiet. She spared a thought for Mrs. Bradley. Richardson must have taken her away with him. But why? Between the rug muffling the sound and her hazy state earlier, she hadn't heard much. Though she did remember... *Middletown.* They were headed for Middletown.

She felt a renewed surge of energy. She had to get out of here.

There wasn't much room, but she tried to roll nevertheless, not sure which direction would free her.

What was that? She stopped shifting and strained to listen.

A man's—men's—voices. Just outside. Her heart pounded. The police?

"Help! Help!" she shouted, hoping she'd be heard through the layers.

The bench made it awkward to position her cords against the rough bolt underneath, but Concordia managed to turn on her side—*ugh,* the floor was sticky—and stretch her arms far enough backward to reach. She bit her lip and grunted as she caught and pulled...caught and pulled... She could barely feel her fingers anymore. Her shoulders ached from the strain.

Oh, David—I've gotten myself in a dreadful pickle this time. I'm sorry.

A bump in the road sent her sliding toward the door again, but at least the wind had whipped it shut. And they weren't proceeding at break-neck speed anymore. Richardson must have realized his horse would quickly tire at such a pace.

She re-positioned herself and doggedly continued her sawing. Catch-pull, catch-pull, catch-pull...

David could barely make out the side lamps of Richardson's brougham up ahead as he followed the conveyance down Wethersfield Avenue. This stretch of road on the outskirts of Hartford was not electrified. With no lantern of his own, David doubted Richardson would see him, but he kept the farm cart a few hundred yards back just to be sure.

Richardson had now slowed his own horse to a trot, which was fortunate, as Domino would need a great deal of coaxing to go any faster than this.

David considered his options. Catch up to him now and perhaps block his path? No, Richardson would hear him coming well in advance. He could harm Concordia.

He would have to bide his time. There might be an opportunity when they reached the populated section of Wethersfield.

Still, it would be wise to close the gap a bit, so he didn't lose them in the dark.

He slapped the reins and clicked his tongue at the horse in encouragement. "Off we go, Domino," he murmured. "Come on, old boy."

"Yes, I'm sure he said Middletown," Madeline Farraday said wearily, for perhaps the third time. She took a sip of the luke-warm tea, served in a faded blue mug, which a kindly station sergeant had set in front of her. Maisie and Trixie sat on either side on the bench across from the precinct captain.

The captain gave her a long look. "You're sure this is not some sort of lovers' spat gone awry?"

Madeline opened her mouth to protest, but the patrolman intervened. "I don't believe we would have found this young lady rolled up in a rug in his office if that were the case, sir."

"All right," the captain said. "I'll telephone the main precinct in Middletown, give them a description of the kidnapper, and ask them to set a watch on the main road. After that—"

"What about the train station in Middletown?" Madeline Farraday interrupted. "Shouldn't you warn them as well?"

"I was getting to that," he said tersely. "Most God-fearing folk are asleep at this hour, my good miss, unlike hoydenish college girls. The station master's office opens in"—he checked his watch —"four hours. We'll telegraph an alert then." He stood.

Maisie raised an eyebrow. "Is that all? Aren't you going to go after them?"

"They're long gone. We've no chance of catching them."

David continued to follow the brougham for the next hour as it kept its steady pace through fields and farmland. What he wouldn't give for a nice, crowded town full of people to come to his aid.

Domino was picking his way carefully but keeping up. The poor horse must be bone-tired. They might have to make a move soon. Cautiously, he tapped the reins to get them a bit closer. They were perhaps a hundred yards away now.

Something was happening. He squinted through the gloom, then gaped as he saw the door of the brougham ease open and his wife step out. She clutched the handle in one hand—a piece of cord dangled from that wrist—and grasped the edge of the frame with the other. She was perched gingerly on the step-up, weaving in rhythm with the trot of the horse. At least, he hoped that was why she was weaving and not because she was about to grow faint.

She hadn't seen him at all. All of her attention was on the back of Richardson's head. Then she turned to survey the gully beside the road.

David winced. It was much too deep. She would injure herself if she tried it. He advanced closer to the brougham.

And in that moment, everything went wrong.

Richardson whipped around in his seat, whether it was from the sound of the cart approaching or because he'd sensed Concordia's movement right behind him, David would never know. At the sight of his escaping prisoner, Richardson pointed his pistol at her. "Stop right there, Mrs. Bradley!" he shouted.

David slapped the reins. "Yah!" The horse surged forward. They were within fifty yards.

Both Concordia and Richardson froze as the farm cart advanced. Richardson's horse slowed of its own accord.

Richardson stood on the bench and pointed his gun close to Concordia's head. "Back off, or I shoot your wife!"

Given a choice between jumping or being shot—though both happening at once was a distinct possibility—Concordia's decision was an easy one.

Now or never.

In one quick movement, she pushed the door at Richardson and leapt toward the gully, ducking her head in her arms.

Behind her she heard the gun go off, then the frightened *whinny* of a horse. She landed with an *oomph* in the muddy ravine below as a jumble of sensations and sounds overwhelmed her senses—a sudden pain in her shoulder, pounding hooves, rattling wheels, confused shouts, a man's shriek. She fainted.

"Concordia!"

She roused herself at the welcome sound of David's voice. "Here," she croaked.

He scrambled down and embraced her, then pulled back as she winced. "You're injured. Did he get you?" He frantically checked her clothing in the gloom.

"No. I seem to have dislocated my shoulder." *Again.* She hadn't the knack for landing gracefully, it seemed. With David's help, she stood. "Did Richardson get away?"

David's expression turned grim. "He's dead."

"Dead?"

"The shot scared his horse, who bolted. You remember Richardson was standing on the bench when he had you at gunpoint. He lost his balance and was caught in the traces before dropping to the road. The back wheels got him. He didn't survive long after that."

She turned her face into his chest. *Thank heaven it was over.*

EPILOGUE

HARTFORD, CONNECTICUT, AUGUST 1900

Great things are done when men and mountains meet.

— WILLIAM BLAKE

The formal opening of the new school at Hartford Settlement House proved to be more of an event than Concordia expected. Vehicle traffic had slowed to a crawl as locals gathered on the sidewalks and spilled into the street.

The crowd on the steps of the school was at least ten people deep, many of them school children and their families. From across the street, Concordia leaned on David's arm as she stood on tiptoe for a better view.

"Do you see them?" she asked her husband.

He tightened his arm to steady her. "I see Miss Farraday and the settlement house director—Miss Newcombe, is that right? Yes. They're about to cut the ribbon now."

A few heads in front of her shifted, and Concordia was able to see at last. "And look, Sophia and the lieutenant are right behind

271

them." Today Lieutenant Capshaw was attired in a pinstripe suit for the occasion rather than his customary uniform. The stiff brown material, however, seemed rather heavy for this time of year. Concordia suspected he owned few suits to begin with.

The crowd broke into applause as the ribbon was cut and the new school was made official. Squealing children were sorted into orderly groups and escorted inside by their teachers as onlookers began to disperse.

"Let's go congratulate them," Concordia said.

Madeline Farraday spotted them first and hurried down the steps. "Mrs. Bradley! I'm so glad you could come."

The young lady looked radiant today, attired in a light summer walking dress of dotted peach muslin and a beribboned straw hat to match. Her blue eyes sparkled with eagerness, and her pale complexion was touched with a flush along her cheeks in the mid-morning warmth.

Concordia smiled to herself. Finally, this orphaned girl had found a path in life that suited her. A far cry from last summer, when she'd lost the man she loved and thought her life was forever tied to domestic service. *Dreams take many forms, Mrs. Bradley.* She was glad Madeline had discovered hers.

"Of course we would come," Concordia said. "We're so proud of what you've achieved." She looked up in appreciation at the building, once the site of a dry goods store and abandoned years before. Now, thanks to Miss Farraday's beneficence, the building had been purchased and restored—its brick front re-faced, steps mended, roof tiles replaced. "The building has never looked better."

"You should see the classrooms," Madeline said. "Freshly painted, of course, and everything's new—floors, books, desks and chairs. It's beautiful. But it isn't *my* achievement. I provided the funds and was invited to sit on the planning board, but greater minds than mine put all this together. I'm still learning about the process."

David smiled. "It's early days yet. You have a bright future ahead of you."

"Thank you, Mr. Bradley," Madeline said.

"I do wish you'd call me David," he said. "We're family, after all."

In the months since Miss Farraday had come into Lawrence's share of Isaiah Symond's fortune, David's father had come to realize that inheriting even half of Symond's immense estate was a formidable sum in its own right and that challenging Lawrence's will had served no purpose other than to widen the rift between Madeline and the Bradley family. Over the past several months, David had tried to ease the estrangement.

"Family?" Madeline gave a wry smile. "Perhaps someday. In the meantime, I hope you both will join us for a celebratory breakfast. Miss Newcombe has a buffet set up at the settlement house."

David grinned. "Wouldn't want to miss that." He dropped his voice as he leaned toward his wife. "Are you feeling up to breakfast, dear?"

She slipped her hand through his arm. "Absolutely." This time around, her nausea was not nearly as profound. She hoped that was a good sign. Only time would tell.

"I understand you're still living at Mrs. Carr's boarding house," David said to Madeline, as they turned down the block toward the settlement house. "I'm curious as to why. You can afford to live anywhere you like."

"And eat something other than mutton stew," Concordia added.

Madeline grinned. "The menu has vastly improved since then. Besides, I've been so busy with committee work I haven't had time to make a decision. And Mrs. Carr has been like a mother to me."

"Perhaps it has something to do with Maisie taking lodgings there as well?" Concordia teased. Miss Lovelace had moved to the boarding house after her graduation from Hartford Women's

College. The two remained as thick as thieves, perhaps more so after their harrowing experience.

"It's good to have a friend," Madeline said.

"How *is* Miss Lovelace?" David asked. "We haven't heard from her since graduation."

"You'll see for yourself," Sophia said, as she caught up to them on the sidewalk, Capshaw close behind. "She and her uncle are attending the breakfast. They've been working to set up the school's new machine shop as part of our mechanical apprentice-ship program."

David's lips twitched. "Sounds perfect for the young lady."

"For both of them," Concordia said. "I'm so glad. That family has been through a terrible experience."

Capshaw clucked his tongue. "It would not have been so, had Lovelace not played at chivalrous knight errant with his false confession. He's lucky it only cost him a few weeks in jail. One should not *meddle* in a police investigation."

He turned a sharp eye to Concordia, who assumed a look of wide-eyed innocence.

"I grant you, jail is not a pleasant place," she agreed.

Madeline raised a puzzled eyebrow.

Best not to share her experience in that regard, Concordia thought. She stifled a smile.

"The outcome isn't entirely satisfactory for Lovelace, poor fellow," David said, "with Miss Phillips gone for good."

"Actually"—Madeline's voice was tinged with excitement —"Maisie and I have a surprise planned. We're taking him with us to Egypt to visit Miss Phillips in the spring."

"How wonderful!" Concordia exclaimed. "So you've been in contact with the lady. How is she?"

"Oh, definitely in her element," Madeline said. "According to her last letter, she just returned from an exciting dig in...Asyut, I believe. She's presently in line for the assistant curator position at the museum in Boulaq."

"Speaking of museums," Sophia said, "what are you going to do with the *Descriptive Catalogue*, now that the college gallery is closed for good?"

"President Langdon suggested a small display in the library," Concordia said. It seemed an apt place.

"Will you continue working at the library this fall, Mrs. Bradley?" Madeline asked, as they reached the front doors of Hartford Settlement House.

After Jane Cowles's "retirement"—only a few knew she'd been dismissed—Concordia had spent long hours helping in the library as the school searched for a permanent replacement. The work was strictly voluntary, which pleased Maynard no end. He rarely stay pleased for long, of course, and the new century would no doubt afford him *may-nots* in plenty.

"Perhaps I will, but not beyond that." She glanced at David, who gave her a warm look in return. "I miss being at home."

He grinned as he held the door open. "Amen to that."

THE END

AFTERWORD

It's a great time to be a historical author, with the wealth of digitized historical material available on the internet. For anyone interested in the background research that went into the writing of this series, I've shared some wonderful primary and secondary sources on my website, KBOwenMysteries.com. I'd love to see you there.

I hope you enjoyed the novel. Please consider leaving a quick review (a sentence or two) on your favorite online book venue. Word of mouth is essential to help readers find books they will love, particularly those written by independently published authors. Thank you!

To order other books in the Concordia Wells series, please visit KBOwenMysteries.com/books, where purchase links to all of the online venues are provided.

ALSO BY K.B. OWEN

From *The Concordia Wells Mysteries:*

Dangerous and Unseemly (book 1)

Unseemly Pursuits (book 2)

Unseemly Ambition (book 3)

Unseemly Haste (book 4)

Beloved and Unseemly (book 5)

Unseemly Honeymoon (book 6)

From *The Chronicles of a Lady Detective:*

Never Sleep (Chronicle #1)

The Mystery of Schroon Lake Inn (Chronicle #2)

The Case of the Runaway Girl (Chronicle #3)

ACKNOWLEDGMENTS

Many people have had a hand in bringing this book into the world, and I want to express my sincerest appreciation here.

Special thanks to Stephanie E. Stillo, Ph.D., curator of the Lessing J. Rosenwald Collection, and her team at the Library of Congress, for allowing me the opportunity to examine an original of William Blake's *Descriptive Catalogue.*

To artist Melinda VanLone, who creates the wonderful covers in this series. I'm grateful for her time and talents. Melinda can be reached at BookCoverCorner(dot)com.

To Kristen Lamb and Jenny Hansen, and the generous community of fellow writers known as WANAs, for their advice and support. We are truly not alone.

To Kassandra Lamb, for her spot-on developmental edits, and to Julie Glover, for her meticulous copy editing and proofreading of the manuscript.

To my aunt, Lorraine Winder, to whom this book is dedicated. Thank you for believing in me.

To my dad, Steve Belin. Although you aren't with us anymore, I know you're still cheering me on. I miss you, Dad.

To my mom, Agnes Belin. You instilled an abiding love of

reading ever since I was little, and you continue to share your enthusiasm for my writing career. Thank you!

To my sons, Patrick, Liam, and Corey, who make me laugh and don't think it's weird at all that their mom makes up stories for a living.

To Paul Owen, my husband and my love. None of this would be possible without you.

K.B. Owen
   April 2019

www.ingramcontent.com/pod-product-compliance
Lightning Source LLC
Chambersburg PA
CBHW031603240626
47153CB00002B/615